AN
EARL
TO
Remember

AN
EARL
TO
Remember

USA TODAY BESTSELLING AUTHOR
STACY REID

Copyright © 2023 by Stacy Reid. All rights reserved, including the right to reproduce, distribute, or transmit in any form or by any means. For information regarding subsidiary rights, please contact the Publisher.

Entangled Publishing, LLC
644 Shrewsbury Commons Ave., STE 181
Shrewsbury, PA 17361
Visit our website at www.entangledpublishing.com.

Amara is an imprint of Entangled Publishing, LLC.

Edited by Lydia Sharp and Stacy Abrams
Cover design by Bree Archer
Cover art by Nikada/Gettyimages
Interior design by Toni Kerr

Print ISBN 978-1-64937-272-7
ebook ISBN 978-1-64937-421-9

Manufactured in the United States of America

First Edition September 2023

ALSO BY STACY REID

Unforgettable Love

A Matter of Temptation
An Earl to Remember

The Sinful Wallflowers

My Darling Duke
Her Wicked Marquess
A Scoundrel of Her Own

Wedded By Scandal

Accidentally Compromising the Duke
Wicked in His Arms
How to Marry a Marquess
When the Earl Met His Match

Scandalous House Of Calydon

The Duke's Shotgun Wedding
The Irresistible Miss Peppiwell
Sins of a Duke
The Royal Conquest

Du'Sean, always and forever.

CHAPTER ONE

*Sometimes revenge can be
too deliciously dangerous…*

Miss Georgianna Eleanor Heyford gasped, the
folded paper with its elegantly flowing script fluttering from her fingers to swish against the
threadbare carpet in the drawing room of their
home.

"What is it? Have you *finally* seen Uncle
Timothy's ghost?" her youngest sister Annabelle
chirped, her cherub's face creasing in a grin. "I
told you I've heard him and Mama singing in the
attic."

"It's not any ghost, Anna. I got the job,"
Georgianna whispered, pressing the flat of her
palm over her thumping heart. "*I got the job!*"

Her sisters were not startled that she'd
screamed joyfully, nor did they celebrate this
opportunity, which was a most wonderful dream
for Georgianna. Young ladies from backgrounds
such as hers were not meant for such a role. She
laughed, unable to quite process the jumbled
slew of emotions rioting inside her chest. It was
surely too much when she had sat on her bed

above stairs only an hour ago, her shoulders weighted with despair and melancholia, fearing that she had failed her family, who greatly depended on her abilities and wit.

Slightly dimming her enthusiasm, Georgianna said, "I have secured the job I've been hoping and praying for."

It was Aunt Thomasina who straightened against the lumpy cushions of the sofa and replied, "It's not right for a genteel miss like yourself to be working. It is just not right! I've told you girls to come and live with me in Kent and leave…" Her aunt looked about the house they had grown up in their entire lives with an acute expression of distaste. "*Leave* this place. I cannot imagine why you girls insist on holding onto it! If the manor is sold, there should be enough money to settle dowries on you and Elizabeth so you girls might marry suitably."

Though there was a painful wrench inside her chest, Georgianna smiled fondly at her aunt. "*This* is where our memories of Mama and Papa are, and we do not wish to leave here…leave them, Aunt. This is our home, Papa left it in my care, and we shall not give up on it."

Aunt Thomasina's mouth flattened. "Working is beyond the pale for a miss of your station!"

Her disapprobation expressed, Aunt Thomasina went back to reading *Frankenstein*. Georgianna swallowed a groan. Ever since her aunt became Baroness Crawley a couple years prior, everything her relatives did was beyond the pale. Georgianna's father had been a proper country gentleman with a distant relationship to a baronet. He had taught all his children the value of working to fulfill the dreams in their hearts and not to be too elevated in their thoughts, which could lead to an excessive, silly nature.

Noting the pinched disapproval about her aunt's mouth, she said, "It is not beyond me to work, Aunt, and once I secure this incredible offer, the monies paid over will see to the many repairs needed around the manor, our larder filled for the rest of the year, new clothes and boots for everyone, and more catering jobs secured from estimable lords and ladies. Imagine it, Aunt, that I might get so popular that I rival those French chefs who serve Buckingham or those elite lords and ladies living in Grosvenor Square!"

"You need to set aside this nonsense about working and procure yourself a husband to help you manage, Georgianna. That is what you girls need, *husbands*."

She barely resisted rolling her eyes in an unladylike fashion, the one her aunt constantly rebuked her for. "I assure you, Aunt, the world is changing, only you seem quite determined to live within the confines of the past."

Her aunt gasped, and Georgianna softened her tone. "I do not *need* a husband to supervise my life or restrict me in any way. If I should fall in love with a man who would love me and support my dreams and passions, that is another matter entirely."

Her aunt harrumphed, and another measure of Georgianna's excitement dimmed as she noted her sisters' reactions, each worried for their own reason. Hurrying over to the youngest, she stooped.

"This is a good thing, Anna," she whispered, tweaking her cherub chin. "You know how much you enjoy my cooking, especially my spiced rum cake and quail roasted with honey?"

Her six-year-old sister's lips trembled before she nodded. "Lizzie especially loves them," she whispered.

"A very important gentleman, an earl, wants me to cook for a lavish party he is hosting aboard his yacht while it sails along the English Channel." Lowering her tone to a dramatic whisper, she added, "This gentleman will compensate me so handsomely, we won't have to eat Hetty as we feared."

Her sister gasped, snapping her head around to peer at the hen who pecked at the earth outside by the water through. Anna looked back to Georgianna, her blue eyes sparkling with that militant determination known to the Heyford sisters.

"Then you *must* go, Georgie. We don't want to *eat* Hetty!"

"Or Midge," eight-year-old Sarah said of their piglet with a giggle. "Though I feel she would be quite tasty."

The girls laughed, and relieved that she had taken some of the worries from their hearts, Georgianna ruffled Anna's tousled dark curls and glanced at the sister closest to her in age, her dearest friend and closest confidant, Elizabeth.

Her sister lifted her chin to imply they should speak in privacy. Georgianna rose and smoothed the wrinkles in her dark, serviceable gown. "I am going to check on the stew and the bread in the oven. Lizzie, why don't you assist me?"

She walked away from the drawing room, knowing her sister would follow. They clambered down the stairs to the large stone kitchen where a savory stew bubbled, the air redolent with the dish.

"You cannot go, Georgie," her sister said as they came off the last step. "It is not safe."

Georgianna whirled around, fisted a hand at her hip, and pinned her sister with a glare. "*Lizzie*! You know this is the chance we so desperately need. We cannot—"

"Is it *him*?"

Georgianna's heart lurched in a most peculiar manner, and she sighed. Him—Daniel Rutherford, the 14th Earl of Stannis, known to her sister only because the man was scandalous in his rakish pursuits and parties. Even buried in Hertfordshire, they received the town news. The earl had made their local papers once because of his unapologetic debauchery. He was a gentleman reputed to be a wicked libertine, but somehow most of society agreed he was one of the prime catches of the season with his debonair looks and wealth. "I am to work for the Earl of Stannis."

Lizzie leaned her hip against the stone counter. "What precisely did the earl say to you in his letter?"

"It is the secretary of Lord Stannis who wrote to me. You know I was not the first choice to cater to this party aboard the earl's yacht, but we must be grateful his first cook fell ill and provided this remarkable opportunity for us. I asked for three hundred pounds and prepared several arguments as to why I am worth this amount."

Lizzie gasped. "Three hundred pounds?"

Georgianna smiled. "Mr. Burnell agreed without any quibble! Though I am confident in my capabilities to amaze the earl's guests' exotic and rich palettes, it was an absurd sum. That they are willing to pay it is beyond what I expected but perfectly wonderful for us."

Her sister sighed. "I know it is a sum we badly need, but—"

Rushing forward, she took her sister's hands in hers. "There is no but, Lizzie! Please trust me."

"Lord Stannis is a rake who does not hesitate to seduce ladies to his bed!"

Georgianna blinked, nonplussed. "What does that have to do with me? I knew of the earl's reputation before I responded to Mr. Burnell's advert."

Her sister sniffed, then sheepishly grinned. "You are *very* pretty, Georgie—what if Lord Stannis...cannot resist being a libertine?"

The notion astonished her so much, Georgianna laughed. "You forget it takes two to play any game of seduction."

Her sister scoffed. "What would you know of it? The earl visited Hertfordshire and our humble town of Crandell, *ravished* Squire Goodley's daughter, and then refused to do the honorable thing. What if he should ruin you, too?"

"Not that silly rumor again! I am not that foolish, and I cannot believe you would think so little of my mettle and character." A spurt of humor shook Georgianna. "I also do not think I would have any cause to encounter the earl to inspire such an alarming sense of ravishment. We had not even met him when he supposedly visited Crandell a couple years ago."

Her sister jutted her chin in that stubborn way she owned. "They say he is so devilishly handsome that even ladies twice his age beg to be his lover."

"I promise to gird my loins and resist the terrible temptation."

Lizzie scowled. "They said no less than *three* maidens have been known to fall pregnant with child with only a kiss from the earl, the only such known cases in all of our kingdom."

"It is rather astonishing, that," Georgianna said drily, terribly amused by her sister. "Somehow I suspect there might be more to it than just kisses, and you should stop reading those nonsensical gossip rags which only know how to publish outlandish speculations."

Elizabeth's scowl darkened. "You do own a naughty and inquisitive soul. I fear you might find his wickedness appealing."

"*Lizzie*," Georgianna said with great exasperation. "You worry needlessly. Mr. Burnell said I will have a kitchen staff of six and an army of footmen at my command aboard the earl's yacht for the few days I'll be there. I cannot see any reason for the earl to seek me out or I him. Truly, it is doubtful Lord Stannis is even aware that Mr. Burnell hired me."

Lizzie sighed and tucked a wisp of hair behind her ear. "I suppose you are correct in that regard. An earl would not dirty his hands by doing anything so normal as looking through the résumés of potential cooks."

Grinning, Georgianna looped her hands with her sister and tugged her over to the stone bench facing the large windows. "Let's be thankful. My compensation is a needed fortune that will set so many things to right, Lizzie."

Her sister hesitated. "Do you not think we should consider Aunt's offer to live with her in Kent? To perhaps have a season in London for yourself, Georgie, and try and find a husband?"

A most peculiar cold pricked deep beneath Georgianna's skin, and she withdrew her hand from Lizzie's and sat. Clutching the apron in a tight grip, she met her sister's worried gaze. "Do you wish to leave here? Sell the manor as our aunt suggests?"

A raw emotion she could not decipher flashed in her sister's blue eyes before her lashes lowered. A hitch darted through Georgianna's chest. Though she could not bear the notion of parting from the home that held so many loving memories, to remain within its comforting and familiar walls could not be her decision alone. She always had to keep her sisters' wishes, hopes, and dreams in her keeping, gently holding their flames alive.

"Please, Lizzie, I am not so decided in my opinions and actions that my dearest sister cannot tell me her thoughts and worries."

Her sister looked around, taking painstaking care to linger on the large table where they normally sat with their parents and laughed and chatted while they baked or cooked together.

"All the memories are here," Lizzie whispered. "Every morning upon rousing, I hear Papa singing in his deep baritone and smell Mama's cinnamon bread baking. And those are just the beginning of the memories that keep me hopeful, Georgie. I do not wish to leave, but staying is *not* the easiest path. The money Papa left us is gone, and we have been terribly worried now for more than a year. It is a *dreadful* struggle, and I see the strain on you."

"Taking the easier path is not always the best," she replied, repeating a lesson their father often imparted. "Aunt Thomasina means well, but I cannot guarantee that we will find husbands to secure our futures when we have so little to recommend us. It is better she provides us with the money to live instead of spending it on pretty dresses in the hopes a gentleman would make us an offer."

A soft longing opened inside Georgianna. "Though I confess it, should you or I ever get the chance to marry, Lizzie, it should only be for love...very much like what Mama and Papa shared. Surely nothing less would do."

Her sister rested her head on Georgianna's shoulders. "I just hate that you are not happy."

Alarmed, she stiffened her spine. "Why do you speak with such certainty that I am unhappy?"

Her sister sighed. "You only live to take care of us, Georgie. I never hear you speak of wants and wishes for yourself. At times I simply find it...sad."

"Do you not think contentment can be found in doing one's duty?" she clipped, feeling a perplexing sense of hurt. "Do not be dismissive of how much I love you and our sisters, Lizzie!"

"I am not dismissive," she cried. "I…I just want you to be *happy*. A husband…children…" A spasm of pain crossed Lizzie's features, and she looked away.

A lump rose in Georgianna's throat. "I am sorry. I do understand more than you know. You wish for a family…a husband to call your own, possible Mr. Hayle?"

She gasped, her hands rushing to her cheeks. "Am I so obvious in my tendre?"

"Only because I know you well, and you look at him with…hunger."

A pretty flush rose in her cheeks, and she groaned. "In church?"

Georgianna smiled gently. "It was at Mr. Tonkin's picnic last Saturday."

Lizzie once again groaned in a rather dramatic fashion, her teeth sinking into her plump lower lip. "I do admire him so, Georgianna. But he does not notice me."

"Mr. Hayle admires you. He is also simply aware that you have no dowry and little connections. He has rather bold ambitions and must think about such things."

Her sister flinched. "Must you be so…so *honest*?"

"I must, Lizzie, so you may understand my hope for you and all of us. Should I become sought after by the lord and ladies of the *haut ton*, imagine the possibilities of how much I could charge to prepare my meals at their balls, garden parties, or scandalous gatherings on their boats and yachts. I could then provide a respectful dowry for you, Sarah, and Anna. And if any of my sisters chose not to marry, I can invest in whatever dreams rest in your hearts."

Lizzie appeared contemplative for several moments. "Did our aunt mention what dowry she would provide should we go to Kent and then London with her?"

"No," Georgianna said, a forlorn sigh slipping from her. "If there is any dowry to settle on us, it will be small. Aunt is hoping for matches for you and me based on the strength of her meagre connections."

Lizzie dropped her face into her palm, a fine tension invading her body.

Georgianna reassuringly touched her shoulders. "I will work, and we will save as much money as we can and make the way for our own futures."

"I—"

"The world is changing, Lizzie. Even in some parts of Europe, ladies are now able to own property, and may open bank accounts without needing their fathers' or husbands' permission. You will continue writing your children's stories. I do believe one day you will be published and under your name, not a pseudonym. We shall be the renowned Heyford sisters because of our wit and skills, much like the Brontë sisters."

Lizzie laughed wistfully, yet a determined gleam brightened her gaze. "Only you would believe it to be possible, Georgie."

"I daresay one day, my name will be on the tongues of many, my food will live in their hearts and invade their dreams. I will build us a fortune through my cooking and even write a book of my own or several. I shall be more renowned than Charles Elmé Francatelli," she said, waving her hand toward his book, *The Modern Cook*, that rested on the large, scarred oak table.

Lizzie's eyes twinkled. "You wish to be more renowned than Mr. Francatelli? Is *that* only your ambition?" She narrowed her gaze. "I am more worried that should you become entangled with the earl, you will become famous like the actress who scandalizes London with rumors of an *affair de coeur* with the Prince of Wales and also an earl!"

"Given the dazzling allure of the *haut ton*, one can understand how she had gotten caught up with a few powerful noblemen."

The prince's rumored mistress hadn't bemoaned the smears on her reputation but had delighted in living life in a manner that made her happy. Georgianna thought she was a lady to be admired, not to be used as a cautionary tale.

Lizzie smiled, and Georgianna was happy to see some of the tension eased from her sister.

"Oh, please promise me you will be very careful. I worry terribly that in accepting the earl's offer, you put yourself at awful risk, dancing so close to the allure of the *haut ton*. Aunt Thomasina did warn us that there is a sort of mesmerizing quality of beauty to that world of extravagance and glamour which has led to many ruinations."

"I will not be tempted by the likes of Lord Stannis, his wealth, or his rumored devastating charm. Now, I believe I can become a superb cook and improve our fortunes, Lizzie... Do you believe I can?"

Her sister turned to face her fully, her expression thoughtful. "I do. You are a wonderful chef and so *incredibly* creative."

Georgianna smiled, her heart squeezing with relief. "Thank you, Lizzie."

Her sister wrinkled her nose. "There is a small part of me that wishes I could be with you aboard the earl's yacht. I can imagine the sleek lines as it cuts and bobs across the surface of the water, hear the strains of the violins as the waltz is played by the deck, hear the laughter of the guests, and taste the champagne and the wonderful food you'll prepare. Imagine it, a grand ball atop the water with the night sky your canopy. And the gowns the ladies will wear, oh, I am most certain they will be astonishing!"

Excitement sizzled in Georgianna's veins. "You could come with me, Lizzie."

"Willingly enter the scoundrel's debauched den? My dear Georgianna, even with my whimsical and oftentimes reckless heart, I am not *that* foolish."

Laughing at her sister's tartness, she tried to ignore the sudden erratic pounding of her heart, reminding herself that she had nothing to fear, especially not a reputation that might not be true.

How truly wicked could one gentleman be?

Simply rubbish, and it has nothing whatsoever to do with me.

Yet somehow, Georgianna could not dismiss the nerves that seemed to slowly unspool inside her belly.

CHAPTER TWO

This is what it is like living a life of wealth, power, and luxury, Georgianna mused from the section of the large deck where she hovered, in the shadows and away from probing eyes. Or more like hid, since she should be below decks in the large and very lush galley area with the rest of the kitchen staff.

Despite the voice of pragmatism that usually directed her course, somehow she had not been able to deny herself a quick peek above deck. The yacht had taken her breath with its beauty and size when she boarded a few hours earlier in Dover. Mr. Burnell had proudly informed her the ship was a cutter and had been built a few years previously on the River Clyde to order by the by the Earl of Stannis.

Georgianna was stunned by its magnificence. The sailors wore an especially designed livery in navy and gray and had carried her luggage on board and shown her to a small but tastefully decorated cabin. The sailing boat had a central mast but had several sails which would enable the boat to tack more closely to the shore for safety and allow it to make use of the slightest winds.

"Oh, I must hurry and return to the galley," she said with a wistful sigh, not wanting to leave. The night was simply decadent.

Surely, she had been standing here for at least fifteen minutes, watching the whirl and glitter of the *haut ton* as they had fun aboard the luxurious yacht as it bobbed on the churning waters. The itinerary of the trip had not been something that the ship's crew had deigned to inform her of, but it seemed that they had sailed down the channel and the distant lights were on the coast of Guernsey. They stopped briefly there, and a small boat had rowed out and delivered various interesting ingredients, among them lobsters, langoustine, cheeses, and many other foods that Georgianna had never had the opportunity to cook with before and now greatly anticipated the challenge of preparing some exquisite meals.

She had swiftly directed her staff to tidy everything away and changed the evening menu to include the most perishable items. Several crates of wine also came on board, but the champagne had been carefully placed in a specially padded contraption and lowered into the chilly water of La Manche or, as she knew it, the English Channel. There was no ice room in the yacht, and so making ices and sorbets would not be possible.

"Oh!" she heard from below her. "Lord Ferguson, do put me down!"

The squeal had her tipping onto her toes to watch a gentleman holding a lady off her feet... and good heavens, the man was kissing her mouth rather passionately. Such a wanton display seemed to be the norm here, though, for no one appeared shocked.

Georgianna observed that almost all the ladies were dressed scandalously with a few in costumes, yet they were also elegant and so graceful. Some wore elaborate wigs and filigree masks while others were not afraid to reveal their identities as they basked in the lush ambience and luxury of the boat. The air was brisk, the wind chilled; however, the ladies and gentlemen laughed, danced, and twirled as if they were ensconced in a London ballroom.

Roped lantern lights hung suspended about their heads, and a string quartet played the waltz or some version of it that allowed the guests to dance outrageously close. No one seemed bothered by the slight motion of the ship as it cut through a surprisingly calm sea. The dancers' bodies swayed together with no respectable distance between them, and a few even recklessly pressed their mouths together. Seeing such eager wantonness did not repulse Georgianna but sent a swirl of longing in her belly and sizzling through her veins.

Once I make a choice to venture down a particular path, I cannot long for the other…

Wrenching her gaze from the dancing belles, she tracked the footmen as they deftly wended their way through the crowd with silver serving platters of her delicacies for the earl's guests' consumption. She watched their expression as they bit into a tart, lobster patties, her spice rum cake, or the shrimp canapés. Lashes fluttered, moans whispered in the air, and food took on the consequence of a sensual delight.

She bit into her lower lip to stop the laugh of happiness from coming out. Their enjoyment and surprise made her want to dance and hug herself, and a few nearby whispering "*compliments to the chef*" sent her heart soaring.

Georgianna had to find a way to capitalize on tonight's success. A peculiar feeling prickled along her skin, as if someone stared at her. Silly, of course, since one could not *feel* a gaze. She scanned the crowd, stilling on a gentleman standing by the bow spit of the yacht, the wind at his back, staring…at *her*.

Her heart lurched. Georgianna held herself still under that unswerving regard. There was no doubt it was she he pinned with that hawk-like stare. Tall, with broad shoulders, he was most outrageously staring.

In the light of the lanterns, she could see his hair, which was ruffled by the slight breeze, was a dark blond and his face classically handsome. However, his most devastating features were his piercing emerald green eyes. Perhaps if he hadn't seemed so enigmatic garbed in black trousers and jacket with only a silver waistcoat to soften the dark image, perhaps if he hadn't watched her too intently and uncaring of its scandalous nature, she could have successfully wrenched her attention away. The stranger drew deep on his cheroot, slowly releasing the smoke, studying her with an air of jaded insouciance.

Why do you stare?

A small, questioning frown split those dark, winged brows, and then his lips quirked. A very small smile, but it was laced with provocative carnality. For a moment, she lost her breath at the wild dip in her belly. Georgianna drew back more into the shadows, grateful that only a crescent moon hung in the velveted night sky, yet this stranger's stare did not falter. His gaze slid across her features, probing and curious. Then wandered down to take in the curves of her figure, which she had taken so much trouble to suppress. Her plain and all-covering gown did much to discourage male attention, but it could not disguise her tiny waist or lessen the prominence of her breasts.

His gaze lingered, and she gripped her clasped hands until her fingers ached.

Oh, do look away, Georgianna!

A lady clad in a vibrant red gown with a revealing decolletage flung herself into the gentleman's arms. He slowly shifted his regard to her, and Georgianna let out a slow breath. Feeling as if she had been unchained, she turned and fled the upper deck, down the stairs, and to the galley where she was meant to exist.

A young footman stomped down the stairs, irritation lining his expression. "There has been a request for food not on the menu. From my lord's lady herself and to be delivered to the master cabin post haste."

This was said with a bit of irritation, as the mistress of the earl had developed a reputation with the staff of being almost impossible to please.

Georgianna held out her hand for the list, breathing a sigh of relief that they were simple yet elegant dishes—smoked salmon and cucumber cups were easy enough, as were caramelized mushroom tartlets, and though the crab tartines would take a little longer to cook, they were all possible to quickly prepare. "I will have everything ready within the hour. Keep serving the strawberry tarts, spice rum cake, and shrimp canapés."

The friendly, talented, and supportive staff went to work while she pulled on her apron, set her chef's hat atop her head, and hurried to make the earl's mistress her canapes, dismissing the way her heart had raced from that unknown gentleman's provocative regard.

• • •

"Oh, Stannis, how *delightful* it has been. I declare you could not have prepared a better gift for me. *Everyone* will speak about this birthday ball aboard your yacht for months…I daresay years!" Lady Johanna Wimpole squealed, rushing over to drop her delicate weight into Daniel's lap.

"Even Duke Beswick complimented my

jewelry, and you know that handsome devil hardly gives out anything as nice as *these*."

Johanna watched his expression, no doubt seeking to flatter her vanity by any show of jealousy and possessiveness on his part. As Daniel did not rise to her lure, she pouted prettily and touched the diamond necklace clasped around her throat.

"Your taste is impeccable as always, my darling; of course the duke could not help admiring me...and the necklace. His Grace even danced with me twice."

"You are beautiful. He could not help it, of course," Daniel murmured, pressing a kiss to the side of her throat, nipping the soft flesh above her pulse.

His lover obligingly arched her slender neck, sighing her pleasure and squirming to get closer to him. "I cannot tarry," he murmured fondly. "I have business to attend."

She swatted his shoulder teasingly. "Now, Daniel, never say it is truly so! Not after the most exciting ending I've planned for us."

He shifted her weight, easing her from his lap. "I've investment opportunities to discuss with Beswick and Moncrieff."

His friends were awaiting his presence before the discussion started, and even if some derided his illicit pursuits and the exorbitant way Daniel spent money, he never placed pleasure before his business interests. Despite all the gossip about him, that was a fact only those close to him knew about. After being his lover for almost a year, this was something Johanna should know.

"Surely it can wait," she said, tossing her mane of blond hair and peeking at him from below her thick, long lashes. "The duke was very occupied when I came down, and the marquess mentioned the meeting is in the morning!"

"I have some market reports to read," he said, amused with her pouting.

"It is *barely* after midnight, and the guests are still dancing under the stars. I wanted you to take me into your arms for every dance, and you've already disappointed me there."

"Have some pity for my feet," he drawled. "You knew my limit was one dance."

Johanna trailed a perfectly manicured finger across his jawline. "You'll miss out on the treat I planned for you. It is *very* wicked."

"Oh?" Daniel said, noting the sultriness of her tone and the gleam in her light blue eyes.

She pressed her mouth close to his ear. "Lady Bonnie and Lady Delilah will join us soon."

His cock, which had been wrung dry by his lover's delightful mouth only a few hours earlier, twitched. "You have my attention, my sweet."

His lover giggled, the sound airy and twinkling. "Will I have it for the night?"

"An hour at most."

She sighed but slinked off his lap. "I know your appetite, my darling. I shall have no less than two hours."

Though he smiled, Daniel made no commitment, watching her with lazy, carnal intent. She sashayed toward the door, knowing his eyes would follow the provocative sway of her lush rump.

Johanna glanced over her shoulder, her lips quirking. "I have ordered the chef to send up some of those titbits that you like with a decanter of whiskey. You must positively try some spiced cake, which is all the rage with our guests. I'm told the secret ingredient is rum. I will…summon my ladies. Await us on the bed…preferably naked."

Daniel lifted a brow, and she tossed him a grin before sauntering from the room, deliberately rolling her hips. He smiled, fond of her antics, the cutting tongue, and the intelligence she often used to flay those who displeased her. Daniel stood and started to remove his clothes, anticipation curling through him at the sexual play he envisioned. He wondered which of his guests were Lady Delilah and Lady Bonnie. Perhaps all stage names or they were some of the elite ladies of the *haut ton* who chose to wear a masquerade mask aboard his yacht for the few days of fun and decadence.

Casually dropping his clothes on the ground, he made his way to the private bath area that had been installed with a convenient shower. He turned the knob and stepped under the spray of the icy water. The music and the laughter drifted through the wood-paneled walls from a nearby cabin, along with a squeal of delight, then a muffled moan. A smile tipped Daniel's mouth as he imagined the nature of that sound and what the scandal rags would print in a few days, given that he seemed to be one of their favorite subjects to speculate on and dissect.

Slicking the soap off his skin, he closed his eyes, staying under the water even as his flesh grew numb, cleaning the sweat of the day and the myriad perfumes from his body. The thoughts of his duties once he returned to town rose in the forefront of his mind. His grandmother's birthday was in only a few weeks—or Nana as he fondly called her. She was one of his greatest loves, and while he could not give her what she had been demanding of late, great-grandchildren to dote on, Daniel wanted to plan a birthday celebration that would please her—the best food, a private operatic performance, élite guests, and perhaps even dance with the lady she had been implying would be perfect to be his countess.

A hiss of annoyance left him whenever he thought about the incessant push from his nana and mother to select a bride soon. It befuddled him that they found it so necessary for him to select a wife at eight and twenty. Daniel would not rush into matrimony because it was expected but planned to enjoy his bachelorhood without remonstrances and knowing his duty would see himself settled by forty.

Not a damn year earlier.

A sound whispered in the air and cut through

the amalgamation of noise. Stepping from the bath, he plucked a thick, white towel from the hanging peg, dried most of the water from his body, and wrapped another towel around his waist before padding toward the room, oddly uneager to meet the ladies his lover had chosen to join them in the bed play.

Daniel suspected Johanna had felt his boredom of late and deduced a more sensual pursuit would perhaps relieve him of his current dissonance. He frowned, for the odd feeling upon him was deeper than boredom… It felt like there was a hole inside of him that was unknown to his senses and waiting to be filled with something… *anything*. Earlier surrounded by the lavish thrills of the party on deck, he had felt alone, uninspired by the glitter and decadence, unable to see the bright lights and colors when everything felt obscured in shadows. He couldn't quite place his finger on when or why they had become less exciting and less satisfying to him. Daniel had silently chuckled at the notion, truly wondering if he suffered from *ennui*.

Perhaps Johanna had the right of it and a night of sensual debauchery and fucking was what he needed. As Daniel ventured farther into the room, he faltered at the sight of a lady balancing a tray of canapés, roasted duck topped with cranberry sauce, and the spice rum cake his guests seemed to love. She placed the tray on the rosewood table near the small stove that heated his quarters before glancing around the lush decor of the cabin.

It is her.

The lady from earlier who had watched those on the deck with an acute stare of longing. It was quite astonishing, the way she captured his regard. A soft tendril of sweat-soaked hair clung to her forehead and flushed cheeks. Her high-necked, dark blue dress was not the most fashionable, but she moved gracefully, like a lady. Her voluptuous figure enthralled him, but now that he could see her face more clearly, he realized her skin was flawless, despite being slightly flushed with her exertion. Her hair, which had been restrained into a plain chignon, was auburn with redder streaks where it had been bleached by the sun. She boldly wore no mask, and her prettiness struck his heart with surprising force. There was a strength of character in her face that was…incredibly pretty if not rousingly beautiful.

"Which are you…Delilah or Bonnie?"

She whirled to face him fully, her hand fluttering to her throat. "You!"

She recognized him. Her eyes were the finest golden brown, very much like the whiskey she held before her in the crystal decanter.

"You are naked!" she gasped, setting down the decanter on the table.

Those eyes, which held a feline slant, widened, slowly caressing over his naked chest, lingering at the knot tied low at his belly. Something about that stare that seemed so innocently fascinated roused his cock with alarming swiftness.

A strangled yelp emitted from her throat at the evidence of his cock stand. He chuckled, the sound low and rough with his increasing desire. She snapped her gaze up from his waist, and her lips parted, but nothing seemed to emerge. Her skin flushed a gentle pink, and her eyes glittered with arousing awareness.

Ah… you like what you see, too.

Daniel found her evident attraction to his body appealing. He prowled over, amused when she retreated a couple of steps until her back was flush against the cabin wall. Her cheeks pinkened even further as she watched his approach.

"Do you like being chased?" he murmured, curious at the type of bed play she liked to indulge in.

God, he hoped it was the wicked, debauched type. A sweet, lush body like hers was made for carnal pleasure, and those pouting lips provoked wanton images of them stretched around his cock.

"Chased?" she croaked, licking her lips.

That swipe had not been a beguiling tease, yet his cock throbbed in a way that felt…new. Daniel ruthlessly buried all traces of arousal, slowly calming the racing of his heart to its normal rhythm.

Who are you?

He braced one of his hands over her head and lightly and gently encircled her throat with his other hand, feathering his thumb over her racing pulse. Daniel tipped her chin upward so he could stare into her eyes. "Yes. What kind of bed sport do you like? Do you like being chased…hunted …tossed over my shoulders, then dropped on the bed and tupped hard? Or do you like it tender and deep…a slow, seductive game of cat and mouse? Your pleasure is mine to satiate tonight, so tell me what you want, and I promise it will be yours."

CHAPTER THREE

Her heart was beating so fiercely, it took Georgianna several moments to gather her composure, and equanimity still eluded her. *Chased? Hunted? Slow and deep?* Good heavens! For the first time in her three and twenty years, she felt faint. Her sister would laugh, considering Georgianna had bragged about her stern fortitude against handsome rakes upon departing Crandell.

Worse, the sensual promise that whatever she wanted tonight would be given hit her low inside her belly, stirring bewildering heat. Her pulse skittered alarmingly as peculiar sensations crashed over her senses. Georgianna needed to step away from his maddening closeness. Perhaps then she could slow her heartbeat and suppress the powerful attraction to his handsomeness.

At her silence, his eyebrows raised inquiringly.

"I only need for you to…" she started to say, then the hand provocatively clasping her throat moved, urging her closer even as his head dipped, and he caught her mouth with his.

Georgianna gripped his shoulders and moaned, the sound muffled against his ravishing mouth. His tongue flicked teasingly against her lips, and she curled her toes into her shoes, alarmed at the throb of heat spearing directly between her thighs to her sex. The sensation made her want to squirm and tighten her legs against it.

His hand slid beneath her hair, cupped the side of her neck, and held her in the most tender yet sensual clasp she had ever known as his lips moved over hers with ruthless persuasion. The delightful shock of his embrace made her gasp, and when a whimper of surrender left her mouth, his groan of approval vibrated from him to her.

Mr. Johnson, a local gentleman in Crandell who made some effort to woo her last year, had stolen a kiss before...perhaps even two. Georgianna knew what a kiss was...and this, with this stranger, was not it. He...he sucked her down into feelings that she had never imagined could be found in an illicit embrace. His tongue glided against hers, and the hand braced above her head had somehow reached around her waist and tugged her against his chest.

He was all but lifting her against his body with a strength that was wonderfully rousing. His height and breadth made her feel entirely too feminine and achy. Georgianna gasped when his hips thrust forward, the thick proof of his reaction almost alarming.

He nipped at her lower lip. For a wild moment, she was rendered breathless, then she started to kiss him back, swept away by the curious heat whispering over her flesh to burrow deep beneath her skin.

She wrapped her hands around his neck,

holding him to her as he seduced her mouth with devastating thoroughness. He gripped her hips, lifted her weight with easy grace, and padded over to the bed, where he dropped her onto the mattress, his weight coming down on her. Holding her hips, he molded her curves to the powerful contours of his body.

Oh God.

"Slow and deep it will be," he murmured against her lips. "But first I am going to lick and tease your pussy until you scream and unravel," he added in a lower, huskier tone.

It felt like fire dropped into her belly at the rough, carnal promise. *What is my pussy?* Even without knowing full well of what he promised, a hot, devasting hunger surged through her body.

He pushed from the bed, unknotting the towel at his waist so it fell to the ground in a soft whisper.

The thick sight of his manhood almost strangled her breath. "Sir!" she gasped, desperately looking above his navel. Georgianna scrambled to her knees. "Wait…I…*good lord!*"

She had never seen a naked man before. And he was… *Oh, my heavens, he is splendid and dangerously virile!*

"Bonnie…or is it Delilah?" he drawled, prowling closer, every languid step revealing a man confident in his raw masculine appeal and sensuality.

"You do not even know who I am," she gasped,

shock stiffening every line of her body. She slammed her eyes shut. *Of course he would not who I am, and how mortifying that he should make me feel so much and easily fall for his wicked ravishment!*

She throbbed and ached everywhere, but especially in that secret place between her legs. Georgianna was repulsed by the ease of her ensnarement and captivated by the whispers of pleasure that still wreaked havoc with her body. The duality of those feelings clashed through her with awful force. She rushed from the bed, almost stumbling in her haste. "I am not who you think I am, sir, I—"

The door opened, the tinkling laughter following that sound abruptly stopping. "*Daniel!*"

That cry pulled a groan of distress from Georgianna's throat.

Oh, please, this is not happening.

How could she have allowed herself to be swept away by a kiss from a stranger? The gentleman glanced over his shoulder at the three ladies who stood in the doorway in sheer peignoirs that revealed more than they covered. Then he looked back at her, his eyes gleaming with dark humor.

He pressed a palm to his chest, unabashed that he was naked before so many.

"A case of mistaken identity, I see. A pity you are not whom I believed you to be."

Someone sucked in a harsh breath at his evident regret. That lady Georgianna recognized as

Viscountess Johanna Wimpole, and suddenly she knew that this man…who had watched her from the shadows of the deck earlier and now almost ravished her, was the Earl of Stannis.

Oh God.

Her sister's warning echoed in her thoughts.

"He is a rake, a despoiler of innocents, and ladies even knowing this seem to willingly fall at the man's feet. It is most absurd!"

"I…my lord…I…" Georgianna's throat closed over the words bubbling inside. What was she to say? The situation was mortifying.

Lady Wimpole rushed forward; her hand lifted to slap Georgianna. The earl grabbed that slim hand in an implacable clasp, the humor leaking from his eyes, an indifferent expression settling on his face.

"What do you think you are doing?" he asked with chilling civility.

The dangerous softness to his tone caused her heart to lurch, though his question was not directed at her. She belatedly realized he had stopped his mistress from assaulting her, but Georgianna could offer no words of gratitude. She only wanted to escape this embarrassing situation.

"Who is she and why do you defend her?" the viscountess gasped, pretty tears pooling in her eyes. "Am I not allowed to vent my anger on this upstart?"

"If you had slapped her, I would have repaid you in kind for your meanness," the earl said, his voice soft yet edged with steel.

The shock of those words settled into the room, and the viscountess stared up at him with large eyes.

"Leave," he clipped without looking at her, still holding his mistress's gaze.

Georgianna did not wait to see any more but skirted around them and the two ladies who still hovered in the doorway. Rushing from the cabin, she realized he had planned a tryst with three ladies at once.

The wicked libertine!

And to think she had acted against her good senses and allowed such liberties. Mortification burning through her, she hastened to the other side of the yacht where the staff cabins were located. Thankfully she had been given a small berth to herself, and she went inside, closed the door, and leaned against it. Georgianna lifted shaking fingers to her lips. They were tender...and still tasted like whiskey and strawberries and something else unknown to her senses.

Closing her eyes, she sagged against the door, her frantic thoughts rushing over themselves. Perhaps this was not the disaster she perceived. Neither the viscountess nor the earl knew who she was. She was just another face in the crowd, and there were dozens of guests aboard, all set to disembark back at Dover in a few hours before continuing onward to the southside of France on the following day.

Oh, why had she been the one to take the tray up when the serving girl assigned to the task complained? Tucking a strand of hair behind her ear, Georgianna took a deep breath and went back outside. The party was not over, and though she trusted the staff would follow her instructions to the letter, she could not be careless with her ambitions and hope.

As I was just now.

Brushing aside the fatalistic thought, Georgianna hurried down to the kitchen galley, hoping the earl and his three ladies would be so enamored with their carnal pursuits, they would not give another thought to her. It was only a wretched pity she would not forget him and his illicit embrace any time soon.

. . .

The following morning, after only a few hours of restless sleep, Georgianna stared at Mr. Burnell as if she had never seen him before. "I beg your pardon?" she whispered, feeling sick.

The portly man sighed and fixed his spectacles atop his nose. "Your services are no longer needed for the rest of the journey, Miss Heyford. Please do not allow me to unnecessarily repeat myself."

"I...I am being replaced?"

He lifted a brow in evident censure. "You are being fired, by order of the earl."

She lowered the knife to the counter, aware of the silence in the galley and that the rest of the staff was careful not to look in her direction. The man had not had the decency to terminate her services in private. "I do not know what to say."

"Nothing is required, Miss Heyford, only your compliance."

He handed her an envelope, and she took it with unsteady hands. Georgianna peered at the contents with incomprehension. "There is a twenty-pound bank note here, Mr. Burnell," she said, struggling to maintain an even tone.

"Yes, Miss Heyford, your wages."

A startled laugh escaped her before she tightened her lips. "The agreed sum was three hundred pounds!"

"For three days of service. You are relieved only after one," he said condescendingly.

"One day service would ensure me a sum of one hundred pounds, sir."

"I merely do my lord's bidding," he said stiffly before walking away.

She fisted her hand at her side, staring at his back. Anger burned through her in fiery waves. Lord Stannis had been the one to kiss her, and for his liberties she should be relieved of her post and deprived of money that she had worked so hard for? Money that her family needed!

How dare he!

Fuming that she had been ensnared in his sensual thrall for even a second, Georgianna ripped off her apron and tossed it into the corner, then marched from the galley, going to the cabin she had left only a few hours ago. She knocked and waited for several moments, frustrated tears burning behind her eyes. The door opened, and the earl framed the doorway.

Recognition and an indefinable emotion flashed in the dark beauty of his green eyes, and he emitted a low sound, one of relief and perhaps pleasure.

"You're here," he said with such satisfaction, she could only stare. "To think I had doubt he would find you."

Georgianna spluttered when he snaked his hand around her waist, tugged her inside the cabin, and claimed her mouth in a kiss that felt wild and hungry and so very desperate. It lasted only for a brief moment, yet the fiery sensations he so quickly and mercilessly evoked shook her. Her nipples immediately felt taut and tender, and there was a tightening low down in her belly. Temptation to lean into his kiss and allow him to have his wicked way with her beat at Georgianna's senses.

"God, the taste of you kept me awake," he said against the corner of her mouth.

She turned her head slightly, bit hard into his bottom lip, satisfaction surging through her when he hissed in pain. He released her, and she drew back, folding her arms and narrowing her gaze on him.

"Should you kiss me again, I will not hesitate to slap you over the head with my skillet, you vainglorious wretch!"

Humor leaped into his eyes, though he did retreat a few steps. "Why do I find your fieriness so appealing?"

She gasped. "You are a right rogue! I have never encountered the like!"

He dipped into a most charming half bow. "Forgive my eagerness. I am not normally so... unrefined when it comes to these matters. I will do better, hmm?"

Do better? "There will be no more opportunity for you to do so!"

An arrogant brow lifted. "Come now, did you not enjoy it?"

"Not enough to repeat the experience," she said tartly.

His lips tugged, and that look in his eyes gleamed even brighter. "I am wounded," he said drolly, pressing a hand over his chest. "I was hoping the reason you are here is because the maddening want was mutual. Was I truly mistaken?"

"Yes!"

A frown flickered over his face. "Are you not here because you received my invitation to drink with me in my cabin?"

Good heavens! "No."

He stiffened, then bowed deeply. "I can only beg for forgiveness."

Her chest heaved with the force of her emotions, and she narrowed her gaze, recalling his words upon seeing her. Was that why he had kissed her so just now? He thought she had sought him out to continue…to continue their supposed madness? "No one found me and relayed an invitation for a dalliance. Even if someone had, I would have rejected it, my lord. The only matter between us, Lord Stannis, is what is owed to me. I respectfully demand the remainder of my wages."

"Your *wages*?" That brow lifted again, and his gaze swept over her in a searching glance. "Who are you really?"

Georgianna took a deep breath. "I…I am the chef aboard your yacht! I have labored for several hours, providing *excellent* food and service for your…your lady love and your guests. Now that my services are being prematurely dismissed, Mr. Burrell is declining to pay the balance owed to me as per your orders, my lord. The balance owed is eighty pounds!"

That admission seemed to render him silent. "The *chef*?"

She offered him a tight smile. "Yes, the head chef, my lord."

For a moment, he appeared shocked, then the earl's expression became inscrutable. "Ah…now I understand why I was unable to find you last night."

The implications that he had searched for

Georgianna without knowing her identity and role on his ship sent her heart hammering. "You searched for me to…"

His expression veiled even further, and a rueful smile tugged at the corner of his mouth. "That I did, like a fool."

Georgianna shook her head, aghast. "The rumors *are* true, and even knowing of them I am amazed at your audacity and capacity for licentiousness. You clearly planned a dalliance with those ladies, *three* of them, and even after, you were not satisfied but thought…but thought that I…"

"Everyone was dismissed from my cabin minutes after you departed," he said coolly, turning away from her to attend to a stack of letters. "However, it does not matter. You are indeed dismissed."

Georgianna fisted her hands at her side. "*Why?*"

He continued in an indifferent tone, without looking up from the correspondence he shifted through. "We are close to Dover. Mr. Burnell will take a small boat and escort you to shore. He will ensure you travel home in a private compartment on the train or a carriage if you prefer."

She took a halting step forward, almost rattled by the change in the earl. His far too alluring mask of sensuality had vanished, and in his place stood a man of refined elegance and chilling civility.

Georgianna chose her words carefully. "What I would prefer, my lord, is that I do the job I was hired for and that I be paid the sum promised."

"Denied."

His polite indifference rankled her. "If you would be so gracious as to inform me of the reason, my lord."

He stilled, before shifting to face her. "My... good friend does not like your food, it seems. A rash appeared on her face this morning, and she spent the night casting up her accounts. The food was tainted."

Shocked concern curled through her. "Is she well? There have been no complaints, my lord. I would have been told."

His gaze hooded. "This was the only case."

Outrage sizzled through Georgianna's veins as awareness dawned. "There was nothing wrong with my food, my lord. Your good friend," she cried furiously, "did not like that you were kissing me, an embrace I did not invite but which was tossed upon me because of *you* mistaking my reason for being in your cabin!"

Her chest heaved with the force of her feelings, and she had to take a deep breath to steady herself. Being rash and angry would not solve anything. "Please remit the money owed. Preferably the three hundred pounds promised, as I am being relieved through no fault of mine, my lord."

I need it...please. Yet her pride would not allow

her to voice that last thought.

He lifted a brow. "Your services are exorbitant, and surely you do not expect to be compensated when the very person you were supposed to please with your skills has suffered deleterious ill effects?"

"If your good friend is still feeling poorly and casting up her accounts, I assure you it was not because of anything I cooked, my lord. As for the money owed, it was agreed upon before I stepped onto your vessel, and I daresay I am worth *every* pound."

"My good friend was the one who in truth needed your services, and it was that sum she determined you were to be paid, Miss Heyford."

"The feast and service I delivered last night are worth more than a third of the money promised," she snapped, fisting her hands at her side. "Even you were in raptures when you took the first bite of my prawns in tartare sauce. I'd even go as far as to say your expression was salacious."

His gaze unexpectedly gleamed. "Ah, you were watching me. This knowledge pleases me."

Even now, the man was indecently charming. Ignoring the fluttering in her stomach, she fisted a hand on her hip. "I do not care what pleases you," Georgianna said frostily. "Only that you remit to me the money owed, my lord."

His gaze narrowed thoughtfully on her. "I do believe that was a genuine statement. How refreshing. You are…different."

Georgianna was all too aware of her rarity in this world, a lady who was not falling over herself in awe of his wealth and handsomeness. She narrowed her gaze, for while she could admit that he was devilishly handsome and her heart had done that silly little skip, it meant nothing. She had a similar reaction when she ate braised pork in peppered sauce. "I was watching *everyone's* reception to the first bite of my food. It is what any reputable chef does."

"What was Lord Pendley's expression?"

She blinked. "*Who?*"

"He has a stiff upper mustache and dark red hair. He was standing beside me for most of the night."

Georgianna could only stare at the earl with a measure of bemusement. The earl's dark chuckle washed over her in an alarming surge of heat.

"My lord, I—"

"You'll depart with Mr. Burnell within the hour, Miss Heyford. There is no room for negotiation. Now you may leave my cabin."

How indifferent he sounded, his bearing growing austere and powerfully intimidating. As if he had not just ruined everything she had been hoping to accomplish.

Panic gripped her chest, squeezing, and for several moments Georgianna felt as if she couldn't breathe. "My lord, please—"

"Out."

The command snapped through the small space with chilly authority. Georgianna could see there would be no reasoning with the earl. Tears burned in the back of her eyes, and she stared at him, breathing rapidly, before clenching her fists and stalking from the cabin. Once in the passageway, she paused.

That arrogant, self-absorbed…

Georgianna slammed her eyes closed, pressing the heel of her palm against her forehead. Her family needed that money, and because of her temper, she had lost the opportunity to bargain for an income that would have seen them comfortably secure for a year or more. The awareness of it almost shattered her heart. Hot tears coursed down her cheeks, and she took several ragged breaths.

No, I lost it because those aristocratic nobs are selfish and indifferent to others' pain and hard work. And why not, when everything they have in life is handed to them?

That terrible feeling of despair once again settled like an immovable anvil on her shoulders.

Oh God, what do I do now?

CHAPTER FOUR

"Why are you not in my bed, darling?"

Daniel stared at the churning waters for a few more moments before turning to face his lover. He'd ventured onto the upper deck for the last hour, content with watching the stars and dark beauty of the water while he mulled over business matters. Daniel leaned against the taffrail, liking the feel of the wind against his shoulders. "I am preoccupied."

Johanna arched a brow and sensually sauntered closer. She peered into the water for a few beats before lifting her regard to his. "What could possibly be more important than being with me at this time of the night? It is after midnight, my lord."

He bit back his amusement, knowing it would prick her vanity. "It is best you return to your cabin. I am…" *Restless*. Yet Daniel could not find it in himself to admit this to her, especially as he did not understand the malady plaguing him.

"Is it because of her?" she demanded tightly.

He lifted a brow. "Who?"

Johanna fisted a hand on her hip. "You know who I speak of. I had such wonderful adventures planned for you last night, and you dismissed me from your cabin. My friends were mortified! You have made no effort to make it up to us as yet."

He considered the pique on his lover's face. "I am not interested in sensual pursuit at the moment because two of the factories I recently purchased in Leeds and Manchester are not operating to the standards that would ensure the workers' safety. I am occupied with thinking about the length of time the factories would need to remain closed while the necessary renovations are done, and I am furious I had to inform the manager that workers should still be paid their full wages while they are away from work. This tells me my manager needs to be replaced, yet he has been with my father for years and has a family to support. When I bought those factories, I vowed to make the workers' lives better. When I promise something, I will deliver on it. Those are the matters in my thoughts, Johanna, not tupping."

She searched his expression before stepping closer, resting her hand on his chest. "I understand." Johanna delicately cleared her throat. "There is a matter I need to discuss. I questioned Mr. Burnell if that...that woman is off the yacht. He revealed that you ordered him to remit another two hundred and eighty pounds to that cook! He means to send a draft to her upon docking. I disagree with this! I forbade him to send that draft and that he must wait for an update before he acts. My lord, her food made me deplorably ill and to reward such—"

"You are acting the jealous shrew, Johanna,"

Daniel growled. "I have already fired the lady at your unproven accusation that your food was tainted. Let that be enough to soothe your ire."

Her eyes pooled with tears. "I am not soothed nor satisfied. You have not taken me to bed since...since you met that serving wench!"

"I believe the lady is a chef, and a rather brilliant one," he said drily. "Stop the theatrics, Johanna. They do not suit you. I have already explained I am occupied with business matters and have little time for diversions."

Her chest heaved with the strength of her passions. "We've been lovers for more than a year."

Daniel pinned her with his regard, baffled by her anger. "I am quite aware of the passage of time. Why is this relevant?"

"I know you will eventually get married. It is an inevitable duty for men of your rank and consequences."

An odd sensation moved through his chest. "What are you getting at?"

She curled her fingers into a fist against his chest. "We are good together... Let us marry. Surely you can tell I have the greatest affections for you."

A chill passed through his heart. He stared down at her in bemusement, for he'd believed they had a mutual stance on the idea of marriage. He always ensured his liaisons were with older ladies who were well-versed in discreet affairs with mutual understanding of what they got from each other. Daniel had always avoided those feverishly marriage-minded young ladies, for he had no interest in the marriage mart. There would come a time a man had to honor his duty and traditions, but by God, when that time came, it would be wholly decided by him.

"You are a widow…with freedom and wealth and beauty. Why would you want to marry again?"

She touched his jaw. "It is only for you I would make this sacrifice, my darling."

"It is a sacrifice not needed," he said firmly.

"Why are you so afraid of marriage?"

"It is an imposition and a restraint for someone like me who cherishes the freedom to do as he pleases. While I must eventually marry for the earldom, I have no wish to do so before I am ready."

Her eyes flashed. "And when will that be? Ten years?"

"Perhaps even twenty," he said with chilling politeness. "Marriage is naught but a duty that I will do in time. There is no reason to mention it between us."

"You unfeeling beast!"

"I made you no false promises," he snapped. "You stepped into my path and gladly vied for the position as my lover. I have never treated you unkindly even when your actions were unworthy."

She pouted. "You are talking about that serving girl again; it was not unkind or unworthy for me to ask that you fire her. Would you want me to suffer the humiliation of every time I see her, knowing how much you wanted her? I saw it on your face... I have never seen such hunger for another...not even me, and I hated it!"

Daniel ruthlessly suppressed the visceral memory of the hunger Miss Heyford had roused within his body. It was already in the past, and he was not the kind of man to dwell on events that had no impact on his future.

"I will not ask for your understanding on that matter again, Johanna," he said with icy indifference. "I believed her to be one of the ladies you intended to join in our sensual play. That is no fault of her own but mine. Mr. Burnell will pay the lady in full. I will inform him of this shortly. Do not ever think to counter my command again with my staff. Now, let's put this matter to rest."

With a sinking feeling, he realized it was time to end their dalliance. Now that she had gotten the idea of marriage in her thoughts, Johanna would not relinquish the desire. The sensation in his gut grew colder. If there was one thing he loathed, it was being pressured into marriage, as if it was some sort of holy grail he needed to reach for. A marriage was simply a damn alliance meant to strengthen connections and produce an heir. More importantly, it was a state he would decide on himself, not be manipulated into by a lover *or* his family.

Johanna must have seen the decision in his eyes, for she blanched and jerked back. "No!"

"It is time we part, Johanna," he said. "Our desires are no longer aligned."

Anger and bitter disappointment contorted her features, and with all the fury of a woman rejected, she shoved him.

What the bloody hell! Daniel toppled against the railing, and it was the horror in her eyes and the scream whipped away by the wind which alerted him that he was about to fall overboard. He tried to lurch forward and grip the railing, but the momentum worked against him.

His head struck something, and agony shot through the base of his skull. Before he could wonder at anything, he hit the surface of the water. The cold stabbed Daniel's body like a thousand knives. He tried to swim upward, but his head felt light.

What did I hit?

He tried to move his arms, but the lightheaded sensation sucked him down, the freezing depths of the water pulling deeper into murky darkness. A dark dread suffocated Daniel, filling his lungs, weighing him down like bricks dragging him toward a watery grave, and before he could feel any sense of regret or deeper despair, icy blackness closed over him.

...

Four days had passed since the Earl of Stannis devastated Georgianna's senses with his illicit kiss, fired her from her dream opportunity, and crushed the hope that had been slowly burning inside her chest like a magical ember. Once in the comfort of her bedchamber, all the anger and despair that had traveled back home with her had been released into a healthy bout of weeping that lasted for far too long. It was not in her character to wallow in a state of defeat or melancholy, not when her sisters relied on her steadiness and resilience in the face of adversity. Should they see her crying or in despair, the heavy burden of worry about their futures would also now rest on their shoulders.

Georgianna had spent a few hours pacing the threadbare carpet in her room, desperately seeking another way for herself and her family. It was only at last night's ball held in the town assembly hall, she had subtly mentioned to a few notable members of their society that she had served as head chef for an earl, and he had been very pleased with her food and creativity. Everyone had been inarguably impressed. Georgianna had been very deliberate in mentioning how much the earl himself had complimented her food, and Mrs. Ford had been quite eager to retain her services for the exorbitant sum of fifty pounds.

Untying the string to her bonnet, she hung it on the peg and skirted past their housekeeper, Mrs. Woods, whom they had only been able to retain on two days a week. When their parents had been alive, their manor had been staffed, with

Mrs. Woods full time, a kitchen maid, a cook, and a man of all work. Georgianna almost told Mrs. Woods the good news that she might be able to increase her daily wage but decided to hold her counsel until she calculated their household expenditures for the next four months, at least.

"Good day to ye, Miss Heyford," Mrs. Woods said, pausing in her cheery hum as she polished the banister. "Miss Elizabeth said to inform you that she had taken a walk with the young Mr. Hayle."

"Thank you, Mrs. Woods. I shall walk out to meet them." Hurrying out without donning her bonnet, Georgianna made her way toward the pleasant grove where Lizzie loved to walk.

She saw Lizzie, Sarah, and Mr. Hayle in the distance, and they gaily waved to her.

"Sarah," Georgianna scolded when she noted her sister held a small piglet in her hand, already muddying her gown. "Only yesterday I mended this gown, and look at it now."

Sarah did not appear in the least contrite, and Georgianna almost threatened to roast the piglet her sister adored. Lizzie came forward, her eyes glittering with excitement, a rosy flush on her cheeks, and lips that appeared as if they had been thoroughly kissed. Mr. Hayle doffed his hat and bowed courteously to Georgianna, and she returned his honor by dipping into a simple curtsy.

He was a rather handsome young man, a very good-natured spirit, even if his humor bordered on scandalous. He made Lizzie laugh…and more alarmingly, despite his reluctance to publicly court her, Georgianna could see that her sister was falling hopelessly for his many charms and perhaps had allowed dangerous liberties.

Oh, Lizzie, please take the advice you gave me and be careful!

It was at moments like these Georgianna desperately wished their mother was alive to provide them with her guidance. Her sister leaned forward, lowering her voice conspiratorially.

"Have you heard the news, Georgie?"

Promptly putting aside her own news that she had been eager to share, she asked, "What news?"

"Mr. Hayle called by to inform us a gentleman was found this morning on the shores on the outskirts of Crandell."

"Good heavens! Was he dead?"

Lizzie cast her an aghast stare. "Why must you be so morbid? It is nothing that dire."

"It is grave enough that this man is said to have lost his memory," Mr. Hayle added, his dark gray eyes somber.

Georgianna gasped. "What do you mean, lost his memories?"

Mr. Hayle nodded. "It is what everyone is talking about. That the man has no notion of even his name. Can you imagine it? To open your eyes and not know who you are?"

She shook her head. "It is most astonishing and inconceivable."

"Your cousin has taken him to his house. I presume he told you of it?"

"I've not been into town as yet," she said, curiosity burning inside her chest. Their idyllic village hardly had anything mysterious or exciting happening, so why would anyone wash upon their shores with such a tragic wound?

They spoke some more of this mysterious gentleman and whom he might be before Mr. Hayle took his leave, mounting his horse and riding away. It was her unchecked curiosity that dragged Georgianna's feet, as if they had a will of their own, through the woodlands, to her distant cousin's four-bedroom house at the edge of Crandell Square.

It was a solid house, square and unornamented, which looked like it had stood there for centuries while it was only twenty or thirty years since it had been built. She had known Doctor Albert Parnell, a second cousin, from her mama's side of the family, since she was a small child. He was also their local physician, a very excellent one. On her walk into town, Georgianna had encountered several people, and it was evident Mr. Hayle had spoken the truth. The entire populace of Crandell seemed to know of the mysterious stranger who washed ashore last night and had been taken to Albert's small practice.

He kept his surgery in a small extension that had been built to the rear of the house, with a number of uncomfortable chairs in a lobby that led to the room. So she slid past the front door and entered the lobby and, as there were no patients waiting, knocked on the doctor's open door. She hovered on the threshold of the room where he attended to his patients, rising atop her toes in hopes of seeing this stranger everyone said claimed to have no memory of who he was. Such an occurrence had never happened in their idyllic town before, it was quite understandable that everyone was agog. Even Georgianna was astonished that there were such cases of missing memories in this world. How would her cousin solve such a malady?

Albert's voice as he questioned his patient was low and soothing, and the stranger's response was just as low. However, something about it felt familiar. Georgianna frowned, stepping forward. Her cousin shifted, rubbing at his nape, revealing the man propped up in the small bed with a few pillows supporting his frame.

Shock darted through her, making her fingers nerveless enough to drop the basket, which held the three pounds of beef, scallions, thyme, and leeks for tonight dinner on her cousin's wooden floor.

It is the arrogant, wretched Earl of Stannis!

Albert snapped his head around, pushing from the chair, and hurried to her, gripping her elbow to escort her from the room.

"Georgianna, is all well? You've gone pale. When did you come in? I did not hear Maria's announcement."

"I...that man..."

He gave her a sharp glance. "Do you know who he is, Georgie?"

"I..." She pressed a hand over her frantically beating heart. "Is he the gentleman everyone is speaking about? The one who was found and is said to have lost his memory?"

Albert heaved a sigh of frustration and raked fingers through his sandy-colored hair. "Those meddlesome busybodies. I told Maria to tell no one of this!"

Georgianna winced sympathetically. "I am afraid this news is on everyone's tongues. Is it...is it he who is without memory?"

"Yes," Albert said gruffly. "He was found ashore only in evening clothes and no shoes! Yet the man had bank notes amounting to sixty pounds in his pocket. I cannot tell if he stole it or if they belonged to him. His mode of dressing suggests a man of some consequences, surely."

Georgianna could only stare at her cousin, her mind whirling. "May I...may I see him?"

He looked surprised at the request, and then his gaze narrowed thoughtfully. He lifted his chin in permission, and she moved forward slowly, thinking perhaps she had made a mistake.

It cannot be Lord Stannis.

She paused in the doorway, a hitch in her heart on seeing him again. *It is definitely he.*

"Albert, is this gentleman not at all familiar to you?"

Her cousin gave a start of surprise. "I have never seen him before, nor has Maria."

Georgianna wondered at the rumor that the earl had once visited Crandell and seduced the squire's daughter. A few voices came from behind, and she glanced over her shoulder to see the town's two most notorious gossipers and busybodies shuffling down the hallway. Albert looked as if he wanted to growl but checked himself for propriety's sake and that Mrs. Goodley was his wife's grandaunt. Georgianna was about to turn around and ask for a private audience with Albert when a sound whipped her attention to the earl.

He was out of the bed, standing with his fists curled to his side, a harsh frown splitting his brow. "*You!*"

She gasped, stiffening. *Good heavens!*

Albert rushed forward, casting a worried look from his patient to her. "Is something amiss, sir?"

"I *know* her," he growled, taking a step forward only to sway, flashing a hand up to grip his head. "I know her."

Georgianna's heart pounded a fierce beat, and she pressed a hand over her chest.

"Upon my word, never say the elder Miss Heyford knows this gentleman," Mrs. Portman gasped, far too dramatically, that glitter in her eyes suggesting she was already envisioning how she would repeat the tale to all those who would listen. Of course she would be celebrated as the first person to provide some insight into this famous situation.

"I suspected you knew him," Albert said tightly. "Please inform us of who he is."

She shook her head. "I do not know him as you suggest, Albert. This man is—"

"I've had you in my bed," the earl said, his gaze pinning her with an almost feral intensity.

Oh God, this is a disaster.

CHAPTER FIVE

The ladies behind Georgianna gasped, then silence fell. Those damning words reverberated in her head. *I've had you in my bed.* She lost the feeling in her legs and sat down heavily on the small chair by the window.

"*What*?" Albert roared, a ruddy flush entering his cheeks.

"No," Georgianna said, blushing. "I have—"

"I am certain of it," the earl said, his gaze raking over her. "The image of you just seared through my mind... I can still taste your mouth on mine, hear your moans, and feel your body pressed—"

"Stop!" she cried, bringing her hands to her heated cheeks.

Oh, this cannot be happening!

Her reputation, already hanging by a thread because she lived alone in a crumbling manor with her sisters, tugged rather violently. Mrs. Portman and Mrs. Goodley stared at Georgianna as if she were a rare creature with three heads, spewing fire from the mouth.

"Whatever is he saying?" Mrs. Goodley demanded.

How could she justify being in his bed? The earl spoke with such certainty that this memory was real, no one would believe her denial.

"Miss Heyford—" Mrs. Portman began in shrill accents.

"He is my husband." Georgianna gasped, then slapped a hand over her mouth, horror burning through her in icy chills. The desperate lie had leaped from her before she had even analyzed the sense of it all. But there was no other way out or she would be irrevocably ruined. "*You* are my husband!"

A choking sound came from the earl, then a harsh bark of laughter. "*Married*? To *you*?"

"Surely this is not true," Mrs. Goodley whispered. "How would she have met him?"

Georgianna surged to her feet, ignoring the tittering ladies behind her, and pinned the earl with a glare. "What do you mean by that, Daniel?"

She was quite deliberate in the use of his name, and he reared back his head as if slapped. The ladies looked between her and the earl, but she kept her regard pinned upon him.

"Is that your name, sir?" Albert asked carefully, as if he did not know what to make of everything.

"It feels right," he said with chilling politeness, his accent clipped and precise. "But I would not have married a woman so…"

"So what?" she asked through gritted teeth.

"So *plain* and obviously below me in every regard."

Her lips parted, but no words emerged. *The*

wretched beast. Georgianna gave him a tight smile. "Oh *darling*, you do recall some things. That my station was below yours in every regard was the main objection of your family. But your aching, *desperate* love for me and my plainness saw us marrying only a few days ago after enduring throes of love and longing for a few days."

The earl looked at her as if she was a raving lunatic, and Georgianna did wonder at her sanity at this time.

"Throes of love?" he demanded in an icy bite, narrowing his gaze.

Mrs. Goodley clapped her hands, her expressive gaze delighted. "Was that why you were away from Crandell, Miss Heyford? We had all wondered about it and made enquiry of the younger Miss Heyford, who remained tightlipped as to the reason for your absence. How terribly romantic, even if a bit hasty."

Her gaze dropped with deliberateness to Georgianna's tiny waistline, and she wanted to cry. There was no doubt in her mind a rumor would start to circulate that she was with child. She cast a beseeching glance at her cousin, and he sprang into action, urging those two meddling wretches from the small space. He begged them to practice discretion for the sake of all parties involved, and if Georgianna had not been caught in the earl's probing gaze, she would have rushed from the room and added her voice to Albert's.

"An aching, desperate love, you say?" he asked

dangerously softly.

She clasped her hand at her waist. "Yes."

He narrowed his eyes. "I say you are a damn charlatan. I know enough of myself that I would not be caught in no damn throes of love."

"Please inform me why I would even need to pretend to be married to a boorish lout such as yourself?" she demanded tightly.

That tart demand seemed to deflate his anger and send him into deep retrospection.

"Who are my family? I must write to them immediately."

Georgianna's heart lurched. "We never got around to discussing your family and their locations, caught in our throes of love."

The earl made a rough sound of disbelief. "What is my name?"

"Daniel."

"All of it!"

"Mr. Daniel Stannis." She waited, holding her breath to see if mentioning his title would jar his memory.

He frowned, then murmured the name a few times before raking his fingers through his already mussed hair. "I presume I am a man of some distinction?"

Good heavens, this was getting complicated. "We never got around to discussing it."

His gaze swept over her, a hard curve touching his mouth. "The implication that I was so enamored by your charms that we spent all our time in bed, hmm? That I find bloody hard to accept. I am not a man led by his cock."

She flushed at his crudeness. "You do have a head wound, so I shall forgive your skepticism and vulgarity, husband, or my heart might be forever wounded."

The sound from his throat was like a growl.

"What attracted me to you, Miss Heyford? You have no elegance or style. You are plainly dressed in one of the most God-awful gowns I am sure I must have ever seen, you wear no gloves, and I can see the callouses on the tips of your fingers from here. You are not a great beauty and from the little I recall from my memory…a mediocre lover. What could have possessed me to marry you?"

Her cheeks heated at the raw incredulity in his tone.

"It's *Mrs*. Stannis," she snapped, hating the thickness in her throat and the burn of tears behind her eyes. Why did it hurt that he thought of her in such an unflattering manner? Was it only the practiced libertine who had taken her mouth with such passion? Was it a mere route for him to kiss ladies and take them to his bed? Even more mortifying, for the last few days, she had to admit that illicit embrace had tormented her dreams.

The rough clearing of a throat sounded from behind her. Albert's expression was carefully blank as he came to stand close to them.

"Mr. Stannis, I could tell from Miss Heyford's

expression that she knew you. And, ah…from what you said…ah…there have been carnal relations between you. So if you are not married to Miss Heyford, I would most certainly insist upon a ceremony for the liberties taken with my cousin," Albert said stiffly. "Honor would demand it, sir."

Georgianna fought the blush with ruthless will and abysmally failed. Her entire body burned.

"She could have been my mistress," the earl drawled, his gaze watchful and indecipherable.

Outraged, she gasped, "Upon my honor, I was not your or anyone's soiled dove!"

He stepped forward. "Did you somehow compromise me? I will not bloody well believe I had my pick of the crème of the crop and chose—"

The earl paled, swayed, and she instinctively rushed forward, catching him against her. "What is it?" she gasped, glancing over her shoulders at her cousin. "Albert, is this normal?"

"I remember your smell," the earl murmured, dipping his head perilously close to her cheek. "The feel of you against my body."

Shocked, she glanced up, their gazes collided, and her heart lurched at the flare of heat in his gaze. Georgianna helplessly stared at him, painfully aware of the power and size of him. Except this close, she could see the curl of uncertainty in those dark green eyes, and perhaps a hint of pain.

Are you afraid?

Of course, he must be. A lump formed in her

throat as she tried to imagine how horrifying it would be should one day she opened her eyes and knew not the world or herself. "I—"

"Prove that I am your husband," he said, lifting a hand to cup her cheek.

"Why must it be proven?" she desperately asked. "What reason have I to pretend?" *Oh God, surely I will burn in the afterlife for this.*

A frown flickered across his features. "Why was I alone in the sea?"

"You went aboard a party...a ball of sorts on a yacht."

"Extravagant," he said with another small frown. "You were there... I saw you just now...in a cabin...on my bed."

Oh God. "I...yes..."

"Our wedding night?"

Georgianna swore an egg could be fried on her cheeks. Her wretched cousin was observing them most keenly. She delicately cleared her throat. "Yes."

"How in God's name did I end up here?"

"You must have fallen overboard," she said softly. "How or why, I do not know."

Awareness flickered in his eyes, and she sensed that felt like a truth to him or he had some memory.

"Why were you not with me?"

"We...we had an argument, and I disembarked at Dover and made my way home on the train," she whispered, so aware of that hand on her cheek.

He pinched her chin, lifted her head up more to meet his. His gaze searched hers, his own dark with cunning and intelligence. "Am I really your husband?"

What am I doing? she silently wailed. "There is a small red strawberry birth mark on…on your… manhood." The words choked from her.

Shockingly, his eyes crinkled at the corner. "That only proves we have been lovers."

"It does not! I would *never*…never," she spluttered, her entire body engulfed in waves of mortification.

Wariness entered his eyes. "You are genuine," he said slowly, "that you would never take a lover without the benefit of a marriage."

She shook her head fiercely, and he released her as if she had been burned. Her heart pounding, Georgianna shuffled away, unable to look at Cousin Albert's dissentingly curious stare.

He stepped toward the earl. "Miss Heyford is my cousin, Mr. Stannis. I can also assure you that a lady with her stiff moral rectitude would not have taken a lover—"

"Good God, stiff moral rectitude?" The earl growled. "I cannot recall my own bloody name, but I would not have married *any* woman owning to a stiff moral—"

Unable to continue, he spun away from them and marched over to the small window where he grasped the edge of the sill in a white-knuckle grip. Georgianna closed her eyes. She could not do this. She had to tell Albert the truth and have him find a way to discover the earl's family. Surely it could not be that difficult. Then she would determine a way to suppress the gossip that was bound to happen.

Should the good people of Crandell think I was this man's lover...all is lost. But I cannot keep pretending...this madness. Oh, this web is too tangled!

An awful sensation entered her stomach, and she knew Mr. Benedict Ford, one of their wealthiest and most connected landowners in Crandell, would no longer hire her to cater for his beloved wife's garden party.

My family needs this money, and this wretch has already cost me a fortune!

"I feel it is best you take him home today," Albert said in a low voice, cutting into her frantic musing.

"Home!" Georgianna glared at her cousin. "I think it best Mr. Stannis remain here until—"

Her cousin waved aside her objection. "Your husband will need the sense of safety and familiarity. The wound on his head will also require diligent care, and I know I can trust you with this, given how often you have helped me here."

"Albert, I—"

"You are clearly...entangled with this gentleman," he said without meeting her direct gaze. "I will hand his possessions over to you, the money, and a lapel pin that seems like it has diamonds. I will procure a pair of shoes for him to wear and have the bill sent to you."

She blinked, looking down at the bank notes he stuffed in her hands. Georgianna closed her eyes and wrestled with her good upbringing and conscience.

He owes me money that my family desperately needs, she reminded herself, *and he is a cruel beast! Not to mention, even if only for a few days, I need to protect my reputation until a better plan is formed.*

"Albert, we…we may not be married," she started to whisper, only to stop when he squeezed her hand.

"I do not need to know the full details or if there was consummation," he said, flushing. "The news will already be all over town that our mysterious stranger is the eldest Heyford's husband. Do not mistake the pointed look my relative did to your belly."

She groaned, hating that her hands trembled. This was a mess, one of her own makings by her damn curiosity. "I…"

"I have never seen you appear so out of sorts," Albert said gently. "I do not know the reason behind the suddenness of your marriage to this man, but I know you to have a sound head, Georgie. This situation might seem frightening now, but his memory will return in due time."

Beads of sweat trickled between her breasts. "How long?"

He sighed. "It could be months…or years… I

have read in some cases never."

"Never?"

"The medical community does not understand the full of amnesia. I cannot say for certain how long it will take Mr. Stannis to recover his memories, nor can I make any guarantees. He theoretically could recover in years or even weeks. I have read about a case study in Edinburgh where the patient recovered his full knowledge and abilities after three weeks."

"Good heavens, are there truly situations like these?"

Albert sighed. "What I do know is that he needs proper rest and to not be agitated. He took a blow to the head, and he was in the water for heavens only know how long. There is no dock nearby, and it can only be a miracle that he lives. There was a slight fever last night that abated this morning, and I can tell he is a man in pain but the proud sort who does not seem behooved to ask anyone for help. He needs your care, Georgie."

She nodded, feeling numb. Albert shuffled from the room, and the earl turned to face her. They stared at each other, Georgianna unable to read his indecipherable expression and she no doubt appearing like a doe caught in a hunter's trap.

Oh God, what have I truly done?

CHAPTER SIX

"I am irrevocably *certain* that I do not live here," Daniel said, staring at the modest white stone-washed manor and the overgrown garden to the side. Incredulity writhed within his chest. "There is a chicken walking about as if…as if it *lives* here, too. There is a certain assurance in those steps that says it knows it will not be eaten."

His bride of only a few days, if the tale could truly be believed, made a sound low in her throat, and her cheeks pinkened. A whirlwind romance, she'd said, throes of passion and love. He might not have his memory, but he was damn certain he was not the sort to believe in any sort of romance. The surety of it settled deep inside his chest.

The damn chicken waddled over and pecked at her shoes, as if in greeting. Daniel made a sound of disbelief in his throat, and Miss Heyford peeked up at him from beneath incredibly long lashes.

"You and Hetty are good friends, Mr. Stannis. I am certain she misses you."

"*Hetty*? The fowl has a *name*?"

"Yes."

He paused and stared at her carefully bent head and subtly shifting shoulders. Was Miss Heyford laughing? He arched a brow but made no comment, relieved she would find some sort of humor from this damn situation when earlier her eyes had been dark with embarrassment at his recitation of all the reasons he would not have married a woman like her, even if she was in possession of some beauty.

Except I did.

She was not at all plain as he suggested, he could admit, even if she was arrayed plainly. Miss Heyford…or Mrs. Stannis, he supposed, was astonishingly pretty. She owned petal-soft skin with a golden hue indicating she spent a copious amount of time outdoors. She also had a lush mouth with full and inviting lips, which evoked too many lurid thoughts.

Daniel frowned when the door to the manor opened, not by a butler or a footman, but by a young lady who greatly resembled his wife. A sister perhaps. That this young lady opened her own door struck him as…wrong.

"I am used to servants opening my doors," he said with certainty.

Miss Heyford's golden-brown eyes widened. "That…that was before the collapse."

His gut tightened. "The collapse of what?"

Her throat worked on a swallow. "Your fortune. You are broke."

He bloody recoiled. "I am *broke*?"

"Yes," she said, careful to not look at him.

Why, what are you hiding from? "I had several bank notes in my pocket," he said gruffly.

"I…I was surprised by the sum that you were found with, Mr. Stannis."

Fucking hell. He looked back at the manor that was in desperate need of a coat of paint, the overgrown weeds, and perhaps a new roof. Daniel knew he was not a man who could exist being damn well broke. The very word offended his senses.

"Is this perhaps a quaint country cottage we visit from time to time because…I might be a tad bit eccentric?"

She glanced up at him, her mouth shaping a small *O* of surprise. "This is your only home now. If you own others, I do not know their addresses or anything about them, sir."

A desperate feeling of unreality crept over his senses. Why could he not recall any bloody thing? Raw frustration and fright surged through his veins, and he took a deep breath to steady himself against the sensation. Anger and panic would do little to solve his dilemma. Daniel believed in calm practicality and logical planning in solving problems.

"I don't…I don't remember anything. You, this house, my name, or even where I am from."

Her gaze softened. "I know. I am terribly sorry… It must feel so petrifying. You need to rest and heal. Perhaps in a few days you could…do more to try and remember. My cousin has recommended nothing strenuous, and I am certain pushing yourself to recall too soon might be detrimental."

Daniel was not at all certain what to say, hence he remained silent.

The lady hovering in the doorway turned around and hurried inside, the door closing behind her.

"Who is that—" Daniel faltered, pressing a hand to his forehead, gritting his teeth.

That sharp pain he'd been experiencing since he woke inched its way up his spine and settled at the base of his neck. His heart drummed hard and fast, and he took a few breaths to steady himself against the feeling of dizziness that stole over him.

"Are you well, my...husband?"

She seemed to choke on that word, and he inferred she had meant to say something else. He cracked open an eye only to slam it closed as the light from the sun pierced his skull.

"What the hell is this?" he hissed.

Miss Heyford leaned against him, pressing a hand to his chest. He peered at that delicate hand that had calluses and a chipped nail, seeing a flash of a manicured finger in its place for a second. Another hand. Whose?

"Are you well? You've gone very pale, and you are trembling."

The soft concern in her tone had him looking down at her. She did appear worried...as if she cared. Somehow this rattled him, and he had to squash the urge to shove her from him. It was damn baffling how familiar yet unfamiliar she felt.

Do I really know you, Miss Heyford?

Yet the moment he had laid eyes on her, he'd been struck by a stunning sense of recognition. And his body had reacted with a carnal thump of awareness, a blistering one that said he wanted her more than he possibly realized. Worse, he could not imagine why she would fabricate a wedding to a gentleman who clearly had poor money management with little in the way of inheritance if this was where they lived.

Throes of love and passion.

Daniel was damn tired, the insistent pain now drummed atop his head, and his body ached all over as if he had gone a few rounds in the fighting pits.

"I need sleep," he said gruffly, knowing he had to be alone.

The desperate feeling of wrongness crept over his senses again, and his heart started to hammer even harder. Daniel wondered if he had made the correct decision to follow her home instead of staying at the doctor's. He was a man who deplored weakness, and that he was so reduced now left a bitter taste in his mouth. The only reason he had agreed was because he'd at least thought a familiar setting would jar his memory.

This place felt strange. "Have I been here before?" he said gruffly.

"No."

"Have I met your family?"

"This will be your first meeting."

Daniel scowled. "So I have not really met

Hetty, have I?"

"I foolishly teased," she said softly.

He pressed a thumb into his forehead, desperate to stop the agony piercing his skull. He took a step—and a peculiar, weak feeling overcame him. "Allow me the honor of meeting my new family after I have rested for a few hours."

The gaze peering at him was very worried. "You also need to eat. Food nourishes the body."

The idea made Daniel feel even more nauseated. "No food."

"Would you like to return to Cousin Albert's home?" she queried hesitantly. "You are his patient, and if you prefer to remain there or go to a hospital instead, he will accommodate it. I shall, of course, visit you."

The heaviness on his head grew worse. *A hospital?* "God, no. This place will do." *For now. Once I have regained my sense of self, I will damn well be leaving.* "I am about to bloody collapse. Take me to our bedroom."

Her eyes widened, and that becoming flush pinkened her cheeks once more. "Very well. I will take you to the…bedroom."

Now why did she sound like a croaking frog realizing it was about to perish?

...

Thankfully, Georgianna had a strong relationship with her sister, enough so that Lizzie had not dashed out of the music room to question the identity of the gentleman entering their home. Georgianna had been able to escort the earl up the stairs and to the bedroom her father had used as his own with little fuss or anyone being aware.

Worry knotted her stomach, for the earl seemed so pale, and deep grooves bracketed the corners of his mouth. He had tumbled into the bed, dragged a pillow over his head, and tersely demanded to be left alone.

Once outside in the hallway, she took a deep breath before making her way downstairs. Lizzie was waiting for her at the bottom of the stairs, her hand and knuckles gripped tightly on the banister.

"Who is that gentleman?" she asked, shock evident on her face. "And why did you take him upstairs? What is happening, Georgie?"

"I am sorry I did not get a chance to let you know of everything that was happening," she said wearily. "Where are Sarah and Anna?"

"They insisted they were responsible enough to feed the chickens. They are outside."

Thankfully their aunt had returned to town, and now that the season was upon them, Aunt Thomasina would not return anytime soon to their idyllic village. Georgianna glanced up the stairs. "Let us withdraw to the parlor. What I have to share cannot be revealed to anyone. Not even our aunt."

"Good heavens," Lizzie breathed, pressing a hand to her chest. "Is it very bad? Of course it is.

There is a strange gentleman in our house." As if it was improbable that a strange man could have been found in town, and another at their home, she queried, "Is it *him*? The gentleman Mr. Hayle told us about?"

Georgianna hesitated, then nodded.

Lizzie's eyes rounded, and she truly appeared on the verge of a faint. "*Why* is he here?"

Georgianna kept her counsel until they were closed away in the privacy of the parlor, and then she told her sister everything. Well, nearly everything…her own embarrassment kept her from mentioning their passionate kisses aboard the yacht.

Afterward, the silence was painful.

"Is this a poorly conceived jest?" Lizzie finally demanded faintly.

"I am sorry, Lizzie, it is not," she said softly. "I have told you everything that happened since I left. Now we have to tell Anna and Sarah and—"

"Good heavens, no!" Lizzie cried. "They are too young to bear the burden and responsibility of this…this mad ruse. They only need to know that in the days you went away, you got married."

Astonished, she stared at her sister. "I…I feel a sense of panic." Pressing a hand over her fiercely beating heart, Georgianna went to the windows overlooking the gardens, peering at her sisters as they played among the high weeds and flowers. The weight of her deception suddenly felt too heavy.

"Where will he sleep, Georgie?"

She turned slowly to face Lizzie. That was not the question Georgianna anticipated from her sister nor one she had even considered. "Oh, dear," she groaned, briefly lowering her head to her hands. "Oh, dear!"

Lizzie pressed a hand over her mouth to contain her sudden laugh that was perhaps edged with hysteria. "*How* could you be so bold and simply outrageous?"

"I confess I am still uncertain how it all happened. Perhaps it is not too late to turn back from this mess."

"It is too late," Lizzie said, fisting a hand on her hip. "Have you forgotten those two nosey bodies who will be telling everyone by now in Crandell that the stranger without memory is your husband? Until the next exciting diversion or scandal comes along, you and this supposed husband will be under much scrutiny. I daresay the ruse will have to go on for a couple of weeks. But how are we to feed him? We cannot add another mouth to be responsible for. Did you think of this?"

Georgianna dipped into the pocket of her dark bombazine dress and withdrew the crushed bank notes. Her thoughts raced, and she admitted she felt unmoored and frightened. "He had this sum on him—it is sixty pounds, Lizzie. We can now use it to see us through for this year and fill the pantry."

"Georgie! That is *stealing*! First such an

elaborate lie and now this? Have you no worry for your mortal soul?"

Georgianna jutted her chin determinedly. "It is not stealing but taking back what is owed. I worked hard for that money, Lizzie, very hard, and I am not stealing from the earl. Perhaps it is providence he washed up here in Crandell. Lord Stannis *refused* to pay what is due to me, and a lot of that money would have seen to procuring much-needed necessities for our family!"

Hating the painful pricks of guilt and worry, she started to pace.

"In truth, when I consider all the anxiety and pain his indifferent decisions have caused us to endure, he can do the damn job as well!"

Lizzie's lips parted, and her eyes rounded. "Do what job?"

"The job of the man of works we had planned to retain with the money he refused to pay over and the job of the maid to help Mrs. Woods. Those jobs he can help with as…as my husband!"

A horrified sound slipped from her sister. "Have you lost your marbles? He is an *earl*! Despite his rakish reputation, he is a powerfully wealthy aristocrat who we should not dare to meddle with, Georgie! Do see sense in what I am saying! He needs to recover and from what you said, in peace, with little to worry his thoughts. Let us accommodate that, and when he is well enough, we send him on his way. We can always say that your husband has gone abroad. Is that not the same reason our local modiste used to explain away her husband's absence these last four years? I urge you to not put him to work doing any menial jobs. The very idea is absurd."

Georgianna waved aside her sister's objections. "The earl is a spoilt, conceited lord with an overblown sense of his own consequences," she cried, pacing even harder. "It is perfect, Lizzie. Not only will he help with everything the monies paid over would have done, but you said it perfectly: the earl's presence at our manor should still the wagging tongues and idle speculation about the nature of my marriage. Mrs. Ford, and the good people of Crandell, will have no reason to doubt my reputation, and I should not lose the income catering for her garden party."

Lizzie fretted on her bottom lip. "Georgie, what happens if he should recall one day that he is an earl and yet he is here doing menial work? We cannot bear such consequences, and you know they will be dire. We have no station or connections to stand up to a lord!"

She straightened her shoulders even as a curl of fright darted through her body. "Cousin Albert said it is unlikely the earl's memory would return so soon. The earliest he has ever read the return of one's memory after an accident involving the head is a *month*. And Lizzie, I will tell Lord Stannis the truth long before that, I promise it, and perhaps he will even see the humor in everything."

Oh, such rubbish, but she had to reassure her-self of the possibility of such an outcome. "I will simply wait until he is more…recovered. But is it not the perfect plan? I get some much-needed help around the manor by putting him to work… and taking advantage of having a temporary hus-band. There are so many people in Crandell who whisper about us ladies living alone. I have even lost a few opportunities to cater to a few of our wealthy local landowners because of this, and I daresay I should now be able to convince Mr. Broomfield to hire me for his daughter's engage-ment ball. That nonsense he has been saying about us being too scandalous can no longer be his reason to refuse my skills and services, and we know that Mr. Broomfield does desperately want to hire me but has been restrained by Vicar Pomeroy and his wife."

Her sister's skeptical gaze suggested she heard the doubt in Georgianna's tone. She sighed, real-izing she needed to admit to the last bit of the story she'd previously tried to keep from Lizzie.

"If I had not claimed him as my husband, Lizzie, we would have been run out of Crandell by tomorrow morning, since he proclaimed in front of the town's most notorious gossip that… that he and I were lovers!" she finally admitted, hating that her palm sweat, and her stomach roiled. "And the earl was distressingly explicit!"

Lizzie gasped. *"No!"*

"Yes, that wretched man!"

Her sister narrowed her gaze, assessing Georgianna too intently.

"You are blushing, Georgie."

She sniffed. "It is the heat."

"Upon my word, something happened aboard his yacht! Why ever did you not tell me? Did the bounder seduce you?"

"Of course not," she said, glaring at her sister, annoyed by the traitorous way her body stirred at the memory of being in his arms. "He kissed me, that is all. And it was this embrace he recalled upon seeing me and said it aloud in Mrs. Portman and Mrs. Goodley's presence."

Lizzie groaned. "This is a very complicated and tangled web you've woven, and I am petrified. What if the earl has family who are worried about him?"

"First, we must stop saying 'the earl.' He is Mr. Stannis. And if he has family who are worried about him, it is their duty to search for and find him. If they do, he will return home."

Seeing how pale her sister was, she ventured closer and touched her shoulders. "I admit I also did not insist on leaving him with Cousin Albert. Mr. Stannis seemed uncertain, very different from the powerful and arrogant man I met."

Lizzie sighed. "Will the earl not demand proof? Such as a marriage license? Once a man and a woman only needed to declare they were wedded, and it was accepted as truth. But I daresay it is not so today!"

"You overthink the matter, Lizzie—why would he ask for such proof? Is there truly any reason to doubt he is indeed wedded? Does he have anyone else presently to rely on so that he can afford to have these doubts?"

Her sister's expression softened. "I can see that you feel guilty. You are worried for him."

Georgianna took a deep breath, not liking she did so after the abominable and conceited way he treated her. "Do not read too much into it. I would feel anxious for any creature who suffered from such an inexplicable malady. And should I truly feel guilty? Does he really not owe me for what his selfish conceit caused?"

"Perhaps, but you are always kind, putting others before yourself, so I know this is also ravaging your conscience, Georgie. There is no need to pretend for my sake. I know you well, sister."

She looked away from her sister's probing regard. "I promise I will venture forward with good sense and know when to stop this…from becoming too tangled."

Isn't it already far too complicated? a small voice whispered in warning.

That vow seemed to release some of the worry from Lizzie's gaze, and not for the first time, Georgianna wondered what madness had prompted her to say he was her husband.

Even at the threat of ruination, I shouldn't have been so reckless. Closing her eyes, she ruthlessly pushed aside all doubts. *But I have already stepped forward; there is no turning back or time for regrets.*

Recalling his haughty assurances that a lady like her could never be his wife, and the prick to her vanity, she took a deep breath, firmed her resolve, then smiled at the thought of exacting her revenge on the far too arrogant earl.

She'd show him what a "plain" woman could do.

CHAPTER SEVEN

Daniel had been staring at the ceiling of his bedroom for the last hour, wondering at the hellish trampling that had jerked him awake at the unholy hour of five in the morning. He had listened to the boots and laughter through the door, wondering exactly who the hell he was and how he had come to wash upon the shore with no memory.

How is it damn possible a man can have no notion of who he is? He silently snarled, resenting the sense of helplessness creeping through his veins.

How old am I?

Who are my parents? Are they even alive?

Do I have siblings?

Am I truly alone in this world?

A dark fear sat upon his heart then, and he hissed, ruthlessly fighting the sensation. *Not alone*, a small voice reminded him, *you have a wife...a home...a place to rest, heal, and recover.*

How do I not know my age or what kind of food I like?

Daniel thought so hard on this matter, he provoked thumping pain at the back of his skull. That was his first warning that the physician's advice might be necessary to follow.

"Do not try and strain to remember. It will only agitate the pain in your head."

"Try not to indulge in any strenuous activity."

The man had said that with a flush about his face, and dark humor had washed through Daniel.

"Miss Heyford has assisted me greatly from time to time here. Her kind, compassionate attentions should speed your recovery."

His lips quirked. What kind, compassionate nature? After escorting him to this chamber, she had turned and fled as if a devil chased her. Daniel had filed away her discomfort and the skittish way she appeared whenever he'd devilishly allowed his fingers to graze her skin or linger on her hips as she assisted him up the stairs.

The final advice had been, *"I believe your memory will return with natural ease. Your only job is to heal and stay in a surrounding that is familiar."*

He turned his head on the lumpy pillow, peering through the small window to the overcast sky outside. There was nothing familiar about this room and the bed he had spent the last several hours sleeping in. While it was tidy, clean, and gave the appearance of being lovingly tended to, the room had no pretensions to fashion, and the furniture could not be worth more than a few shillings. The wallpaper was dingy and must have been at least twenty years old. The mattress and pillows could all do with replacing, and the patchwork quilt on the bed, while beautifully crafted, was not luxurious. Daniel also found it damn astonishing that this confining space would now be his bedchamber.

He sat up slowly, grateful the peculiar spinning sensation had fully abated.

Why can't I remember anything?

He once again waited for a hidden part of him to answer, and when none came, he rose from the bed, padded over the basin on the washstand, and splashed his face with the cool water. The bar of soap provided smelled like lemon, and he used it with the washcloth to tidy his body, a peculiar feeling of being unmoored stabbing through his belly. Dropping the washrag, he used the dental powder someone had thoughtfully provided with the brush to complete his ablutions.

As he made his way over to the large armoire, he spied a set of clothes laid out on the small chaise by the windows, presumably by his Miss Heyford, for last night he had not seen a valet, footman, or a maid.

I am a man used to having servants.

Daniel glanced at the connecting door, which he suspected led to his wife's bedchamber.

There went that odd kick inside his heart again. *I have a wife.* The notion of it felt bloody absurd, and he wondered about that instinctive awareness. Was he a man who had not believed in marriage or this nonsensical throe of love? Or was it simply that he did not think Miss Heyford could have been a right fit as a partner?

Why did I choose you? Was it because I was broke and she had…

Looking around the drabness of the room, he dismissed that thought. A broke man would marry an heiress, unless his reputation was so damn terrible no one would have him. Given her lack of connections and wealth, the only reason he would marry Miss Heyford was as she said, they had been caught in throes of wicked passion or he had irrevocably compromised her, and she might be with child.

Turning back to the clothes, Daniel frowned. They appeared outdated but of his size. Shoes that had seen better days had been polished and also set aside for him. A few minutes later, he was dressed in a white cambric shirt, dark trousers, a striped vest, and a neck cloth. Daniel scowled at his appearance, for while he seemed decently garbed, the overall presentation felt wrong. He looked for the clothes and boots he had taken off last night, but they were nowhere to be found.

Someone had indeed entered the chamber while he slept.

Was it you, Miss Heyford…and did you notice I was in the nude?

Thinking about her supposed stiff, moral rectitude, amusement washed through him. Leaving the bedroom, he walked along the empty hallway and down the stairs, noting the threadbare appearance of the home. Whomever tended it ensured it was clean, the interior smelling of lemon, beeswax, and fresh flowers, but it was in desperate need of... Hell, the place needed a serious injection of money.

But I am broke.

His gut tightened upon recalling that. He needed a swift understanding of his financial background, his family connections, and a conversation needed to be had with his wife without delay.

The house was far too quiet, but he searched the lower floors, first peeking into a music room that held an outdated pianoforte and a harp. The sofas needed to be upholstered, and the rug was so worn, he could see the unspooling of the intricate threading.

He ventured into another room, a small parlor that had a fire going on in the hearth but was once again empty. Daniel took his time exploring the manor, which revealed in its entirety six bedrooms upstairs, and on the main floor, a drawing room, a parlor, an office, a music room, a very small sewing room, a dining room, and a depleted library which also seemed to serve as a schoolroom. Each room was sparsely furnished, well-tended, clean, and empty.

The only place left for him to explore was the attic, which he decided to leave for the next day, and the kitchen below stairs. He ventured farther into the office, glancing down at the stack of papers on the large oak desk. Flicking through the pile, he recognized bills, several unpaid, and invitations to a few soirees. A sound had him glancing over his shoulder to see a rather large ginger-and-white cat veering close to corpulence staring at him from the doorway.

"Whiskers, get back here," a soft voice cried. "Your job is to catch the mouse and...though I agree that you should not kill it, it *cannot* be your friend."

It was then Daniel noted atop the cat's back, a small mouse was perched quite comfortably. He blinked, and the image remained. Miss Heyford appeared and stooped before the cat.

"He cannot be your friend, Whiskers. It will only invite his family to also come inside, and we cannot afford that. Now do not give me that arrogant look as if you are the master here. I will not—"

Daniel must have made some noise, for her words broke off and she whipped her head around.

"My lo...*husband*!" She surged to her feet, flushing. "I had not realized you were awake."

"I have been sleeping since yesterday evening."

She smoothed the flat of her palm down to the front of her dark blue gown that fitted to her curves with mouth-watering sensuality.

God's teeth. Her voluptuous figure was a sight to behold.

There was a cautious look in her golden-brown eyes. "I...yes, of course, you must be well rested.

However, you have been sleeping for two days, sir."

That jolted him. "Two days?"

"Yes, Albert often explains to me when the body needs to heal it slumbers. I did check on you frequently, and you displayed little agitation and no fever. I also fed you some water."

He frowned, vaguely recalling soft hands on his cheek, and the feeling of something cool sliding down his parched throat. Miss Heyford had certainly tended to him like a compassionate wife. "I was not aware of the passage of time."

"I gathered you were…exhausted. Your clothes have been washed and pressed, but I am afraid your boots could not be recovered." A nervous laugh escaped her. "I feel as if I am rambling."

He had nothing to say, for he suspected he had always been a man of few words. They stared at each other, an awkward tension crackling in the air.

"How are you feeling now?" she tentatively asked.

His stomach growled, and she blinked.

"You must be famished. I've cooked some oatmeal."

"You do your own cooking?"

That soft flush spread from her cheeks to her hairline. "I love cooking the most, sir. I shall make you some breakfast. I…ah…it will be simple, I am afraid. Oatmeal sweetened with honey and perhaps some toast with eggs."

"I believe I am a simple man," he replied, noting the air of anxiety about her and the forced nature of her smile.

"If you would wait in the dining room, I shall bring you something to eat right away."

Before he could answer, she darted away, her footsteps echoing on the floor. Daniel strolled forward only to falter as running footsteps approached. Miss Heyford once more framed the doorway. Her cheeks were red from the exertions, and wisps of hair framed her cheeks.

"It occurred to me you would not know where the dining room is located."

"I've already explored the house."

Her eyes widened. "Oh!" Those lush lips curved in a sheepish smile. "My sisters are outdoors with their morning lessons. I shall perform introductions after you've eaten. They are most anxious to make your acquaintance."

He had nothing to say to that, and that awkwardness once more rose between them.

"I hope you are familiar with me enough to shed some light on questions I have, wife."

"Certainly." She took a step into the room. "We could meet in the office after the morning chores are completed."

The expectant way Miss Heyford peered at him prompted Daniel to ask, "Morning chores?"

"Yes. If you feel capable and able to offer any help, we would appreciate it. I have a list with me.

Do you feel capable?"

Daniel frowned. "You expect me to do chores?"

Her gaze gleamed, and there was something provoking in that stare.

"There is no need to sound so aghast, Mr. Stannis. My sister Elizabeth and I do the bulk of it, along with Mrs. Woods, our housekeeper. However, she does not live at the manor and comes by twice in the week."

"Where are the other servants?" Even though the house was not impressive, it still needed a few servants to ensure it was run smoothly. A maid, one footman, a cook, at least.

There was an expression in her eyes he could not identify.

"We cannot afford it, but you assured me before we got married that you are perfectly capable of working on the house and even in the garden if necessary."

He held her regard, and Daniel noted she seemed mortified. He realized then the family's circumstances had been much better in previous years, and they must have had to seriously retrench. Questions swirled inside, but he only said, "And where is this list?"

She dipped into the pocket of her dress and withdrew a slip of paper. Daniel reached for it, reading quickly, carefully burying the outrage snapping through his veins like crackling lightning.

"I presume all of these are my chores," he murmured, dangerously soft.

She pinned him with a bright smile, and it damn well annoyed Daniel that her prettiness sent his heart into a lurch. Long lashes framed bright, golden-brown eyes that were captivatingly tilted and pinned on him with unwavering intent. A memory of those eyes widened and darkened with lust flashed through him, and his heart kicked a furious rhythm. He could feel her body against his...and he closed his eyes, briefly trying to capture the elusive memory. It danced from him, but Daniel was even more certain he knew Miss Heyford carnally.

"Yes, but they all need not be done today. However, for me to prepare a proper breakfast for the family, eggs must be collected from the chicken coop, so do be careful when you deal with Hetty, and fresh milk must be collected from Nellie. I do not wish to exert you much because of your injury, unless of course you believe your state to be too delicate?"

Delicate? He narrowed his gaze at her, feeling the stab she made at his masculine pride. *How interesting.* He wondered what they had argued about that would see them separated only hours after their marriage. There was a look about her that informed him she expected him to make a fuss about collecting eggs and milk.

"I shall see to these chores," he said.

Her lips parted with surprise, and he felt some

satisfaction he had upended her expectations.

Daniel marched out the back door with the basket that had been thrust into his hands and tried to locate wherever the chickens lived. There was a small, ramshackle building that was surrounded by a hedged enclosure. He stared at the building, for a moment wondering why the hell he was truly going to collect eggs. Daniel did not need his damn memory to know this was beneath him.

"Are you going for eggs?"

It was to Daniel's credit he had not startled at that whisper. He glanced down, lifting a brow at the small child perfectly hidden behind an old bale of hay. "What are you doing?"

She peeked out and looked behind him before she glanced up. "I am hiding from Lizzie. I do not want to learn about rivers and mountains today. It is dreadfully boring."

Ah, the words somehow brought back to him the feeling of tortuous days in a school room with tutors. Though he could not see anyone's faces, he knew the boredom the scene evoked.

"Is Lizzie your governess?"

She shook her head, dark curls bouncing on her cheeks and forehead. "My sister."

He considered the child for a moment before dipping into a bow. "It is a pleasure to meet you. I am Mr. Daniel Stannis."

She charmed him by scrambling from her hiding spot to hold the edge of her bright yellow dress with its mud-stained hems and sank into a curtsy. "It is a pleasure to meet you, Mr. Stannis, I am Miss Annabelle Heyford, but everyone calls me Anna."

She had been taught graces and etiquette. When she rose, the child almost pitched forward but caught herself in time. Her cherub cheek dimpled, and dark blue eyes twinkled up at him. She was clearly pleased with her efforts.

"Are you Georgie's new husband?"

He lifted a brow. "Is there an old husband?"

The little girl wrinkled her nose quite charmingly. "Mr. Johnson wanted to marry Georgie, and Lizzie said he made a cake of himself by going down on his knees and spouting nonsense. Georgie did not have him, and he was bitterly disappointed and would no longer sell us any milk. Georgie had to buy Nellie, who can be very stubborn about sharing her milk and is not afraid to let you know."

Daniel blinked at that unexpected information. "We're all mad here. I'm mad, you're mad, Miss Heyford's mad."

The child's eyes lit with delight. "Do you also read *Alice's Adventures in Wonderland*?"

It surprised him somewhat that she knew he spoke of the Cheshire Cat. "I do."

Her smile widened. "It is a most wonderful story, but Georgie had to sell all of Papa's books to a circulating library to fill our larder last winter."

Bloody hell. How bad off were they? "I see."

Seemingly dismissing him from her thoughts, the child climbed the bale of hay, lowered herself to her stomach, and propped her chin on her hands. "Hetty can be scary," she said in a rather dramatic whisper. "Do be careful."

"The fowl?"

The child nodded solemnly, and he smiled, almost against his will. "I am more fearsome than a chicken." Lowering his tone, he said, "I'll spit the fowl on a stick, slowly roast it, and devour it should any trouble be given."

The pitying look the child gave him had Daniel reconsidering that assertion. He approached the coop with determination, aware of the little girl scrambling off the mound of hay to creep behind him. Daniel paused and glanced over his shoulder. She grasped onto his trousers below his knee and whispered, "Is it Hetty?"

Amusement rushed through him. "I am wondering why you are following me."

"To help with Hetty."

He did not reject the offer of assistance, thinking her a most charming child. Peculiar that, for he had never been too fond of children. He stiffened, trying to follow the trail of thought that would lead to more understanding of himself, but the memory eluded him like wisps of smoke. Pushing it aside, Daniel ventured forward and located a gate, which was attached by a loop of twine.

"I'll wait for you here," little Annabelle said. "Do remember that Hetty is still our dearest friend despite her contrary nature. She is the only brown hen."

His mouth twitched, and Daniel nodded solemnly to match her grave demeanor. He opened the gate and refastened the twine behind him. The area of scrubby grass contained a few chickens who ran out of his way, squawking. He moved toward the battered wooden coop and opened the door, which hung crookedly. Daniel had to bend to enter and was hit by a pungent stench that made him cough and his eyes water.

What the hell is this? What Daniel was most certain about was that he had never encountered such a damn horrid scent before. That would have lingered with him, even without his memory intact.

Snapping his teeth in annoyance, he turned away, intending to return to the manor. Daniel frowned. If he did not do this chore, who would? His wife? Her sisters? *Bloody hell.* He could not allow it. They were bloody genteel young misses! How could they be so reduced?

Spinning around, he walked toward the pen enclosure. Blinking, he found the interior dark, and the smell did not get any better. There were a number of roosts with hens sitting on them. Where in God's name were the eggs?

On the heel of that thought, little Annabelle lifted her voice to say, "Hens sit on their eggs, Mr.

Stannis. You should look underneath them. We need about eight!"

He approached the first broody hen, instinctively using stealth. As he slipped one of his hands under her feathered bottom, she squawked and tried to peck at him, flapping her wings. He jerked back and glared at the damn hen. A muffled giggle floated to him, and he glanced over his shoulder to see Annabelle standing on her toes to observe him. Swallowing the sigh, Daniel ventured forward once more and pushed the hen out of the way. There were a couple of eggs underneath, and he picked them up. But one felt strange and when he looked at it, he realized it was made of china. He put the china egg back and the real egg in his basket, then, dealing with the other hens, he collected another seven eggs.

Daniel swore Hetty watched his approach with a warning glare, informing him the hen was indeed a character. When he reached toward her, though, she flew up to his face and pecked at him, making furious squawking noises. He tried to cover his face, to get around her, but the damn hen was relentless with her pecking, allowing him no room to advance and snatch any eggs from her.

Daniel jerked back and scrambled from the coop. He fled, carefully carrying the basket and running for safety, pursued by an indignant Hetty, who was not deterred by the gate and flew over it and viciously tried to peck at his legs.

"This way!" Annabelle cried, her little legs

pumping with impressive speed.

And for reasons that might elude him for a lifetime, Daniel found himself running alongside the child, basket clutched to his chest, and the damn hen giving chase.

How in God's name am I to live like this?

CHAPTER EIGHT

Georgianna stared in astonishment, the mixing bowl and flour forgotten, when the earl sprinted across the back lawns, clutching a basket in his grip, and Hetty chasing after him. A laugh choked from her, and she pressed a hand over her mouth to contain her hilarity.

Lizzie rushed to her side to peek through the windows. "Why is the earl running, and why is Anna running beside him making all those noises of encouragement?"

"I think Hetty might be in a pecking mood," Georgianna gasped, trying to stifle her laugh.

Lizzie groaned. "This is terrible!"

"What is?" Georgianna murmured, leaning to press her face to the window for a better view.

"Lord Stannis is considered one of society's most elusive catches, and you are having him collect eggs from a chicken house! Am I not to emit groans of dread? I cannot escape the feeling that this is a disaster waiting to happen."

"He will be doing much more than collecting eggs. He... Anna!" Georgianna cried when her sister tripped and fell to the ground.

The earl skidded to a halt, stooped, and slung her into his arms before resuming running, Hetty chasing with furious squawks. She glanced at

Lizzie, and they dissolved into laughter. Georgianna felt...oddly charmed.

Noise clattered to the side, and she moved away from the window as the kitchen doors opened and the earl spilled inside with her sister, both pressing their backs against the door as if they expected Hetty to try and break down the oak. Anna's cheeks were flushed, and her eyes twinkled with delight. Georgianna's heart kicked uncomfortably at the way she peered up at the earl. Her sister had lost their parents when she was only two years old and had missed having a father in her life. The manner in which Anna stared at the earl now suggested she was already adoring his presence here.

Georgianna cleared her throat, and the earl straightened from the door. He walked toward her and held out the basket. "Mrs. Stannis, your eggs."

Her throat squeezed. It wasn't an endearment, but the way he said it felt far too intimate. She took the basket and wetted her lips, not liking the dip in her belly or the increase in her heartbeat. Georgianna stepped away from him, and his shrewd gaze noted her actions.

"Thank you. I see you've met Anna; she is my youngest sister. Sarah shall be inside soon. Please allow me to introduce Elizabeth, my sister closest to me in age."

Lizzie came forward and dipped into a curtsy. "I am very pleased to meet you, Mr. Stannis."

He bowed and murmured, "I am charmed, Miss Heyford."

"Oh, please do call me Lizzie."

A quick peek at Lizzie showed that she stared at the earl with wide eyes and pink-tinged cheeks.

"Very well, Lizzie," he said. "I shall continue with my...chores and hope I am spared from further harm." His tone was grave, but his eyes glinted with humor.

It was then she noted the scraped skin on his knuckles.

"You were pecked!"

His gaze lowered to the reddened areas. "I'll survive. I am not so delicate."

Their gazes collided, and inexplicably her heart turned over in response. Georgianna's fingers tightened on the basket, and she hurriedly looked away from him, lest he saw her shattering awareness of him in her expression. She almost groaned at the shocked look on Lizzie's face as her gaze swung between them before shuffling toward Anna and the door.

"Lizzie," she began, oddly desperate for her sister to not leave them alone.

"I must see to Sarah and Anna's education," Lizzie said with a bright smile. "We shall return when breakfast is ready."

Clasping the hand of an evidently disappointed Anna within her own, Lizzie opened the door and escaped with their sister. Georgianna looked up at the earl and stilled. He was watching her, the gleam in his eyes far too perceptive and perhaps a bit cunning. She took a measured step away from him, setting down the basket on the stone island in the kitchen.

Oh, why am I so nervous to be alone with him? "Would you like some oatmeal while I prepare the eggs and toast?"

"Thank you," he murmured and went to sit on the long kitchen bench, folding his arms on the table.

Georgianna almost groaned. The blasted man planned to simply sit there and watch her. A searing flash of awareness burned through her. The earl's eyes were like phantom fingers, caressing over her nape…down to the line of her back, to linger on her derriere. It was so terrible that she could *feel* his stare. Worse, the silence felt heavy with an awareness she did not understand.

Conscious of his gaze upon her, she went about ladling the porridge into a bowl, mortified that it had a small chip on the edge. She searched the cupboard for something better, but they all held one imperfection after the other. Pushing aside the feeling of embarrassment, she took the bowl over and lowered it to the table.

"Where did you sleep last night…and the night before?"

Georgianna could only stare at him with helpless surprise. His expression as he watched her remained unfathomable, but there seemed to only be genuine curiosity in his tone. Of course he would have such questions. She was pretending they were husband and wife. "I…in my room."

He reached for the bowl, his fingers grazing hers. She realized he had been quite deliberate in his touch, perhaps curious as to how she would react to him. Georgianna did her best to not appear skittish. Still, that single lingering caress had her belly knotting with a tight tension.

His eyes lit with a knowing gleam, and she flushed.

"Do you intend for us to occupy separate bed-chambers, wife?" His gaze glowed with the promise of wickedness.

Her knees grew so weak they felt as if they folded beneath her as she sat on the bench facing him.

"It is the way of married couples," she said evenly.

Even her parents had existed so. Surely that was considered the norm, given they had been deeply in love with each other.

"Is that how you wish to exist nightly, sleeping away from my arms?"

Heat swept through her body at the image his words provoked. Her heart stuttering, she said, "Yes. You…you need rest and healing."

His eyes glinted with a far too sensuous light. "After running from Hetty for so long, I venture to say with confidence I am fully restored, wife."

Oh dear.

She delicately cleared her throat. "I am also a terrible sleeper. My toes might end up in your mouth."

"I'll simply lick or nibble them. There is no problem there."

Aghast, she stared at him, glaring at the dark humor in his gaze. "Are you teasing me?" she murmured huskily.

He arched a brow. "Is it not the norm for a husband to tease his wife?"

"I…" Georgianna supposed it was. Her papa had teased her mama often, but they had been in love. She and the earl barely knew each other. Why was he so…frustratingly appealing? "I am not used to your teasing disposition."

"Ah…we only burned in the throes of passion, hmm?"

"Y-Yes."

A considering look entered his dark green eyes. "Are you with child?"

The shock of his question stuttered her heart, and then she realized why he asked it.

"Of course, you are wondering what motivated you to marry me." Why did she feel so mortified and hurt? His opinion of her did not matter! "I am not with child, sir."

"I merely wondered," he murmured, a slight frown touching his winged brows. "How long did we know each other before we married?"

Her heart lurched, and she hesitated for a brief moment. "Only a few days."

He faltered into remarkable stillness. "I married you only after a few days?"

"Throes of passion," she said drily. "Surely you

recall enough of your innate self to know you are a man of…strong emotions and passions."

He laughed, the sound low and almost mocking. "Then why did we argue? I presume that is why you have no wish to share a chamber with your husband though we were so lasciviously caught in our mutual lust?"

Georgianna stared at him, feeling the oddest sense of bemusement. Not once did she imagine they might have a discourse such as this. *At least not so soon.*

"Your mistress did not approve of your obvious desire for me," she said bluntly, feeling heartened that she did not lie.

It should not be so, but I loathe lying to you! Feeling that she was weak-willed, Georgianna crossed her arms at her waist, refusing to soften toward a gentleman who had treated her with such callous indifference.

A harsh frown cut above his brow, and tension invaded his shoulders. "I have a mistress?"

"Yes." She unwaveringly held his stare, wondering at his thoughts.

"Do I still have this mistress?"

"When I left the yacht…you did," she said cautiously. It was such a dangerous path she trotted on, but she preferred to keep to the truth as much as possible.

The earl's expression veiled, and he said no more but attended diligently to eating his oatmeal. He lifted a brow at the first taste, peering into the bowl with a sense of surprise. "A simple dish but quite tasty."

"The secret ingredients are cinnamon, nutmeg, and honey," she said, standing.

"Nutmeg?"

"It is a spice from the east." She went to the stone island, plucked the chopped nutmeg from the counter, and held it beneath his nose.

The earl inhaled and made a low noise of pleasure in his throat. That sound sparked a heated sensation low in her belly, and swallowing, she lurched away from him, hoping her agitation was not evident for him to speculate upon. Georgianna kept her back to him and set about kneading the dough to bake bread for their morning repast. Conscious of his gaze upon her, she did her best to attend to her task without peeking over her shoulders at him.

The bench scraped against the stone floor, and she presumed he stood.

"Mrs. Stannis."

She sank her fingers into the dough and closed her eyes briefly. "Yes?"

"Look at me."

Georgianna took a second to gather her composure then, releasing the dough, slowly turned to face him, clasping her hands together at her waist. Even in clothes years outdated, the earl was dangerously handsome. His lips quirked, and there was a disconcerting hint of sensuality in that smile.

"I will not break the vows made to you. I will honor our marriage."

That unexpected promise struck her heart so forcibly, she flinched. "I…"

What could she say? Georgianna stared at him wordlessly, never imagining such words from a gentleman who only a week ago planned to take three ladies to his bed at the same time.

He took a single step forward. "Do you understand what I am saying?"

"I confess I am not sure I do."

"If I had a mistress before we wed, I'll not have a mistress now."

She swallowed tightly. "Do you remember her?"

He frowned. "I do not. However, I know enough of myself to be sure I would not dishonor my wife by giving to another woman what belongs only to her. Once I have a wife…all past liaisons must end. That is one of the duties of a husband, to honor and be faithful to his wife."

Her heart trembled in response, and Georgianna could only stare at the earl. *Who is he, truly?* And what was this slow pulse of fascinated curiosity wending through her chest?

"You look at me as if I am a creature unlike any you've ever seen."

A shaky laugh escaped her, and she tucked a wisp of hair behind her ears. "You were…the little I knew of you…you were a right scoundrel. It merely astonished me…what you said just now."

He canted his head. "A right rogue, yet you still married me."

Drat. She lifted her shoulder in an inelegant shrug. "Throes of—"

"Of passion," he completed. "I sense perhaps we were both a bit reckless, hmm?"

"Perhaps," she said softly, wondering about the man beneath the power, arrogance, and conceit.

"Sleep with me tonight."

Her heart jolted and her mouth dried. "I beg your pardon?"

An arrogant brow lifted. "Why so aghast? Are you not my wife?"

"I… It is far too soon," she stammered, blushing. *Good heavens!*

His lips quirked at the corners. "For what do I need to wait on to feel my wife in my arms, sleeping beside me?"

This was simply not happening. "To remember me," she said, aware of the terrible thumping of her heart. "Surely you would prefer to recall our…meeting and time together first?"

An unfathomable emotion flashed in his gaze, and she gasped when he sauntered toward her, languid sensuality infused in every step. Her heart pounded so hard, she feared he could hear those beats. It was when the earl used a finger to lift her chin that Georgianna realized she had looked away from him.

"In this way I will know you, Mrs. Stannis," he murmured, his eyes glinting with deviltry.

The earl looked at Georgianna as if he would gobble her up in sweet, delectable bites.

"Is that not the way of it, we use our touch and our bodies to learn and connect with each other?"

Her heart leaped with wonder and something akin to fear, because shockingly, temptation slid against her senses. *Even without memory, you are still a rake!* "I…"

He dragged his thumb sinuously over her chin. "I am not a man who believes in looking back on the past and dwelling there. I cannot even remember it, but I will not panic or lose hope. I refuse to."

The peek at his iron will shook her, for that resolve was stamped implacably on his features.

He continued. "There is something in front of me that I can focus on. You. Me. The future. That is the man I know myself to be. I do not need to wait on memories of the past to know you are my wife or that I need to be a good husband to you. Do you understand, wife?"

"Yes," she said in a voice that sounded faint even to her ears.

"Good."

He dipped and brushed the softest of kisses against her mouth. A warm, fluttering sensation filled her belly, startling Georgianna. *Oh!* His lips on hers was the gentle caress of a butterfly wing, yet she felt destroyed by his tenderness and the assurance in his touch. Her throat ached with emotions she barely understood, and before she could sink into the kiss, the earl lifted his head and walked away.

As Georgianna watched him retreat from the kitchen, she realized that not once in the madness of this scheme had she feared her heart or virtue might be in peril with the earl. How foolish she had been.

Oh God, I must never allow him too close.

CHAPTER NINE

Daniel sat on a wooden stool inside the barn, staring at the black-and-white spotted cow who kicked at him every time he tried to squeeze milk from her udder. He cast the cow a baleful stare, but the creature remained unruffled, chewing her tongue and considering him as if he were an ant.

Should my friends see me now, I would be the joke in all of society's scandal sheets.

Daniel stiffened. "What friends?" he growled, desperately reaching for the line of thought. When nothing came to him, he released his fierce concentration and recalled what he had told his wife only a few minutes ago.

Am I really the kind of man who reaches for the future and does not linger in the past?

That implacable assurance as he said it to Georgianna had felt as if it came from a place inside of him that was unknown, however, most certainly real. The past was hidden from him, and while this morning he had felt a surge of black fright that he might never reclaim it, that fright had melted away and a new resolve had formed in its place.

It was his duty to do the best he could for his new and very unexpected family by making a path forward for them. He only wished he could recall why he chose Miss Georgianna Heyford and what had led him to marry her. Clearly, he was physically attracted to her, but she had no social connections or wealth, nothing to recommend her family to align with his.

Daniel tried to follow that trail of thought, for it felt damnably significant. Who was his family and why was he so certain he should not be wedded to a lady of such inferior circumstances?

He scrubbed a hand over his face. *What is done is done...and I must have made the choice.* Possibly whatever had pushed them together had not been the best of situations. Instead of falling back into the predictable trap of tumbling into these supposed throes of passion, he could relearn her or begin learning about her, since only carnal physicality seemed to have been their bond.

And he understood. Her prettiness struck his heart whenever he looked upon her, and she was stunningly lush with more than a handful of curves. It did not take much effort for him to conjure images of his wife splayed open before him, the pretty folds of her pink pussy, glistening, and ready for his mouth to devour.

Lust curled through him, wicked and insistent. *Bloody hell.* Daniel sucked in a sharp breath, pushing aside thoughts of ravishing his wife. First things first, concentrate on the chores at hand. Retrieve milk from the cow, and then see about compiling the tasks to do about the house in a semblance of logical order.

The house was in disrepair, his wife wore clothes that were probably three seasons old, her boots were scuffed and barely holding on, his youngest new sisters had no governess or formal education, and the quick peek he had seen at the pantry showed it to be almost empty.

I am broke.

Another hiss of irritation left him, and he tipped back his head to the ceiling, noting the missing slats in the roof. The rain would puddle inside when it fell. Not good for the single cow and goat they owned.

"Animals genteel ladies tend to by themselves," he murmured. "Bloody hell, I have truly fallen down the damn rabbit hole." They urgently needed at least a man of all works and a maid to aid them in their daily lives. "But first, the milk."

Daniel pushed to his feet and approached the animal with care. The cow watched him with an expression he could not interpret. "At least you do not peck, but you kick, don't you?"

"Her name is Nellie," a voice whispered.

Daniel looked over his shoulder and chuckled. This time another young girl had joined Anna in sneaking up on him. He presumed this was Sarah. "Have you stolen away from your lessons again?"

They shared a considering glance before looking back at him and nodding.

"I see. What is the subject this time?"

Sarah wrinkled her nose. "Greek literature. *Extraordinarily* boring."

"I thought the same thing when I learned," he said. "So are you to help milk Nellie?"

They share another conspiratorial glance. "Are you to help us hide if Lizzie comes here looking for us?"

"No. One must attend to their education with an industrious attitude, or we disappoint those who care for us."

Sarah sighed heavily and seemed as if she was about to turn around, but Anna gripped her fingers and narrowed her eyes thoughtfully.

"Not only does Nellie kick...very hard, but she also bucks, especially if you hold her udder wrong."

Nonplussed, he stared at Anna, who smiled sweetly at him, while Sarah nodded her agreement most vigorously.

The little hellions.

"What are we bargaining for here?" he murmured, amused by their cunning.

"We will help milk Nellie...and you help us hide from Lizzie?" Sarah asked nervously.

They held their breath and awaited his response.

"I accept this bargain."

Delighted, the girls hurried forward, the hems of their dresses muddied. If not for the difference in height, the girls could be twins with their dark, ringleted hair, blue eyes, and dimpled cheeks.

"Have you ever milked a cow, Mr. Stannis?" Sarah asked, smiling.

"I do not believe I've had the pleasure," he said drolly.

"The teats must be clean," Anna chirped, skipping to the cow and gently patting the side of her face. "We are borrowing some milk, Nellie, and later we will take you for a walk to eat some green grass and to drink water by the brook."

The cow made a sound in her throat, and the girls took that as some sort of permission. He patiently listened as they gave instructions about ensuring the pail was clean, how to use the thumb and the forefinger to squeeze the milk from the udder, and not to be too harsh lest Nellie got hurt.

Daniel nodded, stooped, positioned the pail, and milked the cow. They cheered him on when he got it correct on the first try, and he chuckled at their eagerness. The girls stayed with him until he had completed that chore. They beamed at him as if he had given them some sort of prize when he handed over the pail with milk. "Take it inside to your sister. Do not run lest you spill the milk and waste our efforts."

"Yes, sir," Sarah said, and giggling, they hurried away.

Plucking the paper from his pocket, he analyzed what could be done for the day and set about working. Several hours later, Daniel's muscles hurt like he had gone a few rounds with the devil himself. Blisters had formed on his hands, sweat poured down his body, and he was damn well irritable. With the assistance of Mrs. Woods, he had taken out several rugs and carpets and beaten them, a cloud of dust sending him into a paroxysm of coughing for endless minutes.

Why in God's name they did not toss the damn rugs into a fire eluded him, but he had diligently attended the task before climbing the rickety ladder to take down all the curtains in the bedrooms, the drawing rooms, and the parlor. Apparently, they had not been washed in almost two years. Thankfully Mrs. Woods, Lizzie, and his wife attended to that chore.

Watching how hard they worked, sweating, singing, and laughing with each other had only pushed him to do more, wondering how the hell he would fix this damnable situation for them. Somehow, he could see his wife in a different setting, something more genteel, perhaps sitting in a drawing room taking tea with her sisters and talking about the latest scandal or a book that was all the rage about town. She was not meant to labor away daily to maintain a manor that was clearly crumbling and beyond their modest ability to maintain.

Rubbing the back of his neck, Daniel stared up at the barn that had been mucked and cleaned. Nellie at least seemed like she was happy with his efforts, even if his damn back ached. The sound of footsteps crunching over leaves had him turning around. It was his sister-in-law.

"Elizabeth," he said in greeting.

"I brought you a repast, sir, since you missed

luncheon. It is a beef sandwich. Very tasty."

His stomach grumbled, and he reached for the sandwich, but she withdrew the tray. "Your hands!"

He looked down. "Bloody hell. What are the chances that this is not cow shite?"

A choking sound came from Elizabeth, and he scrubbed a hand over his face. "Forgive me, Miss Heyford, I forgot myself for a moment."

Laughter pealed from her, and he realized he had wiped whatever the hell was on his hand on his face. His mouth curved in an unwilling smile. "I cannot help feeling as if I am in a special hell and wonder what I did, hmm?"

She stilled, staring at him with wide eyes. He bowed, then walked away to the small lake to the east of the manor. Daniel removed his boots and dove deep into the lake fully clothed. He swam for a bit, abusing his already aching muscles. When he surfaced, stilling in the water, he saw his wife walking toward him.

How prettily Georgianna appeared with the wind whipping her hair about her shoulders and back. She stopped at the edge of the lake and tossed something at him. Daniel deftly caught it, smiling when he saw it was a bar of lemon soap.

She held his regard for a bit, a soft smile shaping her mouth. "I will bring out a fresh set of clothes for you, perhaps to your office?"

"If it pleases you," he said.

She hesitated, but instead of saying more, she

hurried away. Daniel watched until she vanished from view, then lathered his face, hair, and everywhere he could touch with the soap, paying keen attention to his chipped nails and the dirt beneath them.

Almost thirty minutes later, he stood in the small office garbed in clean clothes that seemed ill-suited to his frame, a fire blazing in the hearth, drinking the last of the chilled lemonade after quickly consuming the sandwich and orange that had been waiting for him on the tray on his desk.

My wife is considerate.

Withdrawing a sheaf of paper from the top drawer, he selected a fountain pen and wrote a note.

If you are familiar with one Mr. Daniel Stannis, and have business with him, please attend to him in the town of Crandell, Hampshire.

He would make plans to travel to the town square and have this notice posted to London, Manchester, and Leeds. While Daniel would not suffer to be the fool and worry endlessly about his past, he would still take decisive actions in helping his brain to figure out who he was instead of merely relying on fate. Perhaps someone who would be able to better help him understand his financial standing would see this notice and reply, even if they were a damn creditor or debtor.

A knock sounded on the door, and he glanced

up, setting the pen and note aside. "Come in."

The door creaked open, and his wife sauntered inside, two young girls tucked to her side. Daniel stood when they dipped into graceful curtsies. He went around the desk and bowed.

"Mr. Stannis, please allow me to introduce my youngest sisters. This is Miss Sarah Heyford and Miss Annabelle Heyford. Girls, this is Mr. Stannis."

"Pleased to meet you, sir," they chirped prettily.

"Pleased to meet you, Sarah. Anna and I had an adventure earlier escaping Hetty."

He winked, carefully omitting their assistance with Nellie. Anna chortled, and Sarah smiled. She seemed more tentative than Anna, who skipped over and handed him a piece of paper. It was a charcoal drawing of their family.

"I made this before you came," she said, "But look…I added you."

Ah, that she had done, and he peered down into her expectant features, unsure of how he should precisely respond. Daniel cleared his throat. "I am pleased to be here…"

Georgianna's lips quirked, and her eyes gleamed rather mysteriously, as if she knew he fibbed and would rather be anywhere else but this dingy manor. She shooed the girls outside and closed the door behind their departure. Daniel sat on the edge of his desk, casually stretched his legs before him, and waited. She seemed as if she were wrestling with herself, even started pacing before the door, her anxiety seeming to increase with each jerky step. He was a patient man, so he waited without rushing to conclusion, though he did wonder if she fretted about his earlier request to sleep in the same bed.

Her delicate face was set in determined lines. Squaring her shoulders, she faced him, reached into the deep pockets of her gown, and withdrew several banknotes. Georgianna hurried over to his side and placed them on the desk, then stepped back, lifting her regard to his.

"You appear as if you will head to the executioner block soon."

She expelled a shaky laugh, and the tension about her shoulders eased. "My cousin said these were the only items found with you."

He glanced down. A diamond lapel pin and a wad of bank notes. Plucking them up, he counted them. "Sixty pounds. Not a small sum by any means."

"Yes." She jutted her chin out, the move quite defiant. "I...I was going to use the money without mentioning it to you. However, the more I thought about doing so, the more wretched I felt."

Daniel vaguely recalled the doctor mentioning these. He stared at his wife, a curious wrench going through his chest. Given the state of their home, he fully expected her to use the money. Not only was she kind...Georgianna was honorable. He separated the notes into two piles and handed half to her.

Georgianna's eyes widened. "What do you mean?"

"Are you not my wife?"

The pulse at the soft hollow of her throat fluttered madly. "I...yes."

"What is mine is also yours, Mrs. Stannis. There was no need to feel any guilt in using this money. I also gather you had your reasons for keeping it from me, hmm?"

She stared at him warily. "I felt it owed to me...given the nature of our last argument."

Ah, the mistress.

"I would not have blamed you if you spent it all." He added a few more notes to those he held out to her. "This is forty pounds. It should be able to purchase a few necessary items until I have considered our financial situation from all angles."

She took the money with fingers that trembled. "I will make a note of my spending in the household ledger. Thank you."

"There is no need. I trust in your judgment." His observation of the day showed him his wife went to great pains to care for her family. Did he, too, know this kind of love with family? This depth of duty that was willing to sacrifice?

They stared at each other for long moments, and that peculiar sense of unreality crept over him.

What now? they seemed to ask each other with their silent, probing regard. An image of her golden eyes wide and aroused, peering up at him,

rushed through his mind. Daniel gripped the edges of the desk upon realizing he desperately
wanted to kiss his wife. He wanted to see something familiar on her face…and not this wariness
or uncertainty of navigating uncharted waters.

He pushed from the desk and walked toward
her. She took a few steps back, leaning against the
door, yet she did not open it and flee, though she
had ample opportunity to do so.

Curious…and so very interesting.

Daniel placed a finger under her chin and lifted her face so he could see her eyes. He lowered
his head slowly, giving her enough time to protest.
She only watched him, her gaze wide and soft and
luminous. Daniel pressed his mouth to
Georgianna's, and her lips parted on a soft, sweet
sigh. He swallowed that sound, his heart trembling with shocking intensity.

What the hell is this?

He kissed her until she moaned and wrapped
her arms around his neck, holding on as passion
flared far too quickly between them. He sucked
her tongue, arousal kissing over his cock at the
hot, little sounds she made while clasped within
his arms. Their mouths engaged together with
wanton greed. Holding her to him, Daniel kissed
her over and over, losing himself to pleasure.
When Georgianna wrenched her mouth from his,
her breathing harsh and ragged, he did not pursue
her but pushed away, giving her the space she silently demanded.

They stared at each other for long moments. His wife said nothing, merely turned, opened the door, and fled, leaving him empty and damn near desperate for her.

CHAPTER TEN

It was only his sixth day at the manor, yet Daniel felt as if he had been reforged into another being. He grunted as he slammed the axe splitting the firewood. His body protested when he lifted his arm again, but he pushed the pain from his thoughts and chopped the wood until there was an impressive pile.

Thunder rumbled overhead, and he glanced at the sky. Shrieks in the distance tugged his gaze to Sarah and Anna as they chased the hen and a rather fat cat. Smiling at their antics, he lowered the axe and started to cart the wood inside the barn. Almost two hours passed before he took a break, trudging inside to his chamber where he stripped from the sweat-soaked clothes.

Daniel went to the small screen separating the wash area from the bedroom. A large copper tub was filled with steaming water. An odd sensation clutched at his chest, and he knew it was his wife who had labored the pails up the stairs for him to take this bath. He lowered himself into the water, groaning his pleasure as the heat soothed his overworked muscles.

Is it this backbreaking work I have to endure daily?

The work to be done around the manor felt

endless, and a better solution needed to be found sooner than later. Daniel hastened his bath, despite the desire to linger. He wanted to venture into town before the hovering rain fell.

Almost an hour later, he walked along the cobbled street of Crandell, aware of the avid stares of the townspeople. He'd handed off the notice to be posted in the London papers before venturing to the bookstore. It was a small building adjoined to the milliner shop and did not boast many titles with which he was familiar.

He was pleased to see a few works by Lewis Carrol and purchased *Alice's Adventures in Wonderland* and *Through the Looking Glass.*

Daniel visited a few shops, and while the townsfolk stared at him with unchecked inquisitiveness, they did not greet him with any sense of familiarity. He did not linger but trekked through the woods and made his way back to the manor. The sun had lowered in the sky, and the stars and half-moon winked overhead.

He faltered when he saw a lone figure in the distance. It was more a speck of blue slicing through the shroud of dusk. Thunder rumbled once more, and a light misting rain began to fall. He walked toward that figure, and as he drew closer, he saw that it was his wife. She sat on a swing, the ropes attached to a large willow tree. Her hair was loose, the beautiful tresses tumbling over her shoulders and to her waist. She rocked herself on the swing, looking like an enchanted creature, graceful and enticingly feminine.

As he stood watching her, a fierce hunger washed through Daniel with a force that almost knocked the breath from his damn body. His gut clenched when he noted she lifted a hand to her face, wiping away the evidence of tears.

A raw surge of protectiveness went through him, and he stepped closer. "Why do you cry?"

She gasped, snapping her gaze toward him. "You startled me! I thought...I thought you were sleeping."

He heard tears in her voice, and she guiltily swiped at her cheeks. Georgianna's gaze went to the bound packages in his hand. "I walked to the village and back. A few books for the girls."

A small smile touched her mouth. "You...you bought books for us?"

"A few."

The soft light from the moon caressed almost lovingly over her face. Her eyes were soft and luminous with an emotion he could not decipher.

"Thank you, Daniel. The girls will be delighted. We...we have missed reading together by the fire on Sundays."

He nodded and was about to return to the manor but hesitated. There was something about her forlornness that urged him to stay by her side, find her demons, and ruthlessly slay them. "May I join you, wife? Or would you prefer your solace?"

"I do not object to your company," she said after a visible start of surprise.

Daniel went over and sat beside her on the swing, painfully aware of her closeness and tempting fragrance. Though he had teased that he wished to sleep beside her, Georgianna avoided his bedchamber, and he had not thought to question or pressure her. Hell, he was so exhausted each night, even if she were to climb into his bed lush and wanting, Daniel would be too damn exhausted to make love with her properly. "Did someone hurt you?"

The soft hollow of her throat jerked, and he gathered her pulse was racing.

"No, of course not."

"Thunder rumbles, and rain is falling, albeit lightly, the perfect ambience to be sleeping. Yet you are here outside, crying," he said gruffly.

She cleared her throat delicately. "I did not mean for anyone to see."

"Do you come out here often...and cry alone?" An idea that felt unfathomable to him. He could not know for certain what sort of man he had been. What had been his cares? His worries?

Daniel frowned. Whatever did crying solve? Yet he did not say this to his wife, sensing he would injure her pride. Still, he wanted to know what bothered her and fix it. "Tell me, why do you cry?"

"It is silly," she said with a shaky laugh, seeming mortified.

"Silly things do not scare me," he said drolly.

"If you are of a mind to share, Mrs. Stannis, I am here."

"Sometimes…sometimes I feel the weight of my responsibilities, and I get scared," she said softly. "I cannot show my sisters that I feel doubt…and fear because they would then become worried. I do not want that for them."

"I see." From his observations, his wife had been alone for a while, doing everything in her power to see to her family's welfare. Whose shoulder did she cry on when the burden became too much? Who did she share her fears and doubts with? "Husband and wife overcome difficulties together."

She shifted to face him, her eyes wide…and perhaps a bit desperate. "You wish to share my woe?"

How appalled and guilty she sounded. "It is my duty."

The rain was starting to increase, her dress turning alarmingly transparent.

Her teeth sank into her bottom lip. "Until your memory has returned…do not worry much about me, please."

An impossible request, but Daniel only asked, "What do you fear?"

Her throat worked on a swallow. "I dream of a life that feels like it moves further away the more I try," she said softly, digging her toes into the earth and pushing the swing. "There are times I feel as if I stumbled through yesterday and today is just as muddled."

Those words cut through him like a knife, and befuddlingly, Daniel wanted to promise her the world. Using his strength, he pushed the swing, allowing them to soar.

Holding on to the rope, she lifted her face upward. "Perhaps my dreams are as far away as the stars in the night sky. If I do not do everything possible to achieve them, these dreams will disappear like wisps of smoke."

"Smoke eventually rises and reaches the sky," he murmured, unable to tear his gaze from her face.

The swing slowed, and she pressed her feet into the earth to stop it. Georgianna lowered her gaze to him, staring as if she did not know what to make of his reply. "Are you saying you believe in me?"

This was asked with such incredulity, a rush of amusement went through him. "Is the idea so astonishing to you, wife?"

She leaned against the rope to study him, her expression solemn. "You…you do not know me… You do not remember me."

"I have seen enough to know that you have a determined and unflinching spirit."

She smiled, and it lit up her entire face with an alluring prettiness. Daniel reached out and touched her cheek with the back of his fingers. She did not pull away, subtly leaning toward his heat.

By God, he would kiss her, perhaps tug her into his lap and…

The sky chose that moment to break, dumping rain on them. She laughed, jumping from the swing and dashing toward the main house. He watched her run, smiling at how ungraceful she seemed. His wife skidded to a halt and looked over her shoulders.

"I am waiting for you," she cried, pushing a few tendrils from her forehead.

A knot of warmth unraveled just inside his chest. Another peculiar sensation whispered through Daniel's heart, but it vanished before it shaped into a sense of tangibility. He rose, jogged toward her, his heart lurching when she slipped her hand in his, tugging toward the house in a mad dash.

Her laughter curled around him, soft and sweet and alluring. His wife slipped, and he caught her about the waist, lifting her into his arms while deftly holding on to his package of books. She gasped, clutching at his shoulders and peering up at him with wide, shocked eyes. Daniel bit back his smile and hurried inside the house. Her nails sank into his shoulders when he did not set her down upon entering. He padded with her along the hallway and up the stairs. Tension visibly threaded through his wife, and he lowered his gaze to the uneven rise and fall of her breasts.

Once at her bedchamber, he lowered Georgianna to her feet. She leaned back against the door and peered up at him. Desire trembled through him with stunning force, and he briefly looked away from her prettiness. Daniel handed her the books, and she took the package, pressing it against her chest like a shield.

Her cheeks were flushed, her eyes luminous. "Sleep well," she said tremulously. "And thank you for keeping my company."

"Sleep well, Georgianna," he murmured, restraining the need to lift her against the door, wrap her legs around his waist, and kiss her until she was wet with hunger.

She whirled around, opened her door, and slipped inside. Daniel released a harsh breath, went into his room, stripped from the damp clothes, and tumbled into the bed naked. Sleep eluded him, and sounds rustled from the room next door, stoking his imagination with visions of his wife undressing. He rose and padded over to the connecting door. Daniel gripped the knob, tempted beyond measure to open the door.

And then what? The look in her eyes just now had been anxious. He shut his eyes, recalling the set of her soft mouth and just the barest hint of one of her dimples when she smiled, the bold want in her eyes that seemed to surprise her, and the way she had tasted when they kissed. Despite the awareness shimmering between them, his wife was not ready to resume intimacy. Pushing out a breath, he released the knob and went back to bed, knowing for the first time since his arrival he would not tumble into exhausted sleep.

Nay, it would be a long, tortuous night of wanting Georgianna Heyford.

. . .

Georgianna had anticipated that having a gentleman living with them would have set her sisters out of sorts and would see her fielding several questions daily. However, Anna and Sarah had taken the news of a marriage with great aplomb, bowled over by the notion that a gentleman would now be living under their roof for an extended period and that he had lost the memory of his entire life.

They were young enough to only feel a sense of excitement and had asked no questions, simply accepting that Georgianna said she had married someone in a whirlwind courtship in the few days away from Crandell, and he might leave soon to seek greater opportunities.

Georgianna's and Lizzie's faces were pressed to the windows in the kitchen as they watched the earl going about his chores for the eighth day. It surprised Georgianna that he did so with little complaint, even awakening earlier than the rest of the household. The earl would diligently work about the yard, cleaning the barns and the fowl pen, shearing the overgrown bushes, weeding the garden, and now fixing the outhouse so they might be better prepared to store vegetables and fruit. He would work from dawn to dusk before stumbling to the house for supper, then to his bed and to fall into a deep sleep.

Georgianna would gently open the connecting door to their chambers and peek to see if he was well. His fever did not return, nor did he seem to suffer from any nightmares. There were a couple of nights when he would awake before dawn, his pacing rousing her from her sleep. However, he did not disturb her, nor did he test the connecting door. Except for that night on the swing a couple days ago, they'd had no chance to speak alone. Nor did he try to kiss her again. This awareness filled her with an odd sense of relief and disappointment. And that disappointment once again warned her to be careful. Sitting with him on the swing, sharing her intimate fears, had felt too easy and welcoming.

A shout of laughter pulled Georgianna from her musings, and she wondered what the earl said to enchant Sarah so.

Lizzie sighed and said fretfully, "The girls are determined to skip their lessons and join the earl in whatever task he is doing. It is rather unseemly. They are not growing up to be ladies."

"They are young," Georgianna said, moving from the windows. The notion that she was failing her younger sisters pressed against her heart. "Once I secure a few more jobs, I will start setting aside money for a governess to see to their education and comportment."

Lizzie worried her lower lip. "It will be rather expensive, Georgie."

"I will do it," she vowed softly. "Given that the earl gave me some money, I will put aside the funds earned from Mrs. Ford's garden party this weekend for their education. Once we have enough money to pay a governess for a full year, I will seek someone reputable and with suitable references from the papers."

Lizzie nodded and excused herself to work on her book. Georgianna set about preparing lunch for the household. She busied herself preparing boeuf bourguignon, thinking the earl would prefer that to the plain beef stew she had been cooking since his arrival. Yesterday she had ventured into town, putting the money he had given her to good use. Their pantry was stocked for the month, and she had purchased new boots and bonnets for Anna and Sarah. Georgianna had also bought several bolts of cloth, hoping to make them a few dresses for the upcoming summer. Lizzie was superb at needlework and should be able to complete the designs Georgianna had drawn.

She lost herself in her work, cooking and writing down ideas for new recipes she wanted to try for the garden party in her notebook. Her ultimate goal was to publish a book showcasing her recipes, with the promise that once the instructions were followed, every household would be able to create the same tasty, exquisite dishes she made. The door to the kitchen shoved open, and she snapped her head up, the pencil clattering from her fingers.

"My lo…*husband*!" She almost groaned at her slip. "Is all well?"

"Come quick," he growled. "There is a bloody fight, a quite vicious one, too, and we need more hands to part them."

Dropping the notebook, she rushed forward. "Goodness. Who is fighting?"

"Hetty and Midge."

Georgianna skittered to a stop. "The piglet and the hen are fighting?"

Halfway to rushing back outside, the earl glanced over his shoulder with a scowl. "Aye. The stubborn little buggers."

"I…ah…and I am needed to part this fight?" Georgianna began to laugh, and a wry smile curved his mouth.

"I am sorry," she gasped, pressing the flat of her palm over her heart. "This is…"

Daniel's grin widened, and her heart did a somersault. Goodness, her mouth had gone dry, a frisson of awareness climbed down her spine, and fluttering went off low in her belly. *Drat*. She really was terribly attracted to him. *You are far too handsome and appealing*, Georgianna silently moaned.

"Ridiculous," he murmured. "It is, but it is also very important to Anna that we save her piglet."

"Good heavens, the *hen* is *winning*?"

His shoulders shook with laughter, which rolled from him rich and warm. The sound of it did fluttery things to her heart, and way down in Georgianna's stomach, she felt an unknown ache. Aware of the increase in her heartbeat, she glanced away from him, directing too much attention to untying her apron. In her unsteadiness, she nudged the book from the counter, and it clattered to the floor. She stooped, her head almost butting against the earl's. *Oh!* She'd not heard him move.

"I've got it," he murmured, plucking up her notebook.

It was then she noted the redness and scars. "Your hands," she cried, reaching for him. "They are raw…and *blistered*."

"It is nothing."

She snapped her gaze at his. "How can you say so? They are… You must hurt." Her throat ached, and guilt hammered at her heart.

He gripped her elbows and urged her to stand, and it was only then she realized they were still intimately crouched closely together. She rose to full height, unable to look away from the callouses and blisters on his hands. How could she feel so wretched? Of course he had blisters. Before he met her, he'd been a pampered aristocrat who had never done a day's work in his life. She closed her eyes tightly. Yet for the last several days, he had been laboring without complaint, brilliantly fixing all the issues around the manor.

"Open your eyes, wife."

Oh, please, do not call me so. She complied, and his gaze ensnared hers.

"When I promise you something, I will deliver on it."

Georgianna's heart crashed against her chest. "I beg your pardon?"

He lifted a brow. "Did I not promise you that I would fix the outhouse today, clean the pens, and paint the barn and then the house?"

Oh God, the unending list of chores. "I...yes."

She stared down at his reddened palm, a lump forming in her throat. Without thinking, Georgianna lifted his hand to her lips and kissed his palm. The earl faltered into remarkable stillness at the hint of intimacy.

He was so diligent and reliable. Shockingly, at that moment, she felt the benefits of having a companion to share her burdens with.

Husband and wife overcome difficulties together.

Remembering that strong reassurance, longing almost broke her apart.

How can I be so silly to wish that this...to wish that you...were real?

Georgianna released his hand as if she had been burned, appalled at the errant, outrageous thought. Centering herself against the emotions writhing inside her chest, she gently took his hand and tugged him over to the counter. Reaching upward, she plucked a pot from the peg, poured water from a jug inside, then sliced a lemon and squeezed it in the water.

"This will sting a little," she said softly, "but it will also soothe and disinfect the flesh. I will then make a lavender poultice to wrap your hands."

"Thank you, Georgianna."

Her name rolled sensually off his tongue, and that peculiar warmth once again shivered through her heart. She nodded, unable to look at him, afraid he would see the naked longing in her stare. Georgianna wanted to hide this emerging awareness inside…hide it from him and even from herself, for she did not understand it. His presence at her home should mean nothing, nor did she see a future for herself with any gentleman. Buried in Crandell with a few eligible suitors who would never consider the Heyford sisters for marriage, Georgianna had suppressed those dreams before they got the chance to take root. It wasn't a husband and child she had hopelessly yearned for, but the means to provide for her family that did not rely on a gentleman finding her meager connections worthy.

So why did it feel as if each day in the earl's presence, something unknown inside her awoke?

"Why don't you look at me, Mrs. Stannis?"

Mrs. Stannis. He said this teasingly, yet there was a hint of something unfathomable in his tone. She closed her eyes and swallowed tightly before opening them. Yet she still could not look up. The earl placed a finger under her chin, and it took little effort for him to nudge it, bringing her gaze up to his. Georgianna's body surged to life with painful immediacy at his touch. Every breath she drew was rich with his warm scent.

"Your eyes are quite beautiful." How bemused he sounded, as if he should not have noticed. "It is like they hold an inner fire only a few might be privileged to see."

She stared up at him, feeling the beat of her heart in every crevice of her body. The earl stared at her, his gaze kissing over her face with intensity. Georgianna couldn't help noticing that even dressed so casually, the earl radiated a chilling, dangerous elegance. "And your tongue is glib and charming as ever," she said softly, briefly looking away from his intensity.

"Only for you, my sweet, only for you."

Incorrigible and outrageous. "Please, work no more until your hands have healed."

"There is no need for that caution, wife. I am not so delicate, hmm?"

There was a very decided twinkle in his eyes, and she smiled. The door opened, and Lizzie bustled inside, her gaze instantly going to where Georgianna held the earl's hand within hers and that his other hand was on her face. Georgianna could imagine the intimate picture they presented. Surprise widened her sister's eyes, but she wisely held her counsel.

Clearing her throat, Georgianna lowered his hand and stepped away from the earl. "Has the fight ended?"

A muffled laugh came from Lizzie. "Yes, I bravely waded in and saved Midge. When are we going to cook her?"

"Lizzie," a small, hurt voice cried. "We are *never* eating Midge!"

Georgianna groaned when Sarah turned and ran away, forgetting whatever had brought her to the kitchens.

"Lizzie," she rebuked softly. "Please go and soothe her. There shall be no more jesting about eating Hetty or Midge."

Her sister flushed, nodded, and departed the kitchen, closing the door behind her.

"You are good with them," the earl said, his gaze intent on hers.

She glanced up, feeling unaccountably nervous. "They are my sisters. I...I love them, of course."

"You are more than their sister," he said with a considering frown. "You parent them."

"I..." She hurried over to the large iron pot, lifted the handle, and stirred the savory stew. Georgianna answered without taking her attention from the stove. "We lost our mama almost two years after Anna was born...and our papa...I always believed he was not able to live without her. He died in his sleep only weeks later." She covered back the pot, then turned to the earl.

"Why is that look of guilt in your eyes?"

She made a wry sound of disbelief. "I do not think you know me well enough to determine it is guilt I feel."

"Tell me then, wife, what thought made you wince and bite into your lower lip with enough strength to leave a mark?"

Her pulse quickened, and she lifted a hand to her lips, feeling the small bruise surely forming. "I…" Georgianna expelled a slow breath. "I have always felt I gave Papa permission to leave us."

He lifted a brow. "One cannot control matters of life and death. He died in his sleep, and unless you poisoned him, you cannot take that burden on your shoulders."

"You are o-outrageous!" she spluttered, choking back a laugh. "I assure you there was no poison involved. Papa fell into a terrible state of melancholy after Mama's passing, and…and only a few hours before he went to his reward, he asked me if I was capable of taking care of my sisters. I said yes, and he made me promise it twice more. I thought he only needed time to grieve, but my words released him, and instead of fighting, he gave up on life and on us."

"I am damn sorry," he said gruffly.

She had never said those words to another, and that she would share this hidden pain in her heart alarmed Georgianna.

Why is it so easy with you?

He leaned his hips against the edge of the stone counter and folded his arms across his chest. "You have been alone with your sisters for what…four or five years?"

"Five years and two months."

His gaze caressed over her, from the tip of her scuffed boots to her hair bundled tightly beneath a cap and hairnet. "You do not look much above one and twenty. How old are you, wife?"

She smiled. "I am three and twenty, sir." *Soon to be four and twenty.*

"You've done a wonderful job. Never doubt it."

A light laugh escaped her simply because she felt…happy to be having a conversation with someone aside from her sisters.

"You have a lovely smile and even lovelier laugh."

Georgianna made an obvious effort to collect herself, blushing fiercely.

The earl took a step closer, the warmth of him caressing her senses. "Do I not adore you with praises and compliments, wife? Your blushing reaction says I do not; how remiss of me."

A slow, torturous ache rolled through her. "I…"

He touched her cheek with the back of his fingers. "Do I not tell you how soft and sensual your skin is to the touch, how much I ache to kiss this lush mouth of yours, lick the pulse that is fluttering madly as we speak at your throat?"

You gorgeous, rakish beast.

Wicked longing opened inside her like a desperate flower in search of rainfall. If Georgianna was not careful, he would take her virtue and her heart like a thief in the night, leaving her in ruined shambles and heartbreak. Despite knowing this, when the earl lowered his head, a soft sigh of anticipation and need escaped her.

Oh, this is so dangerous.

The clatter of hooves and a loud voice restraining an animal shattered the intimate spell he had been weaving about her. Shocked, she drew away, glaring at him. How had he done it, captivate her so effortlessly?

"You have a caller," he murmured, looking beyond her shoulders out the windows.

Georgianna turned around, conscious of his masculine strength and heat at her back. "It is Mr. Jonathan Hayle. He is a neighbor."

"Is he to come inside?"

Noting the direction Mr. Hayle traversed, she shook her head. "He...it seems he is visiting Lizzie."

"Ah, I see," the earl said, "he is wooing her."

Georgianna cast him a quick glance, and the earl lifted a brow in question.

"Have I misspoken?"

"Mr. Hayle does have a deep affection for Lizzie, and his sentiments are returned. However, the Hayles are an old country family of respectability and large fortune. His parents would have greater ambitions for their only son."

The earl looked away in the distance, his expression inscrutable. Suddenly he appeared more like the powerful earl and not her fake husband who seemed to own a different character from the rakish gentleman she met before.

"Permit me to enquire why do you allow him to meet with her alone?"

She flushed at the cool rebuke of his tone. "Lizzie is one and twenty. I trust her judgment and that she would not be…reckless with her heart."

"Her heart?" He gave a soft, derisive laugh. "When a man pays court to a lady he evidently makes no plan to offer, it is her virtue that is under threat."

A jolt of apprehension went through Georgianna. "Mr. Hayle would not conduct himself so poorly, nor would Lizzie!"

"How innocent…and naive."

He did not mean it as a compliment, and a sense of hurt writhed inside her chest. "I…" But what could she say? Surely, she had not failed in one of her duties to her sister.

The earl turned away. "I will introduce myself to this Mr. Hayle."

He did not await her approval but departed the kitchen, leaving Georgianna feeling wretched and wondering if she had been foolish to not put a stop to Mr. Hayle's visit.

CHAPTER ELEVEN

"Is that the only reason you visited, Mr. Hayle?" Lizzie asked tremulously. "To confirm if the rumors are true? If so, let me assuage your curiosity and you can be on your way. Yes, the stranger found on the shore is my sister's husband, and his memory has not yet returned."

Daniel could not decipher the gentleman's reply, and he shoved his hand in his pocket, wondering if he should interrupt their conversation. It had taken him some time to locate where they strolled, for he had never before ventured to this side of the manor. The fruit orchard was rather large and in desperate need of raking.

The lovers' voices hushed, and he turned away, tipping his face to the sky. The protective surge that had filled his chest still lingered, and he had injured his wife's feelings with his harshness. Georgianna, who seemed to live a sheltered life in the idyllic village of Crandell, did not know there were men ruthless enough to seduce and walk away from a lady without any concern for their reputation or supposed heart.

This is not my concern.

His wife trusted her sister and treated her with respect, so why the hell was he thinking to barge in on their private discourse? He would seek an introduction to Mr. Hayle at another time. Daniel started to walk away, and a passionate outburst arrested his step.

"I do not wish to marry her. It is you I love, Elizabeth! Please do not say I am to never call on you again. I cannot bear it, can you?"

"You plan to marry Squire Tomkins' daughter and wish to maintain a friendship with me?" Lizzie demanded on a sob.

The profound hurt in her tone wrenched through Daniel, and a dark anger took him over.

"I love you. How can I bear to lose you?" Mr. Hayle said, his tone desperate with yearning. "Give me some time and I will… Lizzie, please do not walk away!"

A soft gasp sounded and then silence. A ragged moan floated in the air, and Daniel stiffened. "Bloody hell," he muttered.

The damn bounder had kissed her. Gritting his teeth, he continued on, to grant them privacy, hoping that Elizabeth would have enough good sense to know when to stop Mr. Hayle's amorous advances.

Yet no voice of protest reached Daniel's ear, only soft ruffles…as if clothes were being removed.

"For fuck's sake," he hissed beneath his breath and started to venture deeper into the grove.

Elizabeth would be mortified if he interrupted their expression of whatever desperate emotions they were feeling, but he could not allow this to go any further when Mr. Hayle was clearly promised to another. He faltered when he heard a loud gasp.

"Lizzie!"

Daniel frowned. Where had his wife come from?

"Georgie...I...I..." Lizzie stammered, and then soft sobs sounded.

"Mr. Hayle," his wife said frostily. "Only a few minutes ago, I defended your honor when it was questioned, yet now I've come upon you with your hands...hands...under my sister's dress and your mouth on...on..."

Embarrassment choked her voice, and Daniel sighed. Should he venture farther he would only add to their mortification, but he would listen to the resolution.

"Forgive me," Mr. Hayle said stiffly. "I was overcome by feelings and forgot myself."

"Forgot yourself?" his wife demanded faintly. "Had I been only a minute later, you would have...have irrevocably compromised my sister in the orchard as if she were a doxy!"

"Georgie!" Lizzie wailed, as if she would die from the humiliation of it all. "Please give us a moment."

"Hurry and cover yourself, Lizzie," his wife said. "And Mr. Hayle, I expect an engagement announcement will be made right away, sir."

A tense silence followed, and Daniel arched a brow as he waited for the man's reply.

"Regrettably, I am to be affianced to Miss Ava Tompkins. I… Forgive me, Miss Heyford. Forgive me, Lizzie. I should have never allowed this to go so far. All the blames lie on me, and I ask that you not berate your sister harshly over this matter, Miss Heyford."

Footsteps sounded, and Daniel gathered the man was walking away from the scene. A cold sensation knifed through him, and he prowled forward, no longer willing to hide his presence.

"Jonathan?" Lizzie said, sounding so deeply hurt, Daniel wanted to roar. "Are you leaving?"

She had only been his sister for a few days, yet her kindness, charm, and good-humored affability had endeared her to him.

"You will not just walk away," his wife cried, rushing after Mr. Hayle. "Have you no honor, sir!"

The man had the gall to keep walking without the courtesy of a reply. He stumbled when he saw Daniel strolling toward the tasteless scene. His wife stood with her hands fisted at her side, helpless fury and hurt glittering in her golden gaze. Elizabeth's eyes were deeply saddened, tears tracked down her cheeks, and Mr. Hayle himself appeared to be a man broken by the choices he presumably had to make.

The damned fool was clearly deeply attached to Elizabeth Heyford, but he would act the cad and walk away. A smile tipped Daniel's mouth, and it was perhaps a bit too merciless, for his wife stepped back, her eyes widening in alarm.

He advanced forward. "You will present your-self in a few hours to me with a respectable offer, Mr. Hayle, or we will meet at dawn."

A strangled sound emitted from the man's throat, and his wife swayed.

"Daniel," she cried, hurrying over to stand by his side. In a whispered undertone, she said, "Dueling is illegal. It has been outlawed for many years."

"Is that so?" he murmured, never taking his eyes from Mr. Hayle. "Then murder it is."

The man blanched and tugged nervously at his neckcloth as if it choked him. "I…I beg your par-don?"

"I am not a man who likes repeating himself," Daniel said, his tone implacable. "I will make an exception for you, because it is important you understand what is at stake should you act dis-honorably with my sister. It is your life, Mr. Hayle, the freedom to live it healthily, or merely live it at all, that you gamble with. An honorable offer will be forthcoming, or I will put a bullet through your heart."

The man whitened even further, and Daniel held his stare, letting him see the ruthless nature he'd not been aware lived within him. Yet at this moment, he knew it to be a real, tangible part of his character. Mr. Hayle saw it, for he swallowed and bobbed his head twice.

"It was only a misunderstanding, Mr. Stannis."

"Of course it was," he smoothly said.

Mr. Hayle glanced at Lizzie. "Miss Elizabeth is my fiancée, and we…we were only overcome just now."

"Very well, my good lad, I am acquainted with throes of passion and its danger."

His wife made a choking sound at that, and for just a second, Daniel's anger was replaced with good humor. He continued, "You will await me in the house, in the study, Mr. Hayle. Lizzie, go inside and wash your face."

His sister-in-law appeared to be in a daze, but she nodded and darted forward, careful to not peek at the man she loved. Mr. Hayle looked at her retreating figure, regret and longing evident in his features. He hastened after her, calling her name. However, Lizzie did not pause but broke into a run, with Mr. Hayle foolishly chasing after her.

Daniel glanced down at his wife. Tension crackled in the space between them. Her hands were clasped before her at her waist, her eyes bright with unshed tears and emotions he could not identify, yet they plucked a chord deep inside his body. The need to comfort and wipe that agony from her eyes twisted through him. "Wife—" he began.

She hurtled herself in his arms, slamming her mouth to his in a kiss. He stumbled, but he caught her about the waist, steadying them, while deepening their embrace. Her tongue glided carnally against his, and she cupped the side of his jaw with a tenderness at distinct odds with the tempestuous way they kissed.

He couldn't understand the feelings writhing inside his chest. *What the hell is this?* That they did not feel familiar told Daniel he had never felt like this for another woman. Had he not known anger and fear and laughter despite the memory loss? Yet this sensation piercing his chest for this woman was unknown yet so sweet…tender… desperate…and visceral. A painful ache rushed to his cock, hardening his length, and wicked darts of lust tore through him.

By God, I want her.

She wrenched her mouth from his and lifted shaking fingers to his mouth.

"Why do you cry?" he asked gruffly.

Georgianna placed a light, trembling touch on his jaw. "I…I was frightened just now," she whispered against his mouth. "So frightened for I did not know how I would have brought Mr. Hayle up to scratch or how I would have healed Lizzie's crushed heart…and then you came…"

The wealth of emotions in her voice made his damn chest ache. "I am your husband. I will always be the rock you need, wife. There is no need to fear."

Something wild and desperate and afraid flashed in her eyes before her lashes fluttered closed. Shards of ice seemed to pierce Daniel's chest. "Look at me."

Georgianna shook her head, and he leaned his

forehead against hers. "I can feel the tension in you…and the fear. What is it?"

Georgianna shook her head once again.

"Look at me wife," he said, his tone brooking no argument. He did not like the restless edge suddenly digging into his chest. Something was frightening her; even now small tremors went through the body flush against his.

Her eyes snapped open, and there was a hint of vulnerability in that defiant stare.

"Tell me," he coaxed.

"One day I shall find the courage," she whispered, "but not today. Now I must go to Lizzie."

He searched her gaze, and assured by the steadiness he saw, Daniel dipped and kissed her forehead. Her breath hitched, and a sigh flowed from her before she curved her body within his. He held his wife like that for long moments, then she moved from his arms and hurried toward the manor without looking back.

An odd tenderness stirred within, and he pressed a palm over his chest. *What is it that I am feeling for you, wife…and why does it feel so new…something never before a part of me?*

• • •

Several hours later, that kiss from Georgianna haunted Daniel's sleep. He looked around the small bedchamber, a keen sense of dissatisfaction filling him. Why was she not in here, sleeping beside him and in his arms?

Because it has only been several days and she is still waiting for you to remember her, a small voice reminded him. Daniel padded over to the windows, peeking out into the night. The stars were hidden, and rain seemed to be imminent. Mr. Hayle had departed hours ago with the understanding that his engagement to Lizzie would be announced to his parents and the good people of Crandell.

Thankfully, the attachment he claimed to have formed with Miss Tompkins had not been formalized, more of a suggestion between the parents that an alliance should be cemented between the families, in spite of the fact that no affection existed between the children.

Lizzie had been too overcome to dine with the family, and his wife had joined her sister in her chamber while he had dined with Anna and Sarah, entertaining the little hellions by teaching them how to play whist. He had not seen Georgianna since but had heard when she entered her bedchamber almost two hours ago.

Somehow, knowing she was beyond the door turned the soft want into a razor-edged hunger. He had only emerged from the bathroom, standing to wash in cold water instead of warming water for a bath. It had not helped the arousal thumping through his body and settling against the base of his cock like the most brutal aches.

Do you sleep, wife, or are you also restless and

desperate for more?

Had he ever desired anyone or anything this badly? Daniel somehow knew he had never been an indecisive man, nor had it been his nature to want something and not pursue it. Absorbing that knowledge of himself, he padded over to the connecting door and wrenched it open.

CHAPTER TWELVE

Georgianna's heart started to pound, and for a moment her thoughts scattered. Somehow, she had known the earl would come to her tonight. There had been something in his stare earlier at the orchard, and though she had not understood the intent behind his regard, her body had warmed, and how her heart had pounded.

Taking a deep breath, she slowly rose from the bed, almost giggling to realize her knees were knocking.

"I…" The word stuck in her throat.

The bedroom was dimly lit by a small blaze on the hearth, leaving much of the room in shadow, yet his gaze arrowed in on her with arousing precision. The look in his eyes told her exactly why he was there, but surely, she could be mistaken in her naivete. "Why are you here?"

"A husband and wife should sleep in each other's arms," he drawled, his fingers deftly unknotting the towel at his waist, allowing the material to fall to the floor.

Her breath hitched and tangled inside her chest. "Daniel!" Greedily, she drank in the strong, powerful lines of his torso, the rigid sculpted muscles, trying to ignore the heat surging through her limbs and the thick stalk jutting so unabashedly at her.

"Ah…you are blushing, wife, how delightfully quaint."

She backed away from him, watching his gaze flicker, his expression turned almost mocking. Georgianna stiffened her spine. *Is this a test because he doubts me?* That thought vanished almost instantly at the raw hunger she spied in his gaze.

He all but prowled into the room. He was beautiful in his nakedness, sensual, and so graceful.

"I have a question. Have we never shared a bed, my lady wife?"

"I… Please do recall we are very newly married," she said shakily, feeling rather foolish, for she had never imagined in her mad ruse that *this* would be a possibility, even with all their illicit and so very tempting kisses. Georgianna licked her lips that had gone dry; even without his memory, the earl was a randy libertine.

"Newly married, hmm? Is that to say I've never had you even with our desperate throes of passion? Not even on our wedding night?"

A wicked dart of heat curled low in her belly. "Yes."

His eyes gleamed with carnal deviltry. "My memory says otherwise, wife."

Her entire body went hot, especially the place between her thighs. "We…we did not get to consummate our union." Oh God, her heart was beating too fast.

"Now, why does that not sound like me? Why did we not consummate? You said we married in a mad dash of burning passion." His gaze swept over her body, searching and dissecting.

Georgianna lifted her chin, bracing for words of disbelief that she could have roused him in such a primal way.

"I believe you," he murmured, taking another step closer. "Even standing in this goddamn awful cotton contraption you call a gown, you are an ache in my head and heart, and my mouth is watering for a taste of you, wife."

Oooohhhhhh! She bit into the soft flesh of her bottom lip, desperate to stop the rush of warmth trickling from her belly down to her thighs. She clenched them tightly as if that would stop the evocative sensation, and his beautiful eyes gleamed with sudden heat and humor.

She stared at him in mute shock, unable to proffer any reply that would make sense to a man of his...experience and worldliness. "I... Our quarrel on the yacht halted your amorous advances."

His lips quirked. "We have recovered from that quarrel."

Georgianna cleared her throat. "We have. However, my menses have arrived," she said in a desperate rush, hating that she had done this.

Another truth hovered on her tongue, pushing her to tell him they were not truly husband and wife. A black fright swept through Georgianna.

And should I tell him the truth now…what then?

Her chest lifted on a ragged breath, her heart increasing its speed with every measured step he took closer. Then he was right there, with hardly a scant inch between their bodies, the sensual heat of him wrapping around her like a warm blanket. Daniel lifted his fingers, the backs of them brushing against the mounds that rose above the lowered neckline of her nightgown.

"How bloody pretty," he breathed.

The wretched libertine! Georgianna's breathing fractured. *Not a libertine…my fake husband.* Oh God. What had she gotten herself into?

"You are wounded, sir," she said huskily.

"Daniel, my sweet…or husband…or dear…or my darling," he drawled, his eyes darkening. "I think any one of those words I would like to hear from your lips."

"But Albert…" She cleared her throat of its hoarseness. "Dr. Albert said no strenuous activity. It is not wise in any regard for you to agitate yourself."

"Agitation?" He laughed, a low sound that warmed Georgianna, resonating deep inside her body. "Ah, my wife, sliding my cock into your pussy will be sweet and damn easy. There will be nothing taxing about it." He glided a finger to her jawline. "If you are worried…I'll accept you being on top."

The rough, erotic words kindled an odd spark low in her belly. Georgianna didn't know who she was when she was around him. Her thoughts tripped and stumbled over each other. *On top of what?* She must have asked it aloud for the corner of his mouth hitched in a smile so sensual, she felt the pull of it from below her navel.

"On top of me, wife, seated on my cock."

His tone was mild, but deviltry danced in his eyes. She took a shaky breath. Why did her belly feel so hot...the flesh between her legs achy?

Daniel cupped her cheek, feathering his thumb over her flesh. "What I cannot understand is the sweet innocence I see in your eyes. Have I not introduced you to any sort of pleasure? With my body I thee worship, and with all my worldly goods I thee endow," he said, trailing his fingers over the hollow of her throat. "Did I not say these words to you, wife?"

Something warm and heady unfurled inside her chest, alarming her. *It matters not if he calls me wife... It is all fake...*

He lowered his head, brushing the softest of kisses across the bridge of her nose. Georgianna could not explain the inexplicable sensation scything through her heart. Her breath hitched, and an impossible pain pierced her chest. *Oh, why do I now want things that are just not possible?* "I..."

"Even if we did not consummate, did I worship you with my body, Mrs. Stannis? Did I kiss and tease and taste you, hmm? Did I make these pretty lips wrap around my cock and suck and madden me with delight?"

His forehead brushed across hers, and she felt the restraint in his touch. "Did I splay you naked atop our bed and kiss every inch of this delectable, lush body? Did I linger over your pearl?"

"My pearl?" she asked hoarsely.

He arched a brow, his mouth quirking in a shadow of amusement, then he reached between the tight fit of their bodies and pressed two fingers right on her mound. Georgianna's knees weakened and she clutched at his shoulders. A terrible quiver of excitement filled her belly.

"Are you really seeing your menses, wife?"

The tightening of her belly was equal parts anticipation and nervousness. Still, she whispered the truth. "No."

A low, sensual chuckle vibrated from him. "I assure you, given the work I have been doing around our home I am quite fit for all types of strenuous activity. In fact, I'll relish this one."

Oh God.

This close, she could feel the thump of his heart against hers, the heat that poured off him and wrapped around her. Daniel arched her, lowered his head, and drew her nipple into his mouth. Georgianna felt the heat of his mouth even through the nightgown, and she whimpered, feeling almost bewildered by the twisting knots of sensation which started in her chest and shot to her belly, then settled lower. He sucked harder until her nipples ached, and she cried out when he rubbed his two fingers over her mound down over the throbbing folds of her sex.

Those wicked fingers caught on her nub and pressed hard. Georgianna cried out, jerking onto the tips of her toes, so acute and destructive were the sensations. He released the tip of her breast from his tormenting mouth and dragged his lips up to her clavicle, where he sucked at the pulse beating madly at her throat. She held him to her, trembling as he started to drag his fingers back and forth, over and over along her sex until she grew so wet and desperate, she was mortified. Georgianna pressed her face against his chest, biting into his muscles to stop the wild sounds escaping her throat.

He grunted...or was it a growl? The sound only served to enflame her senses more.

"Fuck..." he hissed. "I need to feel you..."

"Yes," she breathed.

With violent sensuality, he shoved her nightgown up, delving his fingers between her legs and finding her slickness. She sank her teeth even deeper into the muscles of his chest when his bare fingers found her folds. There was no hesitancy in his touch, just a bold carnality that sent her senses reeling and a desperate sob to lift from her throat.

Those fingers pinched her clitoris, rubbed, circled, drove her mad with delicious want. Shocks of pleasure raced from her throbbing nipples to her aching nub. Georgianna released his flesh from her teeth, fearing she would break his skin.

His head dipped, nudging against hers in a sensual stroke.

"Daniel," she whispered his name, when the coil of sensation drew too tight and desperate.

"Kiss me, wife."

Georgianna lifted her mouth at that rough command, spearing her fingers through his hair and pressing her lips to his, allowing their mouths and tongues to tangle in a passionate kiss. Regret and fear already beat at her senses, but she felt almost helpless against his ravishment, hooked by the unfathomable desire coursing through her.

He glided his fingers down, nudged her thighs wider with his, and pushed two of those fingers deep within her body. Her mind blanked, and she whimpered at the burn of pain and agonizing pleasure. He used his thumb to press and circle her nub while stroking hotly in and out of her. Georgianna shattered, screaming into his mouth, and he swallowed down the sound, emitting a groan of his own.

Oh God, I am so wet, she silently wailed, feeling the blush over her entire body. He dropped to his knees, gripped her hips, and dragged her sex onto his mouth.

"Daniel!"

Fire coasted over her body in wicked, undulating waves. *Surely this is too indecent!*

She gripped his hair, her legs weakening until she collapsed against the post of the bed. His masculine chuckle vibrated against her mons. He did not lift his head but opened her legs wider and licked along her folds. Her entire body shook, and all her awareness contracted to his mouth licking hotly over her most intimate flesh. He worked her clitoris with his tongue until she unraveled yet again with a keening sob.

He pushed her nightgown farther up, licking upward, biting the flesh of her lower belly, flicking his tongue over her navel. Daniel rose, one of his hands sweeping up her thighs, the other gripping her hair in a possessive clasp, angling her head for his mouth.

She groaned, unfettered and wanton, when a long finger pierced her sex.

"I want to sink my cock so badly into you, wife," he murmured against her mouth before pressing a soft kiss there, a diabolical contrast to the fingers that evoked such wanton longings within her soul. "Though you are so wet…I'll need to prepare you more…another two fingers…"

She gasped at the stretch and sensuous sting as he followed through on his carnal purr. He swallowed her sounds in a kiss of such hunger, Georgianna almost felt scared, mostly by the sheer intensity of the chaotic sensations cresting through her body. He dragged her release from her, and this time when she shattered, Georgianna felt as if she floated on clouds of bliss.

He swept her into his arms, bearing her down on the bed. She'd passed the point of discretion and good sense. This moment was ill-judged, yet Georgianna felt it too late to turn back. Still, a sense of unalterable consequences beat at her, and her fright grew more pronounced. "Daniel," she gasped. "Wait, I—"

The words caught in her throat when he recoiled, slapping a palm over his forehead. This time his groan was rough with pain, and he stumbled backward. Georgianna scrambled onto her knees, staring at him.

"Daniel?" When he made no answer, she rushed from the bed, almost stumbling in her haste. "You are in pain," she whispered, coming over to stand beside him. "What is it?"

The earl held his body tight, grooves of pain bracketing his mouth. "I will not spend this night in your arms, wife. I bid you to sleep well," he said tightly, turning and walking away and through the connecting door.

The door closed with a soft *snick*. That sound seemed to release her, and she breathed raggedly, pressing her hand against her stomach.

Upon my word, what did I just allow?

CHAPTER THIRTEEN

Daniel sat on the edge of his bed, gripping his forehead, hoping that a tight pinch would ease the sudden pounding in his skull. What the hell had brought it on? He'd been about to make love to his wife, soothing the tormenting hunger that had been plaguing him these last few days. He closed his eyes, even now, and despite the pain in his head, he could marvel at her softness, the sweetness of her taste, and those hot, wanton sounds she made as she came undone.

His heart lurched again, rattling inside his chest like a thing not a part of his body. And as if to punish him, the pain in his head sharpened. Groaning, he lowered himself to the bed, closing his eyes, trying to allow the pain to pass through him. The connecting door opened, and he heard the whisper of his wife's feet over the carpet as she came toward him.

A sheet was tucked up to her chin, and he almost smiled. She then climbed into the bed with him, and he felt the cool touch of her fingers on his nape. His wife did not ask any questions, simply started to knead and massage away the tight knot of muscles he'd not realized existed along his shoulder blades.

"Keep your eyes closed," she murmured.

With each sink of her fingers, the pain eased, and she diligently attended to him even when he suspected her fingers cramped.

"You are very stiff," she murmured. "I am sorry."

"The fault is not yours."

"I will try and help more with—"

"I'll not have my wife doing these labors anymore," he growled. "I alone will attend to these until I have found a solution."

"Turn onto your stomach," she said softly.

There was a smile and a wealth of emotions in her voice he could not decipher. Daniel complied, curious as to her intention.

"Do not move. I shall return shortly." The bed dipped, and he listened to her footsteps as she hastened from his chamber. A few moments later, she returned.

Something warm touched his shoulder blade, and the scent of lavender floated in the air.

"I warmed it by the fire." His wife cleared her throat. "I...I...need to straddle your hips or back for what I have in mind."

Bloody hell. The image those words evoked hardened his cock, pressing it into the mattress below him. Unable to speak past the swell of arousal, he merely grunted. Georgianna slung a leg across his lower back, the feel of her bare skin against him a sweet torture. He held himself still as the aching throb returned at the base of his skull.

Seated atop him, her knees cradling his hips, she started a slow and deep knead of his shoulders and neck. He groaned. *Sweet mercy*. This was good. Too good. Tension Daniel hadn't known he was holding drained away from his shoulders.

She massaged him in silence, working magic with her fingers on his overworked muscles. Her touch as it glided from his shoulders down to his back felt explorative, and more than once her breath audibly hitched and then a soft sigh left his wife.

The darkness that enveloped them in the bedchamber seemed to heighten every sense. The heat of her core as she sat on his lower back was unmistakable. His groin tightened to excruciating hardness, but Daniel gave no indication of it.

His wife rubbed and kneaded his muscles until the dark pull of sleep beckoned. "The pain has eased," he said gruffly. "Thank you. I never knew I needed this."

"Good," she whispered. "Would you like some tea?"

Another almost smile hitched at his mouth. Only his nana fussed over him so when she thought he ailed. Daniel frowned. *My nana?* An image started to form, but frustration snapped through him when it vanished like wisps of smoke.

His wife's weight shifted from his body, and he tensed. "Don't go. Stay with me tonight."

He felt her hesitation, then she touched his arm. Her body lowered and her mouth brushed against his ear. "I'll stay, but no agitation of the body."

Dark humor flowered through him. "I promise, no agitation."

He felt her smile, then she shifted her body away.

"Though it is barely burning, I will put out the fire in the hearth. The smallest of light can increase the pain in your head."

"The night will be cold," he murmured, anticipation already curling through him.

"We'll have blankets," she said, sweet amusement rich in her voice.

"They won't be enough. You'll be cold, wife."

He could feel her stare on him.

"I'll have you to warm me," she finally murmured.

There were several rustles in the room, then she slipped beneath the coverlets beside him. Daniel felt for his wife and drew her into his arms. She fitted against him with such perfection, he had the inane thought that this woman was fashioned precisely for him. "I've never slept with a lady before."

She stiffened. "Surely you cannot know that for certain."

"I know it," he said, feeling the truth of it resounding inside. "I've had lovers...but not this..." Intimacy, this sharing of oneself by allowing vulnerability. He thought then that sleeping with someone felt like a simple notion, yet it required implicit trust.

How curious.

"I've never slept beside another, either," she said, almost shyly.

He opened his eyes and encountered the pitch-black room. His wife had closed the drapes. Shifting slightly, he smelled her hair, liking the hint of lavender…and sun-ripened peaches. How he wished he could remember her. What had their first meeting been like? Their first kiss…or the first moment they acknowledged they wanted to be with each other in a permanent union? She did not look at him with love or affection…more hunger and wariness. Was it because he did not remember her or was there more to it? Why the hell did she agree to marry him?

Do I even want her to look at me with affection?

Daniel frowned, wondering why even the hunger in his heart felt so elusive.

"Your heart is pounding," she said softly, pressing the flat of her palm against his naked chest.

"I am wondering about you."

Thud. Thud. Thud. Her hand jerked against his chest. "What do you wonder?"

"How did we meet?"

Her fingers curled into their side, and he wondered if she knew he could not feel her erratic heartbeat.

"I was hired to cook for a special birthday event." She delicately cleared her throat. "You were there, standing in the shadows…and the night we met, I felt your regard upon me before I saw you."

The memory of seeing her wended through him, and without recalling the full picture, he remembered his visceral reaction to her sensuality and lush loveliness.

"Did I introduce you to my family?"

She turned her face to bury it against his chest, as if she wanted to hide from his questioning.

"I never met any of your family," she said, emotions he could not identify thickening her voice.

Daniel could not promise that he'd not been ashamed of her or offer any reassured explanation of why he'd not allowed her to meet his family, so he remained silent. *Hell, do I even have family?* The gut-wrenching dread tried to grab hold of him, and he ruthlessly pushed it down.

Do not fear what seems undefeatable, but patiently wait and work at a solution.

Those words were a phantom whisper, and unaccountably, he understood it had been a lesson from his father. Daniel closed his eyes, holding his wife close to his side, and allowed himself to drift into a deep slumber.

• • •

A couple of days later, Daniel lowered the brush he was using to paint the side of the manor, working at the pain in the back of his neck. His wife had summoned Dr. Albert, who had reassured them that the head pains were normal for an amnesiac, and the reason for the malady and side effects were not known. Though the doctor had ordered more bedrest, and Georgianna had also implored him to rest, each day Daniel laboriously worked at fixing issues around the manor, yet the work seemed never ending. His wife appeared appreciative of his effort; however, Daniel was not satisfied with their lack of resources. Something bloody well needed to be done, and a hiss of frustration slipped from him, for the solution was not coming his way.

Only yesterday, his wife had spent the day at some local landowner, cooking for their garden party for the miserly sum of fifty pounds. He stiffened on the heel of that thought. What kind of life had he experienced to presume such a sum to be negligible? Daniel scrubbed a hand over his face. *Bloody hell.* He only knew he loathed the exhaustion that had lined his wife's body as she trudged home. Anger had surged inside that the Fords had not the courtesy to send her home in a carriage, but after her back-breaking work, she'd had to walk miles through the wood.

Georgianna had been exhausted, but he had watched her at the kitchen table, making her notes in her ledger, practicing careful economy on how the money would be spent to improve their family's circumstances. It had not even occurred to her to purchase new boots to replace the scuffed ones on her feet. A smile touched his mouth upon recalling her falling asleep at the table, and he'd taken the privilege of lifting her in his arms and taking her up to her chamber.

"*Are you going to ravish me?*" she'd asked sleepily, snuggling into his body and filling his chest with perplexing tenderness.

"*You are too exhausted for that,*" he had gently replied.

And no answer had come from her, because his wife had been deeply asleep before he reached the landing. The provision for his family could not rest on his wife's shoulders. It was his duty to care for them in all ways and to ease her care and worries.

But how do I do that?

Footsteps rushed over to him, and he turned to see Anna and Sarah. They beamed up at him, tripping over each other in their excitement to speak at the same time.

"Ladies," he said, "one after the other. Who will speak first?"

"I will," Anna cried, twirling about. "Will you come with us to pick wildflowers? Lizzie and Georgie said we are never to wander so far into the woodlands alone."

"Why are we picking wildflowers?"

"It is for Georgie. Today is her birthday."

He stilled. "It is?"

"Yes, Lizzie says she will be four and twenty

today, and Georgie loves flowers."

He had not known it was his wife's birthday. Daniel raked his fingers through his hair. "What else does she love?"

Sarah's brows puckered. "Food."

Ah…that much he knew. He glanced behind him toward the kitchen, noting no smoke billowing from the chimney.

"She is still sleeping," Anna chirped. "Lizzie always tells us to allow Georgie to sleep on her birthday, but she will soon awaken to cook us something special."

He arched a brow. "She will cook something special for everyone else…on her birth celebration?"

The girls nodded with great anticipation.

"Why does Lizzie not cook for her?"

Anna's eyes rounded comically, and Sarah made choking sounds.

"I gather Lizzie cannot cook," he said drily.

"She is terrible," Sarah said, making a face.

"What does Georgie get to do for fun on her birthday?"

The girls thought about this and said in union, "Cook!"

Daniel bit back his frustration. She should not be in the kitchen. His wife should be pampered. Bathed in rose water. Massaged with lavender oil, presented with the most scrumptious golden dress, silver dancing slippers, her hair brushed until it gleamed, and then he would take her to a duchess's ball and dance the night away with her.

He stiffened as the vision flowered through his mind, the settings so real and breathtaking that he knew he had attended grand balls before. *How?* Aware of the sudden pounding of his heart, it took him a while to relax.

Anna tugged at his trousers. "Are you going to help us pick flowers for Georgie?"

"Better," he said, "I am going to cook for her. She should not be in the kitchen today."

"Cook what?" Sarah gasped, her eyes rounding.

"You tell me of her favorite meal. I am a learned man, and you are brilliant girls. I am certain that among us, we can figure it out."

They cast him dubious stares, which soon melted into looks of wonder and fierce determination. They followed him inside to the kitchen, where they rummaged through the larder and pantry.

"Georgie specially loves stewed hocks."

"What is that?"

"Stewed pigs' feet," Sarah said, patting her tummy, a dreamy look in her eyes. "It is quite tasty."

"My wife eats pigs' feet?" He hoped the horror did not sound in his damn voice.

Feet? Of an animal that sleeps in the mud?

The girls giggled infectiously and nodded.

"Does it actually look like the pig's feet or is it only the flesh from that part?"

Laughter pealed from Sarah and Daniel ruefully smiled. "Never to worry," he said with a
mock flourish, grabbing up the apron. "We will
delight Georgianna this day!"

And it would most certainly not be with pig's
hooves.

• • •

Almost three hours later, his wife skidded to a
halt upon entering the kitchen, her golden eyes
widening. "Daniel?" she called his name tentatively, venturing further inside, glaring at the mess
they had made. "I overslept! I was aghast to see it
was almost four in the afternoon!"

He ran his gaze over her, noting she appeared
bright faced and refreshed, a far cry from the
deeply exhausted lady of last eve. Georgianna
wore a bright yellow dress with its narrow-pleated
skirt and long sleeves, which sensually clung to all
her curves. Her hair was caught in a loose chignon
with artful curls dancing over her cheeks, and
even so unadorned, her prettiness glowed.

One day I'll wrap you in diamonds and silk.

"You needed it, wife. You are beautiful."

"I…" She smiled and tucked a wisp of hair behind her ear. "Thank you. What is all of this?"

Cooking was rather more involving and chal-
lenging than Daniel had allowed, but he was still
damn proud of their efforts. He lowered the
wooden spoon and padded over to her. Uncaring

of their audience, he cupped his wife's cheek, lifted her face, and lightly brushed his mouth over her lips, then kissed her forehead. "Happy birthday to you, wife."

"*Oh!*" she whispered, her eyes gleaming with delight. "How charming you look in my apron, Mr. Stannis."

"I know," he murmured. "I am of a mind to wear it alone for you."

A choked sound came from her, and he smiled.

"We cooked for you, stuffed roast veal with creamy potatoes," Anna said, skipping over to hug her sister's thighs. "Happy birthday, Georgie!"

Sarah hastened over and hugged her sister, chirping her greetings.

"Thank you," his wife said laughingly, the prettiest color blooming on her cheeks.

"Come, see what we cooked." Sarah held one of her hands while Anna held the other, then they tugged her over to the island where he had just ladled the food on their finest plates.

"You did this?"

"*We* all did it," Anna said proudly, puffing out her small chest. "But Mr. Stannis was the head chef!"

The door opened, and Lizzie burst inside, clutching a basket to her chest. "You are awake!"

"I overindulged," Georgianna said, smiling. "You went into town?"

"Yes," Lizzie said sheepishly, coming over to hand the basket to Daniel. "I was trying to make it back home before you ventured down."

"*Mesdames, emmenez votre sœur à la salle à manger*," he said with a dramatic French accent, startling himself that he could speak French. Daniel frowned, wondering if they even understood that he had asked them to escort Georgianna to the dining room. His heart beating a harsh rhythm, he continued, "Go, I shall present our meal shortly."

Sarah and Anna chortled.

"*Oui, monsieur*, to the dining room we go," Lizzie replied with a similarly exaggerated French accent, giggling as she tugged his wife away.

Georgianna glanced over her shoulder, and their gazes collided. There was a tenderness there he had never seen before, and it rendered his mouth dry. Beyond that tenderness, he saw regret...and sorrow, and Daniel frowned, a tight feeling twisting inside his chest. A soft smile touched her mouth, and she looked away, leaving the kitchen.

His wife had looked at him as if she believed he would soon be lost to her. His gut tightened and something inexplicable inside him recoiled. What was she thinking?

Lizzie returned to help him take the serving platter upstairs to the dining room where his wife waited. He lifted a brow when he noted Anna and Sarah were missing.

"The girls and I decided to take our meal in the parlor," Lizzie said, her eyes gleaming with mischief. "We thought it best you and Georgie enjoyed this time together."

A delicate blush stole across the high ridges of his wife's cheekbones, her eyes gleaming with that sensual allure. Lizzie continued on with a platter, and he set his fare before his wife. Daniel reached for the bottle of wine he'd asked Lizzie to procure for him, opened it, and poured two generous portions in the crystal cut glasses on the table.

"Thank you," she said with a smile. "The last time a birthday meal was cooked for me, it was Mama and Papa who prepared it."

He nodded once and, with surprising eagerness, reached for her plate and ladled the stuffed veal onto it. He shared the same onto his plate before reaching for his glass.

"A toast to you, wife. I am…awed by you."

"Sir?"

How alarmed she sounded, her delicate fingers tightening over the stem of her wineglass.

"I see hardship around you, yet you live and love life vibrantly. You are kind and selfless. You work tirelessly for your family without worrying about your own welfare. At first, it incensed me, but then I see how happy Anna, Lizzie, and Sarah are. You devote yourself and thrive despite the odds because you love your siblings deeply. I admire you. You are without any adornment from me, yet you exist with good humor and cheer. You walked almost two hours yesterday to someone's home, prepared a lavish feast, and then walked back home, and still you pattered about cooking for them and telling Anna stories before her bedtime. I vow, one day, I'll buy you a lavish carriage, and you'll have a cook, a maidservant, a footman, and a butler."

His wife stared at him as if he were a creature she had never before seen, the pulse at the hollow of her throat fluttering madly.

Her lips parted, and Georgianna blinked away at what might have been a sheen of fresh tears. "Daniel I do not know what…"

"Happy birthday, wife. You need not say anything—simply believe in me and my promise."

She nodded wordlessly and took a swallow of her wine. Lowering it to the table, she reached for her knife, tucked into the tender veal, and took a hearty bite, her lashes fluttering closed.

"The girls recommended pigs' feet as the best meal you would wish for," he murmured.

She swallowed, and a light laugh left her. "In truth, I enjoy food so much, I do not have a favorite. There are so many delights I have never experienced for me to decide on a dish as the one I prefer above all."

She took another mouthful, chewing slowly.

"Is it good?"

Her eyes sparkled. "Hmm."

The sound was arbitrary, but Daniel took it as confirmation that his dish was indeed tasty. "Good. Then I shall make you dinner at least twice each week."

She stilled and met his stare. "I am terrified at the notion."

His wife sounded appropriately horrified. Considering the rich humor gleaming in her gaze, Daniel glanced down at the stuffed veal he had diligently prepared according to her recipe notebook. Lifting his fork, he took a mouthful and choked, regret and horror scything through him. "Bloody hell! This is awful."

She laughed, the sound so damn sweet he wanted to hoard it and make it a part of himself.

"You only used too much salt and herbs."

Reaching over, he removed her plate and set it aside. "I do not care too much of what I used. You will not eat another bite."

Setting her elbows on the table, his wife propped her chin on her open palms. "A chef must always taste as they cook."

He lifted a brow. "I never tasted once."

"I know," she said tenderly, that enigmatic glow in her eyes.

Daniel lifted the bottle of wine. "At least I got the best wine in town, hmm? We shall drink until we are foxed."

Her eyes widened. "The best wine in town? Nay, husb..." Her breath stuttered, and Georgianna lowered her lashes, hiding her expression from him. "Husband," she continued softly, as if she savored the word. "You've not had the best wine until you've tasted mine."

His wife rose and beckoned him to follow her.

She ran ahead of him, looking like a woodland fairy whenever she glanced over her shoulder to ensure he followed. Daniel was curious and enchanted. He ran after her until they reached the orchard he'd never explored.

Dozens of orange and peach trees were in bloom, and as they walked deeper into the grove, the fallen leaves shuffled around their feet. A stone bench with a fountain was within the heart of the grove, and she motioned for him to sit. He obliged, watching as she took a small shovel, went under one of the peach trees, and started to dig. A few minutes later, she withdrew an earthen jug. Rising, she stared at it for a long time, a poignant expression on her face. She walked over, sat beside him, and held it out.

"I daresay this will be the best wine to drink today."

"Indeed?"

"Mama and I made it," she said softly. "Then we buried it out here. Mama always said the best wines are stored in mud jars, buried in soil for years. The wine is then sweeter and more flavorful and intoxicating."

"How long has it been buried?"

"Almost six years. It was one of the last things my mother and I did before…before she died in the train accident."

A memory pricked at him, that one of his good friends, an earl, lost his parents as well in a horrific train crash. Daniel tensed, scrubbing a hand over his face. He was good friends with an earl? The very idea was preposterous. Shaking the elusive memory away, he peered down at his wife. The sadness on her face cut into him like a knife. He wanted to wipe it away and replace that look only with contentment. Daniel lowered his head and kissed the corner of her mouth.

A soft shudder went through her. "Will you drink it with me?"

"I'd be honored, wife."

She smiled, opened the lid of the jar, lifted it to her mouth, and drank. Georgianna handed the jar to him, and he took several healthy swallows, almost moaning at the rich, lush taste.

"What kind of wine is this?"

"Peach and orange wine. It's Mama's secret recipe."

"You would make a bloody fortune selling this." He took several more swallows before handing the jar to her, and they sat there in the grove, drinking wine, leaves falling around them like soft clouds to settle on the ground.

"I daresay this is one of my best birthdays," she said, smiling, leaning over to rest the side of her head on his shoulder.

Yet the day has been so simple.

"It is only the beginning of many, wife," he said gruffly, wanting to lay the world at her feet.

His wife lifted her head to stare at him, and the yearning he spied in the depths of her eyes stole his breath.

A sad smile touched her mouth. "Daniel... there is something I have to tell you. I..." She closed her eyes, biting into her lower lip with such force, it would surely bruise.

He cupped her cheeks, and she hugged the jar of wine to her chest, as if holding on to it anchored her against whatever tore at her.

"Look at me."

Her lashes fluttered open slowly, her regard lowered to his mouth, and her cheeks pinkened prettily.

"Ah...wife, I will happily oblige."

"I said nothing," she gasped, her eyes sparkling with wicked allure.

He kissed her mouth, flicking his tongue over the spot she had bruised, then sucked at the flesh there. She moaned, and he kissed her deeper, licking along the seams of her mouth before gliding his tongue over hers.

"Tonight...I am going to make love to you, wife... Then I am going to fuck you."

She gasped again, the soft sound traveling down his body to settle against the base of his cock. "Are they not the same?"

He tilted her head, thrusting his fingers through her hair, kissing the corner of her mouth down to the curve of her throat where he grazed his teeth over her pulse. "Nay. First, I am going to savour you...lick and taste you everywhere, delight you with such pleasure, you'll writhe and beg me to end the sweet torture."

"I would never beg," she said huskily, arching her neck and giving him better access to her flesh.

"We'll drink more wine…take a bath together…and then I'll place you on your knees, arch your back, admire and nibble at your lush arse… and then I'll tup you, wife…hard and deep. That is the fucking part, my sweet."

"My imagination is sorely lacking." She took a deep breath. "Show me."

That hot, little purr did incredible things to his damn heart, for it pounded as if he had no control over his emotions. Daniel groaned and bit harder on her throat and then sucked. The jar dropped from her grasp, and with swift reflexes he caught it, leaned away from her, and drank. She watched him with eyes dark with arousal and indefinable emotions. When he tipped his head back to consume more of the wine, she dipped forward and flicked her tongue, gliding it from his exposed throat up to his mouth.

It was her turn to kiss the corner of his mouth, tasting the wine there. He handed her the jar, and she drank several more gulps until it was empty. His wife stood, almost stumbling to the center of the grove, lifting her hand and twirling.

It must have been some sort of magical alchemy, for at that moment the wind stirred, and her hair tumbled loose from the chignon, spilling over her shoulder to her mid back, the leaves stirring at her feet.

She was simply breathtakingly lovely.

And you are mine.

Possessiveness and something more profound hitched through his heart, and Daniel wondered if he had ever given her soft words and tender moments, or if he was even a man capable of it. He wondered what precious things had been lost in the mire of forgotten memories. It was as she stumbled in her second twirl that he realized his wife was well and truly tipsy.

Amusement washed through him. Daniel rose and went over, clasping her about the waist and pulling her close to his body. She tilted her head up, searching his face. "Make a wish under the stars and take me into your dreams, Daniel."

He was bemusedly aware of the odd plucking at his heartstrings. Right at that moment, Daniel knew he was not a man given to sentiments, and whatever feelings his wife roused within him were wholly unfamiliar and unknown. "You are already there," he said.

Briefly, she closed her eyes. "Do not hate me," she whispered, her lashes fluttering open.

"I can never hate you, wife."

"You only say that because you do not know the truth." Her eyes shadowed, and she tenderly touched the underside of his jaw. "I wish you were real."

There was an odd note in her voice.

"Woman—"

"The truth is I am not your wife," she said in a rush, relief filling her golden gaze. "You would *never* have married someone like me, someone so below your station and regard in every manner."

"You are tipsy, wife."

"*Nay*," she gasped. "Do we not tell the truth when we are in our cups?"

He smiled, loving the red rosiness of her cheeks and the wild glitter in her eyes. "We also tell our fears. I suspect my family might have been wealthier than yours. It does not mean I am unhappy with you. Far from it."

She made a slashing motion with her hand, toppling and landing on his chest with a hiccup.

"You cannot know that!" she said, tears pooling in her eyes. "You poor, wretched soul…who cannot recall his past and his family. How tormented you must be!"

"Poor, wretched soul am I?" he asked drily.

Her head bobbed with her frantic nods, tumbling her hair about her face and shoulders in a cloud of waves.

"Then kiss me," he murmured roughly.

"And what will that do?"

"This poor, wretched fool will feel delighted and—"

Her mouth mashed against his, her efforts at best laughable. He smiled against her mouth, wondering at the profound tenderness wrenching through his heart. The hellion bit his bottom lip.

"Oh, I do so want to be wicked with you," she murmured against his mouth, kissing him with hot, urgent nips. Her eager sensuality only enflamed his lust, and he deepened their kiss, sucking on her tongue with lazy carnality.

Their lips parted, and she whispered, "I like your kisses, and I have been imagining them everywhere on my body. I want everything you said… I want you to love me slowly…and then tup me."

His wife reached for his hand and wedged it between her thighs, and he groaned feeling the heat of her quim through her drawers and petticoats.

"Especially here," she whispered. "Ever since you placed your mouth here and teased me so mercilessly…I have been wanting you back there. But surely, I cannot be so reckless and wanton when we have yet to be married and will never be!"

He groaned. "Woman, we are married!"

She gasped, pushed away from his body, grabbed his arm, and tugged him. She had no strength to move him, but he followed her from the orchard and into the house. Georgianna marched them down the hallway and into the drawing room where Elizabeth, Sarah, and Annabelle rested by the fire, reading one of the books he brought home.

"I have told him everything," she cried. "He is a duke!" His wife canted her head and frowned, another small hiccup bursting from her. "Oh, no, not a duke…a viscount or an earl! Yes, an earl, and we are not married in truth!"

She whirled, and he clasped her gently about the waist lest she fall, and she gave him a very smug nod. He glanced up at her sisters, who peered at her with rife concern.

"Is she foxed?" Lizzie asked, astonished.

"What is foxed?" Sarah asked.

Anna merely yawned and rubbed her eyes, evidently trying to stay awake.

"We have been drinking wine," he murmured.

"Please do not take her words to heart," Lizzie said, her eyes wide and imploring. "Georgie…had always felt that…she was not the type of lady a man of your…elegance would marry."

"I am beginning to realize it," he murmured, peering down into her lovely face.

"But you *are* married."

"Lizzie!" his wife wailed. "I am trying to tell him the truth."

Daniel placed his hands under her hips and back, lifting her into his arms. "It is time to get you to bed."

Delight lit in her eyes, and she slipped her hands around his nape. "Are you about to ravish me, my husband? Perhaps lick—"

He captured her mouth with his, lest she say something far too wicked in front of her innocent sisters. Lizzie's gasp echoed around them, and Sarah giggled. He lifted his head, walked away from the drawing room, and made his way down the hallway, then up the stairs. A soft snoring came from her, and Daniel glanced down.

His wife was sound asleep in his arms, her forehead resting on his chest with utmost trust.

He took Georgianna to her chamber, gently placing her in the center of the bed. She murmured something indecipherable and kicked at his hand when he tried to remove her boots.

"You are just as cantankerous as Hetty and Nellie," he said, chuckling.

Daniel removed her boots and stockings, then, shifting her with ease, unbuttoned her dress. He allowed Georgianna her modesty by leaving on her shift. She rolled onto her belly, her lush arse tempting him to join her, even if only to sleep with her snuggled into his arms. He breathed out deeply, tucking the thick coverlet up to her chin, before going over to the fireplace and stoking the logs. Once he was assured of her comfort, he went through the connecting door and sat on the edge of his bed to remove his boots and clothes.

Naked, he reposed on the bed, lacing his fingers behind his head to stare thoughtfully at the ceiling.

"He is a duke...a viscount...an earl!"

Why was it that this assertion from his wife had not felt strange...but confoundingly right? A thump through the connecting door had him lurching up to investigate. He opened the door and paused to see his wife in the center of the room with the coverlet and pillows tossed about on the ground.

"Georgianna?"

"Cold," she whispered, looking like a lost waif, but so damn lovely and tempting that his teeth ached.

He ventured forward, plucked up the coverlet and pillows, and tossed them on the bed. "You are still unsteady on your feet; let's get you back to bed."

"That is not where I want to be."

Their gazes collided, and though her eyes remained glossy, there was an unspoken need there that viscerally tugged at his chest. Daniel opened his arms, and she stumbled forward and sank into his embrace, as if it was only there she belonged.

"Why are you naked?" she muttered, burrowing her face even more against his chest, then yawning.

Amused, he said, "I always sleep in the nude; there is just something decadent about feeling silk sheets on my arse."

She giggled, the sweet sound piercing him.

"We have no silk sheets."

"No…you do not, do you?" he murmured. *Yet it is what I am accustomed to sleeping on.*

Those delicate fingers skimmed over his chest, the callouses on the tips raking wicked sensations through him. When her fingers clasped around his cock, his damn knees almost buckled.

"This is so thick," she whispered. "And why is it so hard but smooth?"

Sweet mercy.

Her fingers dropped from him, and another

soft snore lifted, and he peered down at the top of her head. Was she truly already asleep? Daniel smiled. It occurred to him then that she found some sort of comfort in his arms, enough where that might be the only place she could rest tonight. Overly indulging in liquor could leave one restless and unmoored. Perhaps she felt this, too, and only in his arms she deemed herself...safe?

His heart started to drum, and he gently shifted and lifted her up, taking her back to her bed. She mumbled irritably and kicked at the sheets, but this time he slipped under the sheets with her, tugging the coverlets around them. Instantly the fight went out of her body, and she rolled into his side, tossing a foot over his hip and perilously close to his cock that responded with alarming swiftness. She draped half of her body over his chest and buried her nose in the hollow of his throat. His wife made a little purr of satisfaction in her throat before her breath rose and fell with her deep, contented sleep.

It is going to be another long, torturous night.

Daniel smiled, wrapping his arms around her, and smiling, for something also inexplicably warned him that it would also be one of the most wonderful.

CHAPTER FOURTEEN

Georgianna slowly woke, yawning indelicately behind her palm. Her brain felt foggy, and her head slightly ached. The events of the past evening came rushing back, and she surged into a sitting position, gripping the sheets tightly. *I confessed to the earl we are not married!* It took considerable effort, but she calmed her heart and looked around her bedroom, unable to dismiss the impression of being wrapped tightly around a muscled, perfectly proportioned body.

Daniel spent the night in my bed.

Georgianna's entire body burned. Had he... had he made love to her as he wickedly promised? Georgianna closed her eyes and tried to recall the evening with some clarity. Her breath released on a rush of relief upon remembering that she had merely fallen asleep in his arms.

"Oh, Lizzie, I was indeed trying to tell the earl the truth." Still, relief filled her veins that he had not believed her, for heavens help her, Georgianna was not yet ready to lose him from their life.

She pressed trembling fingers to her mouth, recalling the feel and taste of him. A wanton burst of heat spread from her stomach to her suddenly aching breasts. She would have allowed him to take her to his bed and destroyed all her sensibilities. Her heart stuttered hard, and she dropped her weight back onto the bed, staring at the ceiling.

Who am I when I am with you?

Reckless and intemperate, no longer the sensible, dutiful, and practical girl her parents had raised.

"I am going to make love to you, wife, and…"

Georgianna groaned, closing out the memory of that carnal promise and the hot sensation of want it provoked.

I have lost all of my good senses, and they must be reclaimed.

The earl was not really her husband, and that he admired her should have no bearing in her life. One day he would walk away and never look back—or worse, he might be vengeful enough to demand recompense for having worked about her yard so tirelessly. Yet even knowing this, Georgianna wanted to touch him, kiss him over and over, hold him tight, and never let him go.

She felt caught between such terrible longing…and fear.

I am so silly and selfish!

The self-approbation hurt her chest, for she had always placed other needs before hers. *And that is what I am doing*, she insisted stubbornly, *as without the earl's help around the manor, our circumstances would have been even more dire*. If she were to calculate the labor he owed for the monies he had not paid over, that would be at least two years!

Why was she faltering in as little as two weeks?

Georgianna scrambled from the bed, a quick glance at the clock on the mantel revealing it was almost six in the afternoon. *Good heavens!* She'd slept for the entire day! *For a second time!*

"I shall never drink again so recklessly," she muttered.

Georgianna hurriedly performed her ablutions, taking a quick bath then dressing in a simple pale green day dress with several buttons to the front. She gathered her hair in a plain chignon, frowning at her reflection in the cheval mirror. Her eyes gleamed with awareness and her cheeks were flushed, and inside she ached.

Silly!

Georgianna hurried from her chamber to below stairs, calling for Lizzie. No one answered, and hurrying to the kitchen, she found it frightfully clean and empty, the fireplace lit, shaving off the chill in the air. There was a pot on the stove, and her recipe notebook opened beside it. She walked over and lifted the lid.

It was curried rice. The smell was divine, and her mouth watered. A very simple but tasty dish she often prepared when their larder ran empty. She noted a slip of paper with presumably the earl's handwriting.

Boil the rice and drain the water. Slice one large onion very thinly and fry the pieces with a little

butter; then add the boiled rice, a tablespoon curry-
powder, and a little salt, thyme, bell peppers to
season, then mix all together in a skillet for a few
minutes. Remember to taste with each dash of sea-
soning.

Georgianna smiled. She felt foolishly charmed
by his efforts. It was her recipe, but he had removed all the flowery creative prose and
descriptions she had placed in her notes, making
her directions simpler to understand. She plucked
up the paper and read it again, wondering if she
should write two different instructions in the recipe book she crafted, one set for those of advanced
cooking like herself, and another set for those
who were ignorant of cooking and would require
very simplistic and precise instructions like the
earl.

Reaching for a wooden spoon, Georgianna
tasted the curried rice, humming her pleasure at
the flavorful taste. Setting down the spoon, she
peeked through the windows, where she spied
Lizzie strolling with Mr. Hayle and the girls.
Georgianna bustled through the side kitchen
doors to outside, gaily waving.

"Georgie," Anna cried, running over to her.
"You're finally awake! How you slept and slept
and slept! Mr. Stannis promised us two new reading books if we allowed you to rest without
disturbance. He said you needed it, and we should
care for you, always."

There went that tumbling warmth inside her

chest again. Georgianna tousled the top of her sister's head and warmly greeted Sarah, Lizzie, and Mr. Hayle. He bowed courteously, reached into his pocket, and extended to her an envelope. Lizzie, who seemingly knew the contents, waited beside him rather breathlessly, her blue eyes glittering.

Georgianna opened the folded note and read, surprise darting through her. "It is an invitation to your mother's annual spring soiree."

Mr. Hayle beamed. "Yes. I...ah...I will make an official announcement of my and Miss Lizzie's engagement right before supper."

Stunned, Georgianna stared up at Mr. Hayle, swallowing all the fright and doubt rushing up inside her. Lizzie was also glowing, but in her eyes, Georgianna saw a similar uncertainty. She gave her sister a reassuring smile. That Mr. Hayle had come this far now, would he dare turn back? Even though it was the earl's threat which had brought him up to scratch, she knew Mr. Hayle adored her sister. It was evident in every stare and "accidental" touch. However, she felt certain his parents would never allow him to see through with marrying her sister.

"It would be my pleasure to attend," she said. "I shall respond right away to Mrs. Hayle. Please allow me to enquire, sir, do your parents know you plan to make an announcement?"

He flushed, tugged at his neckcloth. "I..." Mr. Hayle raked his fingers through his sandy hair and looked away from them, as if he were mortified.

"Mr. Hayle?" Lizzie asked tremulously, her eyes wide and uncertain. "Do you mean to surprise your family with our news?"

Georgianna's fingers tightened on the envelope, understanding that a public declaration would be hard to deny later on without stirring a scandal. He was deliberately shoving his parents into a corner. As she stared at Mr. Hayle and her sister, Georgianna realized how young they were, and her throat ached because she had no notion of how to help them secure their happiness without causing distress to others.

How long would she have to work for to provide a suitable dowry for Lizzie? Would Mr. and Mrs. Hayle ever understand that their daughter-in-law was a passionate children's author and she hoped to one day publish a series she had been diligently working on for the last two years? Would they find the connection forged through Aunt Thomasina's marriage acceptable?

"Mr. Stannis has returned," Sarah cried, delight lighting up her features. "He has with him a pony!"

Georgianna whirled around, pressing a hand to her chest. "A pony?"

"That is no pony," Lizzie gasped.

The earl was indeed walking toward the stable with a beautiful brown-and-black horse with sleek lines and powerful muscles.

"I will speak to my husband," she said to Mr.

Hayle. "If you will excuse me. Sarah and Anna, please keep Lizzie's company."

The girls nodded enthusiastically, and Lizzie blushed because she understood, given the prior conduct of Mr. Hayle, that Georgianna would no longer allow them to walk alone. She hurried toward Daniel, who paused when he saw her, nerves fluttering in her stomach at his unwavering regard. The earl was dressed in tan trousers with a blue waistcoat and matching tan jacket, absent a neckcloth, revealing the strong columns of his throat. His dark blond hair was tousled, as if he raked his fingers through the strands several times. His gaze hooded as he observed her approach. "Who is this?" she murmured, patting the horse's side.

He pinned her with an indecipherable look. "He is yours, wife."

For a moment, Georgianna stared at him with incomprehension. "I beg your pardon?"

"This stallion is yours. Mr. Boucher will deliver a new adjusted harness and saddle. Once he arrives with them tomorrow, whenever you venture into town, you will not have to trample through the woods for hours."

A thrill burst inside her chest as warmth spooled through her entire body, her tongue suddenly feeling thick in her mouth. Georgianna whispered, "It is an extravagant purchase, Daniel." A horse this exquisite would cost more than a hundred pounds. "We cannot afford to keep a stable and a stallion."

"I've calculated it and will see it done," he said, staring at her with his usual intensity. "I have also arranged for a lad to clean the stables, the fowl pen, and the cow enclosure for a year."

Astonished, she was at a loss for words for several moments. "How can you afford this?"

"I sold my jacket pin."

Georgianna made an incredulous noise in her throat. "A *pin* allowed you to purchase a horse and arrange for its feeding for a year?"

The earl lifted a very decidedly arrogant brow. "The local pawn offered three hundred pounds. I believe it worth more, but I did not haggle."

He walked over to her and brushed a kiss across her forehead. "I forbid you from worrying about it in any manner. It is my duty to provide for you and our family."

Oh God, this is going too far. She had never anticipated the earl would be such a considerate and giving gentleman. "I…" She looked beyond his shoulder at the horse, her throat tightening.

"Do you know how to ride, wife?"

She pushed a few strands of hair from her cheeks. "Yes…we…Lizzie and I were taught by Papa. We had a carriage and a mare before Papa died. We had to sell them when we retrenched."

"Good. When you are not riding, I'll start teaching Anna and Sarah. It would be best if they learned on a pony; however, I shall be very careful."

Harsh emotions wrenched through her heart,

and Georgianna wanted to run away from him and the helpless feelings digging so relentlessly beneath her skin.

"Wife," he said, his gaze narrowing. "Why do you look at me with such fright—"

She jerked one step closer to him and fit her mouth against Daniel's, kissing him with desperation and longing she had not thought herself capable of.

"I believe we are scandalizing our audience," he murmured roughly against her lips.

A laugh and a sob escaped Georgianna, and she pulled away, burrowing against his chest to hug him.

"You are squeezing me, wife."

Georgianna was, and she could not stop, because too many yearnings were breaking her apart. *I want this to be real.* And for the first time since her aunt's constant reminder of procuring a husband, Georgianna thought a gentleman to call her own would be a fine thing indeed. What would it be like to have someone to hold when the nights were cold? Someone to share dreams and fears, joy and woes? Someone whose kiss set her heart and senses aflame?

Perhaps a gentleman like you.

Pulling away from his embrace, she hugged the neck of the horse. Georgianna cleared her throat, which had thickened with emotions. "Does he have a name?"

"The gentleman who reared him gave him the

name Montgomery."

"Montgomery," she whispered, combing her fingers through his mane. "It is a good, strong name, and you and I are going to be the best of friends."

"Would you like to go for a ride?" he asked.

Her heart soared, but she glanced behind her to her sisters.

"Ease your worries. Mr. Hayle is already leaving."

"Yes, I would like to ride with you," Georgianna said with a laugh, noting Mr. Hayle indeed went toward his horse and her sisters walked toward the main house.

The earl launched atop the horse with seamless grace and held out his hands to her.

Their gazes collided, and in his, she spied a wicked spark of challenge. "Are you comfortable riding astride, wife?"

Thankfully, she wore no bustle under her simple day gown. "Yes."

She placed her hand into his and allowed him to haul her upward, his strength almost shocking as he swung her into the saddle. Georgianna's gasp turned into laughter.

"Good," he murmured at her ear. "Now split your legs and sit astride."

Her heart thumping, she complied, aware of the scandalous way her dress rode up to her stocking-clad knees. She held onto the bridle when he surged the stallion forward. It felt like

Georgianna chased the wind, and she relaxed against him as they rode for endless minutes, running toward the lowering sun.

"Isn't it glorious?" she cried, staring at the vermilion-hued sky.

Daniel tugged on the reins when they approached the small cliff abutting their woodlands estate, the wild ocean crashing against the cliffside below them.

"It has been an age since I've been out here," she said softly, lifting her face to the wind and inhaling the crisp air into her lungs.

They stayed like that atop the horse, staring out at the abyss.

"I am thinking of venturing to London soon."

Her belly tightened, and she wordlessly nodded.

"Do you not question my reasons, wife?"

"I know it must be in pursuit of your missing memories," she said in a quiet tone. "You've been in Crandell almost three weeks. It would be foolish to not expect your heart to restlessly wonder about your background and identity."

He made a soft noise, then fell into a striking silence.

"The manor will not fall apart without me taking care of the most difficult chores." He nudged the horse closer to the cliff's edge. "The lad I hired will arrive tomorrow. The local baker recommended him, and he is reported to be a steady man of all works."

She lowered her gaze to the hand wrapped around her middle. Her skin beaded with awareness, and Georgianna ran her fingers over his scarred knuckles before taking his hand into hers. How his hands had changed; now the tips of his fingers had rough callouses and red abrasions. Her throat ached, and she looked away into the sun sinking behind bloated clouds. "Thank you for all the work you've done around the manor, Daniel."

He nudged the side of her neck, the move sensual yet playful.

"There is no need to thank me. It is my duty. I also travel to London to seek investment and work opportunities."

Her heart jolted. "Work?"

"Hmm, I must think ahead of how to provide beyond a year for our family. I searched my memories until my head damn well ached, but I cannot recall if I have monies in any bank, real estate holdings, or investment. Yet I am a learned man, at odd times knowledge raking at me without any true understanding of where it originated from. Perhaps in visiting a few places in town I might jar my memories and a clearer understanding of who I am. The greater opportunity would be to seek chances to improve our lot. The manor is crumbling and is in desperate need of an injection of money."

Tears burned behind her throat. No triumph burned inside of Georgianna, yet this was what she had wanted. For him to repair all the harm denying her the job had done, yet this was certainly too much, and it would now be her in the earl's debt. A thing she suspected would be a most merciless place to be, especially when the earl's memories returned.

They might never do, the selfish, desperate heart of her whispered. "I have tried to procure loans to aid in fixing the manor, but I was denied, though I presented credible projections on repayment," she said, leaning her head back against his chest, a keen regret alive upon her heart. "Had I been born a man, I could have gotten a loan with less to recommend me. Isn't it outrageous?"

"It is," he said. "I've known many men who had access to thousands of pounds on the basis of a name and title alone."

Daniel stiffened, and she turned her gaze to meet his. Something stark and raw flared in his eyes. She used the tip of her finger to smooth the savage frown from his brow. Georgianna's heart beat a furious rhythm, and she parted her lips to inform him that he was an earl. Yet the words stuck in her throat and terrible fright swept over her body, leaving her chilled. It was difficult to admit she felt scared that he might not remember his life and past, yet she was just as scared that he *would* remember.

How do I tell you…but how do I also continue keeping your identity from you?

In good conscience, she had to tell him. "Daniel," she whispered, her throat closing over the words trembling to escape.

One day, I'll merely be a passerby in your memory.

A frown cut into his brow, and he placed a finger under her chin, lifting her face. "I hate seeing this fear in your eyes. It makes me want to kill whoever put it there."

A shaky laugh escaped her. "It is not fear I feel."

His gaze flashed with emotions she was not able to understand. "Then what?" he all but growled.

"Have you ever wanted something so much it hurt to want it, and you also feel incredibly foolish because you know it is not yours to have and it will never be?"

The lines of his face sharpened as he leaned in closer. "Tell me what it is you want, wife, and I will give it to you," he vowed, his gaze steady on hers.

It is you. Foolishly, impossibly, her heart was leaning only toward him even though she knew wanting this man was like reaching for the moon in the sky: it was untouchable.

"I…I want to know the world through food," she murmured, instead of laying her reckless heart open.

He lifted a brow. "You want to travel?"

She turned around, leaning back against him to peer up at the emerging stars in the evening sky. "I have only ever been fortunate to leave Crandell once."

"Blasphemy."

Another laugh escaped her at the incredulity in his tone.

"I once spent two years touring the continent, the east, and the West Indies," he said.

She felt the thump of his heart against her shoulder and waited silently for him to try and capture the memory.

"Where do you wish to go, wife?" he murmured after several moments.

"I could not truly leave Crandell," she said with a wistful sigh.

"Whyever not?"

"My sisters are here. Should I be so privileged to see a bit of the world, even for a brief moment, I would wish for them to come with me. That I daresay might never be possible. I am content with experiencing life and travels through food and my cooking. That would be most incredible."

"I have never seen you this animated."

"I…" She wrinkled her nose. "I can get passionate about cooking."

"I see." His gaze searched hers, as if he wanted to discover all of her hidden depths. She almost looked away but forced herself to hold still under his probing regard.

"How do you travel through food?"

"My mama would make the rich and decadent *Tiremesù*, and I would experience and delight in Italian cuisine, then another time she prepared a dish known only to the east and suddenly I am in Shanghai. We can travel the world through food, enjoy the other side of the world and other cultures through taste."

"It is a whimsical and beautiful notion."

"One day, I shall be able to prepare all the delicious delicacies I have ever dreamed about."

"I will ensure it."

Georgianna gasped. "No, I will not—"

He kissed away her protest, and she moaned softly against his mouth, hating the hunger that crested through her with such eagerness.

"Georgie!"

She pulled away from him, laughing shakily. Looking over his shoulder in the distance, she saw a few hands waving. Daniel wheeled the horse and trotted back to her family. Upon arriving, she saw they had laid out a large blanket on the lawns, and a small picnic basket with plates and a jar of large lemonade was waiting. She dismounted with Daniel's aid, and Georgianna introduced Montgomery to the girls.

Their excitement brought a lump to her throat, and she met Lizzie's gaze over their heads. Georgianna saw a similar unspoken wish in her sister's eyes that the earl could always stay in their lives. She sat on the blanket, laughing when Anna barreled into her arms. The earl allowed the horse to graze and lowered himself on the edge of the blanket, resting his shoulders against the large tree trunk.

"How is it that we were not at your wedding, Georgie?" Sarah asked, reposing on her stomach, and propping her palm on her chin.

Drat. She stared at her sister wordlessly. "I…it was hasty," Georgianna murmured, blushing.

"The girls witnessed Mr. Johnson and Miss Bevins wed in church Sunday," Lizzie said, looking almost guilty between her and the earl.

"We caught some of the rice," Anna chirped, her cheeks dimpling.

"I have an idea," Sarah cried, scrambling to her knees. She reached for the earl's hand and placed it on Georgie's.

She stared at her sister, nonplussed, but did not have the heart to steal the delight from whatever she pretended.

"Mr. Daniel Stannis," she said with a wide smile. "Does thee wed my sister Georgie…and… and will you cherish her forever?"

Georgianna instinctively tried to snatch her hand from his, but he tightened his grip on her fingers, the corners of his mouth hitching in a smile.

"You should press your palm over your heart," Sarah instructed.

"I do not recall that being in any vow," Lizzie said with a nervous laugh.

Did her sister perhaps sense the way Georgianna's heart tumbled over inside her chest?

"Aye," he murmured, placing his palm on his chest. "I do."

Her sister squealed like she had been given a

gift, and Sarah seemed to have forgotten to ask Georgianna for her vows. Anna and Sarah dashed off toward the manor, claiming they were going for rice to toss over their heads. Georgianna felt silly for blushing fiercely.

"I shall go and monitor the hellions," Lizzie said, scrambling to her feet and chasing her sisters.

Alone with Daniel, it took considerable effort for her to meet his gaze. His lips were curved in a sensual smile, and his stare held his wicked intention. She made to scramble away, and he lunged, grabbing her around the waist and tumbling her to the blanket.

"They can see us," she cried, her laughter bubbling.

"They are too busy looking for rice. Only a few kisses," he murmured, capturing her mouth with his.

Georgianna's heart thumped inside her chest, every beat echoing the longing he awoke inside of her with his far-too-sensual kisses.

I am sinking too deep, she dazedly thought, wrapping her hands around his neck and kissing him with fervent passion.

This desire was a burning flame that had the power to destroy her heart, for Georgianna knew that she would eventually surrender to this madness between them, knowing he was the wicked darkness that could swallow and consume her. Yet she did not push him or wrench away from his illicit embrace, only allowing herself to tumble and fall more into his dangerous allure.

CHAPTER FIFTEEN

Daniel strolled through the small town of Crandell, almost amused by the blatantly inquisitive glares the townspeople settled on him. This was the third time he had ventured into the heart of the village, and their curiosity only seemed to increase, their avid stares crawling over his skin like ants. He'd decided to travel to London without delay and was here in town to rent a carriage. Traveling by train would be more expensive even if it would take him half the time.

His wife had watched his departure with that mysterious shadow in her eyes, and he had felt damn regretful he'd not taken her to his bed last night. A pounding headache had attacked him on the edge of the cliff, and he'd surmised whenever his cock got too eager, the headache appeared. A portly gentleman dressed in the heights of fashion strolled toward him with mincing steps.

Daniel slowed his walk, understanding the polite courtesies and niceties required of him. Another gentleman strolling to the left of the squire snagged Daniel's attention, and he stiffened, wondering at the inexplicable way his heart started to pound. The gentleman dressed well, tapping his gold-and-white walking stick on the ground, was extraordinarily familiar to Daniel.

As if the gentleman felt his regard, he paused and looked directly at Daniel. The man flinched, then shook his head as if dazed.

Who is that man, and why does he seem to know me?

It did not come to Daniel in a tidal rush but as a gentle waft of breeze, gliding across his thoughts in a kaleidoscope of memories pouring inside him to fill the empty void. His heart lurched and his mouth dried. *I have a younger brother.* "Stephen?"

His brother rushed to him, grabbing Daniel in a fierce hug.

"By God, it is really you, Daniel?"

He returned his brother's embrace for several beats, then stepped away. "What the hell are you doing here in Crandell? And why do you appear so haggard as if you've not been sleeping?"

"That is the question for you," Stephan said, searching his face. "London is all in a tizzy, and the newssheets are all wildly speculating about the fact that you have been bloody missing from society events for almost three weeks. Both the Duke of Beswick and Marquess Moncrieff called for you to no avail. There are even some whispers you might be…*dead.*"

Incredulity scythed through him, and for a moment, Daniel had no idea what to say or how to say it. "Missing?"

"For nineteen bloody days! I have been worried sick!"

Missing…for nineteen days…London abuzz

with the news. He stiffened, thinking of one of the women who loved him more than anything in her world. "Nana?"

His brother closed his eyes briefly. "She tries not to act out of sorts, but Mother has rallied around her, assuring Nana that you are just being your usual debauched self and will soon return to town. But she has hired men to find you, and I have seen her sobbing in the gardens."

Daniel scrubbed a hand over his face, the memory of that night aboard his yacht washing over him in chilly waves. There had been an argument with his mistress, and she had shoved him. He could not tell if her intention had been to send him overboard or not, but that had been the result.

How long had he stayed in the water? By what grace had he washed ashore in Crandell? "By God," Daniel muttered, scrubbing a hand over his face. "I fell overboard my yacht."

"You were damn well shoved overboard." His brother grimaced. "Lady Johanna came to my lodgings only last week and tearily confessed to her part in the entire affair. The lady had been living in dread that she had killed you."

"She could have," Daniel hissed, fury raking like talons through him. "Did she alert any of the people aboard my ship that I had fallen?"

His expression grave, his brother said, "No. But she is a wreck and remorseful. Since she told me, I have been searching for you, then I saw the notice in the *Morning Chronicle*. Mr. Daniel Stannis. The coincidence was just too incredible to dismiss. Now what the hell are you doing here? And what in tarnation are you wearing?"

Daniel faltered into remarkable stillness as the import of everything washed over his senses. Miss Heyford claiming him as her husband, setting him to work around the ramshackle manor, doing all sorts of menial work including mucking cow dung every day.

He had no wife…no new sisters…and he did not live in that manor. Every touch, longing stare, and wicked kiss had been a fabrication. A peculiar, yet profound sense of loss and emptiness tore through Daniel. All of the contentment he'd felt, the hope and determination to make life better for his family, was not real. *She is not really mine and they are not my family.* A knot tightened and grew into a painful lump inside. The anger that lit in his veins felt cold and unforgiving. A lie. *It is all a lie.*

Then another realization slammed inside his chest. "I am bloody filthy rich," he growled under his breath.

"Of course you are rich," Stephan said with a frown. "What are you about and why are you here in Crandell?"

What a petty, vengeful scheme, Daniel thought darkly.

The audacity of the chit was astounding. *So this is your revenge for me firing you, is it?*

Now he understood the nerves she'd displayed
when he touched and kissed her…when he had
first suggested she join him in bed. His heart
started a harsh drumming. What the hell did she
mean by the liberties she accorded him? Did she
not worry that his memory might return, and he
would flip the scheme and enact his own brand of
revenge?

"I will leave for London tomorrow," he said.

His brother frowned. "Why not now? We can
take the train to—"

"Tomorrow, Stephen. I have some business to
take care of that cannot be delayed."

"You are angry," his brother said slowly.

The smile that curved Daniel's mouth did not
reach his heart or his eyes. "I am uncertain as to
what I am. Send a notice to the papers. I took
some time to holiday in Crandell. I was not lost or
missing. See it done."

His brother nodded, and as Daniel walked
away, he heard his soft mutter of, "What poor fool
has crossed you now?"

What poor fool indeed, only he was the simple-
ton in this matter, to have so easily trusted a
pretty face and laughing golden eyes.

Aye, a damn fool I am.

Even with cutting through the woodlands, the
walk back to the manor took him almost an hour.
Georgianna was in the woods near the brook,
picking berries and humming sweetly beneath her
breath. He stood for unknown minutes simply

watching her and her alluring sweetness. Sensing him, she looked up, a radiant smile curving her mouth.

"Daniel!" She lowered the basket to the ground and hurried over to him. Her hands came up, hovered a moment, and then settled lightly against his chest. "Is everything well, Daniel? You seem pale. Is your head hurting? Is that why you've returned?"

How sweetly worried she appeared and sounded. He wanted to wrap his hands around her pretty little neck and... Daniel took a steady breath, ruthlessly pushing the anger aside.

"I am quite well, wife," he murmured, pressing a small kiss to the corner of her mouth. "I am merely anticipating spending the night in your bed."

Her eyes widened, and she gasped. "Daniel!"

"I prefer to hear 'my husband' from these sweet lips," he murmured, rubbing his thumb across her lush mouth.

What a scheming little hellion you are.

"I want you in my arms the entire night, wife, not only for a few minutes or an hour." And by God he would sate this maddening hunger he had for her and get this little witch out of his blood and the space she had already started taking up inside his heart. The honorable provision would be to walk away...to refuse the taste of her lips and the pleasure of her body. However, he would not deny himself.

Daniel had always been a ruthless man, and now…he was even more ruthless in his persuasion, knowing he would walk away after. A part of him acknowledged he had a weakness for her… something he had never before endured even though he was a man of strong carnal appetites and had always been the master of himself and his desires, not the other way.

Her eyes were wide and vulnerable…trusting, stirring something deep and untouched inside of him. Almost angry, he thrust his fingers through her mass of hair, tugging her close. "Will you not deny me?" he asked roughly, a part of him waiting for her to push him away because surely she would not take her ruse this far.

Her delicate fingers trembled, a tip brushing like a butterfly's wing over his brows. "No."

Bloody hell. "I'll not leave until you are sheathed on my cock and screaming your pleasure."

"I know," she gasped, her breath trembling against his mouth. "It is what I also want."

He stiffened, shock and lust hammering at his chest. "*Why?*"

Was this all to further her damn plot? Why would she give him everything, knowing he would damn well walk away and never look back once his memory returned?

Her golden gaze grew somber. "Because I know one day you will leave," she said, her tone ravaged with want and some inexplicable emotion he could not identify. "And the way you make me feel, *husband*…I know I could live a dozen lifetimes and never feel like this again."

Daniel felt wrecked, and hating the inexplicable feelings tying in him knots, he slammed his mouth on hers, ruthlessly taking everything she offered, feeling as if he would also leave a part of himself with her, a part he would never be able to reclaim. Her soft moan whispered through him like an arrow pierced with warmth and desire. He felt the pounding of his heart, that wicked urge to coax and ravish sliding through his veins.

She pulled away from his embrace, laughing. "Lizzie has taken the girls down to the lake for an evening picnic and then a swim."

So they would have hours to themselves in the house. He and his wife…*no*, he silently growled, *Georgianna*. "I cannot resist you," he hissed, wrestling with himself.

She gave him a smile of such breathtaking sweetness, he wondered for the first time in his life if he could be a man who truly fell into the throes of love and passion.

What an utterly ridiculous thought to have.

He took a steady breath, sucking deep inside these jumbled feelings twisting through him. Georgianna grabbed the basket, then held his hand and tugged him toward the house in a run.

A raw regret pulsed through him as he peered down into her prettily flushed and laughingly sensual face. Daniel hesitated, and he was not a man to doubt himself.

*What if I should stay for a few more days...
weeks?*

He gritted his teeth until his damn jaw ached.
And do what? Keep pretending to be a husband
to a lady in an idyllic town called Crandell? Nay,
his real life with his immeasurable responsibilities
as an earl, and his true family, awaited him.

They entered the empty house, the door slamming behind them. She gasped when he lifted her
into his arms, dropping the basket of berries to
clasp his shoulders. He lowered his head and
pressed his lips to her forehead before drifting his
mouth down the bridge of her nose to settle
against hers. Daniel closed his eyes as he kissed
her, breathing in her scent and trapping her
unique fragrance into his lungs.

*After tonight, I will never see you again,
Georgianna Heyford...*

Farewell.

• • •

Georgianna was on the verge of doing something
remarkably wicked. *No...I am already doing it.*
Flames of excitement coursed through her, prickled along her skin, and sent her heart into a
frantic gallop as her fake husband climbed the
stairs with her in his arms.

His mouth ravished hers with deep kisses, and
her chest ached with unfathomable want and

impossible wishes, her heart tumbling over in a manner it had never done before. Daniel stumbled with her into the room, setting her feet down, still kissing her. He coasted his hand over her back and shoulders before exploring the soft lines of her waist, hips, and tracing a sensuous path to the globes of her buttocks.

She felt so…*alive*.

As he undressed her, Daniel touched her everywhere, each caress eliciting whispers of moan and gasps, his intensity fanning the flames of her desire. It did not take long before she was gloriously naked, and though her entire body blushed, she did not hide from his ravenous stare.

His chest rose on a deep inhalation, pleasure and admiration burning in his green gaze. He trailed a finger over the curve of her shoulder down to the underside of her breasts. "I've never seen another equal to your incredible sensual lushness. My God, you are unspeakably lovely."

He sucked in an audible breath when she removed the pins holding her hair until her tresses tumbled over her shoulders, breasts, and back. She was wicked, recklessly wanton at heart to act so, but Georgianna did not shy away from the desire for him, sensing that if she did not reach for this moment with her entire soul, she would dream forever of him when he walked from her life and be haunted with regrets.

Georgianna cried out when he arched her, took a nipple into his mouth, and sucked, the deep pull reaching down to her belly and even lower. He lifted her in his arms and tumbled with her to the bed. A heady feeling rushed through her, a hot and delicious tingle low down in her body. His knee slid between her legs, pressing against the sensitive mound at the secret heart of her.

"Daniel," she raggedly moaned, gripping the sheets at her sides until her knuckles ached.

His powerful body came over hers, and he kissed the corner of her mouth. "I am so damn desperate for you, I tremble."

His voice was a rumble of carnal want. Her lover wedged one of his hands between the tight fits of their bodies, smoothed down her belly, brushed lightly over the curve of her hips, then delved between her thighs to pinch her clitoris. A weak scream left her, which he caught with his mouth in another evocative kiss. Swirls of sensations pulled in her belly as his mouth moved over hers with passionate demand. Releasing the sheets, she slid her hands around his nape, responding to his embrace with wanton greed.

Georgianna arched her neck, her hands falling from his body, when his lips left hers to trail over her, licking and nibbling along her throat, then to the underside of her breasts and down to the soft spot of her lower belly where he nipped. His tongue glided over the bite, soothing and arousing all at once, down until he reached between her thighs.

Georgianna held her breath, keeping the air trapped in her lungs, afraid to exhale, and then his tongue touched her sex. She sobbed, slapping a hand over her mouth to contain the wildness pulsing through her body. His tongue curled, flicked, and tormented her flesh until sweat slicked her skin. She cried out at the sensations that poured through her like a honeyed blade, cutting deep with its erotic sweetness.

"Daniel," she gasped, arching her hips more and reaching down to thread her fingers through his hair.

He broke her apart with his tongue, and a dark, wanton lust rose inside of Georgianna, shocking her with its intensity. Instinctively, she lifted her legs and placed them on his shoulders, his purr of approval vibrating against her clitoris.

This position was wicked and lascivious, and she wanted more. He slipped two fingers deep inside her body, then a third, stretching and preparing her. Sensual pain sizzled beneath the pleasure, and when she whimpered, he sucked her nub into his mouth. Georgianna cried out weakly, her entire body trembling as heat crested through her, ecstasy drawing in a tight coil.

"Daniel!"

He flicked his tongue over her clitoris and thrust his fingers deep, hitting a place deep inside, shocking her with arrows of exquisite sensations. Those sensations peaked within her belly, and with a keening cry, Georgianna shattered, shaking as pleasure broke her apart.

He pushed from her and with evidently trembling fingers undressed. Coming up onto her elbows, she watched as he revealed the striking beauty of his body to her gaze. Sharp and svelte muscles delineated his chest down to his waist, powerful thighs, and well-toned calves.

"You are so lovely, Daniel."

A rough, low, and hungry sound spilled from him, and a raw emotion filled his gaze before his eyes shadowed. "Don't say this to me."

A lump formed in her throat at the rough emotion in his tone. "Why not?" she asked softly, almost afraid of the answer.

He prowled over, coming down over her with his weight, his move almost angry...and desperate. Daniel thread his fingers through her cascading hair, lifted her face, and took her mouth in a bruising kiss. It felt almost like a reprimand... a punishment, yet she felt the painful longing in his embrace, and she responded to it with all the impossible yearnings awakening within her soul for him.

Without releasing her from his intoxicating kisses, he reached between their bodies, and then something hard and heated pressed against the opening of her sex. His hips pushed, and her mortifyingly wet flesh yielded to his invasion, accepting the hard, thick length that surged deep inside, but even so, she gasped at the harsh bite of pain.

"Oh God!" she gasped when he sank even deeper. "Daniel…I…too much! It hurts."

Regret darkened his gaze, and he stilled, giving her time to adjust to the feel of him within her body. He kissed the corner of her mouth, crooning soothing nonsense, while he reached between their bodies once again.

"It will soon pass, I promise it, and you'll only know bliss," he said, pressing those small, tender kisses over her lips.

Georgianna whimpered almost brokenly when he started rubbing his thumb over her clitoris. Ripples of pleasure began to throb beneath the pain, and Georgianna gripped his shoulders at the delicious friction, blushing as wetness rushed from her body to bathe his cock.

"That's it," he murmured tenderly. "Soak my cock."

Another fiery blush engulfed her body at his provocative whisper. He moved again, and her flesh burned as she adjusted to the thick feel of him so deep inside, yet he never stopped his ministrations against her clitoris. The sensations evoked felt almost agonizing, yet she grew wetter and wetter with each press and rub of his thumb, with each slow recoil and thrust of his powerful hips. It felt like an erotic dance, a mating, as he dragged his cock from her sex and then plunged deep. Again. And again. And again, until she lost even the ability to moan.

He kissed her, and every instinct in her body

screamed for release as with each thrust he drove her higher, until she ripped her mouth from his and bit into his shoulder. Daniel's hiss was a sensual sound that edged her closer and closer to madness.

He dragged his lips along the exposed line of her neck. "I've never felt anything as sublime as your pussy strangling my cock," he gritted out at her ears. "So wet...yet so tight."

Oh God! She bit the inside of her lips, swallowed the moan welling in her throat. His mouth was provocatively filthy, the words dropping like molten fire into hidden depths of her body, stirring a wanton creature she'd never imagined existed. Georgianna arched her hips, silently begging for more. He shoved his hips deeper, and she cried out against his mouth at the exquisite pleasure. How long they slid against each other she would never be able to say, for Georgianna became lost, enslaved to sharp crackles of pleasure piercing her body. Each deep shove ignited a burst of fire deep down, driving her wild with the need for more. Sweat slicked their skins, trailed down his nose to drop on her lips. She licked over the parted seam of his mouth before sucking on his bottom lip. Then suddenly the tight coil snapped, and Georgianna's release swept through her like a storm, pleasure tearing through her body and pulling a sob from her. With a deep groan, Daniel pulled from her before releasing his seed on her quivering stomach.

Panting, he dropped his forehead onto hers. "Bloody hell," he muttered, visibly shaken. "I... *hell*."

Her heart beating impossibly hard, Georgianna reached up and lightly touched his jaw. He caught her hand and pressed a hot kiss to her palm, closing his eyes for a brief moment. Her heart hitched, for she felt his regret. Daniel shifted, their gazes collided, and for the space of a heartbeat, she could not speak. His eyes were the same beautiful green, but now they glowed with a worldliness...a hardness that she was not used to seeing.

"Hold me closer," she whispered, not understating this inexplicable need to feel his arms around her.

He kissed the corner of her mouth. "You make me yearn for foolish things."

His voice was edged with suppressed emotions, and a sweet, sharp pain throbbed in her chest as her heart started to hammer. Daniel moved off the bed, retrieved a handkerchief from his trousers, and brought it over to tenderly clean her quivering belly. He tossed it aside on the bed, climbed over her, and caught her mouth with his, the strength of his hunger catching her unawares, for they had just burned with passion.

"So soon?" she gasped against his lips when he nudged her legs apart so that he could settle his weight between her legs.

He slipped one of his hands beneath her hips,

arching her to his body so no space existed between them. Daniel squeezed her buttocks, sending a quiver of sensual shock through her.

"I plan to make love to you for the entire night, Georgianna, and I might still never be free of this hunger I have for you."

She touched his mouth with fingers that trembled. "Perhaps I do not want you to be free, so that in that way, you will never forget me."

Daniel stilled, his eyes darkening.

"It would be impossible to ever forget you," he said gruffly, shaking his head, almost as if he was in denial of his own words.

I know I will always remember you, she silently whispered.

As he took her mouth in a deep yet tender kiss, Georgianna curved her body into his, surrendering to his charm, knowing she might never have the chance to indulge so wickedly ever again.

Her lover gave her no time to recover from her earlier orgasms before he began devastating her sensibilities. Daniel flipped her onto her belly, arching her hips into the air, sinking his teeth into the curve of her buttocks. She gasped, moaning when he licked her sex from behind, forcing her to scream her pleasure into the sheets for fear her voice would travel through the stone walls to outside.

"By God, there is a part of me that damn well wished you were real."

It was said in a low whisper that sent her heart into a frightened gallop.

"Daniel?" Georgianna asked shakily. She turned her head against the pillows, and he blanketed her frame, coming down on his elbows to kiss her mouth, sinking into her body in a move that felt hard and desperate, yet so deeply sensual.

Had he truly said those words?

She had no time to ponder as he obliterated all thoughts with pleasure for the long night.

CHAPTER SIXTEEN

Georgianna shifted, turned over in the bed, softly sighing at the ache in her body. She smiled, for they were also wonderful aches. That smile dimmed, and she sat up in the bed, drawing her knees up and resting her chin there. How wicked they had been for the long night, spending hours in bed. She blushed and with a soft snort wondered at her capability to do so, given the wanton way they had joined together in her bed. It was at the warm drop on her knees Georgianna realized silent tears coursed down her cheeks. She sighed and wiped them away, bravely acknowledging the shattering truth stirring inside.

I am falling in love with the earl.

Worse, she had no notion of how to tell him the truth, knowing it was necessary given their new intimacy.

My husband…no, Daniel…we are not married in truth. I am not your legal wife nor are you my husband.

Could she dare say these words to him without the benefit of liquid courage? Georgianna blew out a steady breath, wondering if the closeness that had formed between them would allow the earl to forgive her the deception. She shifted, and a small, folded paper on the pillow next to hers caught Georgianna's attention. Frowning, she plucked it up, flipping it open.

Let me simply be a passerby in your memory, Lord Stannis.

Georgianna jerked, alarm shocking her heart, the paper falling from suddenly nerveless fingers. Her heart was a such terrifying tattoo against her breastbone, for a petrifying moment, Georgianna thought she would faint. She read it again, the import of his words settling against her chest like a boulder.

Let me simply be a passerby in your memory.

Tears sprang to her eyes, and Georgianna tried to swallow past the lump forming in her throat.

"Oh God," she whispered, glancing around the room. She pressed trembling fingers to her lips. "He knows."

What a splendid fool I've been.

Georgianna fought with the raw feelings of fear, heartbreak…anger. *He made me no promise, and I gave him none.* Swallowing down all the feelings trying to push against her chest, she clambered from the bed and went about her morning ablution, blushing as if the sun had burned her when she saw all the strawberry marks his mouth had left on her breasts, belly, and thighs. Almost an hour later, she was freshly bathed and dressed in a warm yellow gown, perfectly buttoned up to her throat, allowing her to hide the marks he had placed on her neck.

The ghost of his lips as he sucked at the flesh there, his large palms gripping her buttocks as he urged her up and down on his cock as she had rode him only a few hours ago, were already a haunting. On the cusp of leaving her room, she closed her eyes, gripping the doorknob until her fingers ached. He had devastated her senses with his dangerous sensuality three times before he had written that letter and vanished.

Georgianna hastened from her room, heading to the music room where someone determinedly tried to play the harpsichord.

"Oh, Sarah, you are hopeless," Lizzie said laughingly. "Is this your way of telling me you are not interested in playing?"

Georgianna eased open the door, smiling at her sisters. "Hullo," she greeted.

"Georgie," Anna cried, leaping from the carpet and running over to hug her around the waist.

She returned her sister's embrace, ruffling her tousled hair. "Good morning."

Sarah giggled, hurrying over for her hug. "It is no longer morning. Mr. Stannis said you were exhausted, and we were to let you sleep. And Georgie, he made us oatmeal!"

Her heart lurching, she glanced around. "Is…is he here?"

Lizzie frowned. "No, he has left for London, remember?"

"I…of course." Her throat tightening, she spent

a few more minutes with her sisters before excusing herself to the kitchens. Once there, she stared out the windows at the young lad walking the horse across the lawns.

Let me simply be a passerby in your memory.

What did he mean by not even offering a rebuke for her ruse? Footsteps whispered over the stone floor, and she turned around, pressing the flat of her palm against her stomach.

"Lizzie," she said with a smile that wobbled. "I thought you planned to take the girls outside for a lesson in geography."

Her sister's clear gaze assessed her with a measure of concern. "Your eyes are ravaged by tears. Is…is everything well?"

Georgianna took a moment to breathe past the emotions tearing through her. "The earl is never coming back, Lizzie."

At first Lizzie seemed confused, then she gasped. She pressed a palm over her heart. "What do you mean?"

Even though Georgianna felt mortified, she held out the note he had left behind. Lizzie took it, her gaze scanning the contents. "He has recalled he is the earl!"

"Yes," she said hoarsely.

Lizzie shook her head. "This morning when he bid us farewell, I thought he seemed a bit contemplative, but not distressed. Did he not confront or accuse you, Georgie? He just left?" Incredulity rang in her tone. "This is most astonishing and unexpected. I have been in dread of his reaction should he ever recall his identity."

Georgianna closed her eyes, hating that her heart twisted at hearing those words. "Perhaps it would have been best if he *had* been angry or given me a chance to explain…even though I do not know what I could have said. His indifference is… painful, extraordinarily so, and I feel wretched that I am affected in such a manner, Lizzie."

Silence fell, and when she met her sister's gaze, Georgianna flinched from the pity she saw there.

"Did you fall in love with him?"

"*No!*" She recoiled from the very idea of it. But she could not bear lying to herself or even her sister. "I was halfway there, Lizzie," Georgianna whispered. "Foolishly, and against my good sense and better judgment, I was halfway there."

Her sister rushed over and hugged her. It felt like a warm, soothing blanket was placed on her cold shoulders, and she returned her sister's embrace, grateful for her love and understanding.

"Come, let us tell Sarah and Anna that he has left for better opportunities and should not expect his return."

"It will break their hearts," Lizzie murmured, shaking her head. "They were halfway in love with him, too, and were saddened when he bid them farewell this morning."

Georgianna hardened her heart under the lash of guilt. "He has only been with us for three weeks.

Not enough time to take root and indelibly change our lives."

Liar, a silent wail ripped through her. *I am forever altered*.

"Still, let us give them a few days or perhaps allow them to ask about the earl before we explain he will never return to Crandell."

She nodded, and Lizzie hesitated, anxiety darkening her eyes.

"What is it?"

"Are you worried the earl will seek some sort of retribution?"

Georgianna wiped her palms on the skirts of her gown and walked toward the kitchen windows. "I...I am not sure what to fear. Perhaps he will simply forget about us. That he left without any sort of word surely reveals that we had an insignificant impact on his life."

That awful pain stabbed at her chest once again.

Her sister came to stand beside her, resting her head on Georgianna's shoulders.

"We knew it would have ended, and we can only be grateful it was not concluded with any sort of animosity."

Yet his indifference is like a knife upon my heart, digging deeper with each passing minute.

She nodded, determined to go about life as if her world had not been indelibly altered, unfortunately by a gentleman who might never think of her again.

Let me simply be a passerby in your memory.

• • •

It had only been two days since Daniel left Crandell, yet it felt like a lifetime had passed. He'd returned to town and his townhouse in Berkeley Square without fanfare, ignoring the pile of letters and invitations that had awaited him on his desk. The first morning he had tried his damnedest to sleep beyond five, absurdly restless, for he had fallen into a routine of waking up at dawn to complete menial labor.

Daniel had summoned his secretary and had spent the day attending to his various correspondence, investment reports, and estate holdings reports. He was pleased by the report that the workers in his factories had been paid despite being sent home while renovations were completed. He was never the type of man to trust easily, so he wrote a letter to his man of affairs to confirm that the workers were paid in full and the safety repairs were underway.

He'd also written to Mr. Burnell, ordering him to immediately remit the two hundred and eighty pounds owned to Miss Heyford. He had not ventured out in the evening, instead retiring to bed early, only to lie in that bed for hours, replaying scene by scene every interaction with Miss Georgianna Heyford.

He'd forced his mind to recall every instance, her fieriness aboard his yacht, how wary she'd seemed when she claimed him to be her husband, that defiant triumph in her eyes when she'd first sent him to do chores, and then the foolish ways in which he had started to want to be in her presence.

Daniel had barely received any sleep before his body roused this morning at half after five. He'd went to his exercise room and pounded away at the mounted sandbag until his muscles ached, reminding him of how he would feel at the end of the day working about the manor. He took a long, hot bath before venturing downstairs for breakfast. The palatial townhouse had felt empty and cold without the sound of laughter and stomping feet following him around.

His cook presented him with thinly sliced ham, kippers, eggs, and toast with three cups of coffee, yet Daniel thought he would have preferred oatmeal with nutmeg and honey. Irritated, he left the dining room and retired to his library, completing the reports he'd not finished the day before. Daniel spent several hours responding to political correspondences about the bills that needed to be debated at Parliament's next sitting. After attending to those letters and invitations to political dinners, he went over the reports from his estate steward on his principal estate in Berkshire.

Hours passed, and Georgianna lingered in the back of his thoughts, a sensual shadow with gleaming golden-brown eyes. Blowing out a deep breath, he tossed the pen across the table, watching as it skidded across the smooth surface.

What had she thought upon waking and reading his note?

I wish you had been real.

Had he really whispered that nonsense in the soft curve of her throat, or had he merely thought it, drowning in the desire she'd evoked within him? Daniel scoffed, reaching for the decanter and pouring himself a drink. He knocked back the glass of whiskey in a long swallow, appreciating the fiery trail from his throat to his stomach.

He stood, walking over to the windows overlooking the side gardens. Daniel scrubbed a hand over his face, an annoyed sound hissing from him. Georgianna Heyford had invaded his mind, filling him with dual needs of anger and aching want. He hadn't experienced this burning hunger for a woman before, and it annoyed the hell out of him that it was for one who had deceived him with unchecked audacity.

What a damn fool he had been, spouting nonsense about it being his duty and honor to care for her. How she must have laughed at him, delighting and relishing in her revenge. Yet when he recalled that curl of hunger in her eyes whenever she looked at him, the sweet way she responded to his kisses, and the breathless way she'd moaned as he had taken her three times for the night...

What the hell was that, my little schemer? Surely not revenge, even one that might have been just deserved.

Georgianna Heyford did not fit into any facet

of his life, so it was damn nonsensical to be thinking about her this much. He summoned his butler and advised him to call around the mews for his town carriage to be prepared. Perhaps what he needed was a night about town with his cronies to retrieve his sense of normalcy and to forget Crandell and all its inhabitants. He ruefully accepted her brand of revenge, for it had been unfair and unjust for him to fire her merely to soothe his mistress's anger and petty jealousy. Now that the monies due had been sent, Daniel acknowledged they no longer owed each other anything. She had been a fleeting yet beautiful fancy, nothing more.

Daniel reached for the pen, intending to summon his brother, for he required him to visit a smaller estate in Northumberland. The report from the steward had been missing for the last six months. He plucked up the fountain pen, and the curled edges of this morning's paper caught his gaze, especially the bold print calling out his good friend Simon Loughton, the Earl of Creswick. Lifting a brow, Daniel paused, pen in mid-air, and reached for the paper.

Lord Creswick has boldly declared his support for the reform of the Marriage Act. This author wonders if because the earl has seen success with the Reform bill which he had so publicly and fearlessly supported last year to the dismay of many. Creswick is arrogant enough to think his support could impact the deeply entrenched view of this society which mercilessly upholds that women should have little to no autonomy and monetary power. The support for the reform of The Married Women's Property Act would grant women far more rights than what they are allowed today have garnered little support in the Commons, with many noting the earl and his party fight an impossible battle that may never see the bill argued in the House of Lords.

Daniel lowered the paper, wondering when the houses had called for this particular reform. The current act already permitted married women a small measure of financial independence where they were no longer wholly dependent on their husband's goodwill and could even work. Whispers had abounded for the past couple of years that necessary reform was much needed, but those whispers had hardly caused any ripple.

Last year in the house, Daniel had given his full support of amending the Reform bill to ensure the working men of Britain had the right to vote. He had not supported the bill from a place of caring, but merely to stand by his good friend, Creswick, in his political fight. Daniel grimaced, lifted the decanter of whiskey to his mouth, and took a healthy swallow.

Why in God's name was he even thinking about this?

Because a bill like this is damn well important, especially for ladies like the Heyford sisters. Why did he feel so altered, only after spending a little over three weeks with a woman who had pettily deceived him? Glancing at the newssheet once more, Daniel made a swift decision. Setting down the crystal cut tumbler, he called for his coat, top hat, and horse, informing his butler the carriage was no longer needed.

Only a few minutes later, he was being admitted to Creswick's townhouse in Grosvenor Square and led to the elegantly furnished drawing room. The door opened, and Simon entered, his eyes crinkling at the corners with his smile when he saw Daniel.

"Stannis," he murmured. "Some said you were dead. I am relieved there is no truth to those rumors."

"I for one never believed it, Lord Stannis," another voice said brightly.

The earl shifted to reveal Creswick's wife, her belly high and rounded with their child. The countess was scandalously bare feet, her mass of vibrant red hair tumbling about her shoulders down to her back. When she noted Daniel arching a brow in question at her feet, she grinned and tossed him a wink.

Bloody incorrigible, he thought with amused fondness.

Daniel pressed a hand over his chest. "I am heartened to hear of your faith in my abilities, Mina."

Her eyes widened with false innocence. "When

I thought back to the first time I met you and the…debauched state you were in, I assured Simon you were of course somewhere with a lady love."

Daniel chuckled. He had come to love Simon's wife's bold vivacity, earning his admiration after he had learned it was her who had defeated his friend in a fencing match a couple years ago and not her brother as everyone had previously assumed. Creswick had always been a man of unfathomable depth, indifferent to many pursuits others reveled in, and was even icily reserved, but then he had met Miss Mina Crawford. It was as if she had bewitched his body and soul, for Creswick wore his heart on his sleeve for his darling wife and the entire *haut ton* to see, uncaring about their whispers.

Daniel could not imagine owning such affections and emotions for another, worse that he would walk about appearing like a besotted fool. Marriage alliances had little to do with love and were more practical arrangements, yet Creswick had finally married only for this whimsical thing called love. Cynical amusement twisted inside Daniel. The earl had always been an unusual man; it made sense he finally put the noose around his neck for a reason as whimsical and eccentric as himself.

"You are contemplative," Creswick said, lifting a brow.

"I read that you have put your full weight behind the call for amendment to the Married

Women's Property Bill."

"Aye." Creswick's gaze sharpened. "Are you interested in joining me?"

Daniel's mouth hitched. "I am."

The countess cast her husband a delighted glance. "You are *deplorably* popular, Lord Stannis," she drawled. "Your move into the current political ring would awe and alarm many in the *haut ton*. A dangerous move, my lord, but very welcomed."

He walked over to the side mantel and poured himself a glass of brandy. Daniel took a few sips before he murmured, "I've always been a Whig Liberal."

"But very indifferent to political power moves and machinations," Creswick said, his brilliant gaze piercing and cutting.

Daniel lifted a brow, amusement scything through his chest. "I see the wheels turning in your head, Creswick. Does my reason need to be analyzed and dissected? Have I not always supported your motions, hmm?"

"Yes, but without entering the fray. We both know the political underbelly can be dangerous... with deadly enemies to be made, especially those who will oppose the bill."

A sort of savage thrill moved through Daniel, and Simon's eyes gleamed.

He lifted his glass to him in salute. "I look forward to the fight."

"Welcome, friend."

Daniel tossed back his drink and set it down on the walnut table, moving over to the fireplace.

"I shall check on dinner with the cook, my love. Lord Stannis, please stay and join us." The countess brushed a kiss over her husband's jaw, and his lashes fluttered close as if he savored that small caress.

Daniel closed his eyes as memories of his wife...no, not his wife, Georgianna wafted through him. The way her eyes had danced as she'd watched him taste the birthday meal he'd prepared, and the incandescent way she had shined when she spoke about her creative art. The way she'd tasted, and how her shaking fingers had touched his mouth with hunger and stirring tenderness.

"You've fallen in love," Simon said, coming to stand beside him.

Bloody hell. Daniel snapped his gaze open, recoiling from the nonsensical idea. "Don't be ridiculous."

"You have that deep contemplation in your eyes, an expression I have concluded can only be brought on by the madness of loving another."

A hiss of irritation left Daniel. "I would not love that deceiving little vixen for any damn reason."

Yet longing for her crashed over his senses and almost broke him. What the hell was this? He'd never believed missing someone could swallow him whole. He was being fanciful, and he was not that sort of man.

The butler interrupted to announce that the Duke of Beswick and the Marquess of Moncrieff had come to call.

Daniel lifted a brow, and Creswick lifted a shoulder. "A happy coincidence."

He grunted, and soon their two friends entered the library, their elegance of dresses and rakish air about them suggesting they meant to carouse around town tonight. Beswick's green eyes gleamed when they landed on him.

"I heard you were dead, Stannis. I am relieved it was just a damn rumor." The duke poured himself a drink while running his gaze over Daniel as if to ensure he was indeed well.

"Where the hell were you?" Moncrieff growled, coming over to slap him across the shoulders. "I bloody hired men to investigate after you missed my third card party. It was too unlike you to go missing without any word."

"I was shoveling piles and piles of cow shite, while at times being chased by a hen." He held up his arm. "I have muscles in places I had not thought possible and callouses on my palms."

Beswick choked on his whiskey. "The hell you say!"

Creswick's eyes gleamed, and Moncrieff glared at Daniel.

"Surely you jest," the marquess said. "Shoveling cow shite? *Where?*"

"In a little town called Crandell."

Beswick shook his head. "Never heard of it. How the hell did that happen?"

"Johanna shoved me overboard, and I lost my memory and washed up ashore there. A scheming little hellion contrived to pretend that we were married and set me to work about her manor."

His three friends stared at him with varying degrees of shock and amusement. Then laughter rumbled from the duke.

"Yet you do not seem angry," Moncrieff said, a smile hovering about his mouth. "A great beauty, is she?"

Daniel frowned, shoving his hands deep into his pockets and walking over to the windows. "She is lovely."

He could feel his friends stare upon his shoulders, yet no one said anything else.

Finally, Moncrieff drawled, "We are visiting a pleasure party in Soho. Care to join us for a night of wenching?"

An illicit pursuit a month ago, he would have been the one to suggest it. "Aye," he said, turning around. "I will see you in the Commons, Creswick."

His friend nodded, his gaze unfathomable as they left the townhouse. Instructing one of the footmen to see his horse delivered to his house, he boarded Beswick's palatial carriage, curious at his lack of eagerness for a night about town.

"You've inspired me to host my own midnight yacht soiree," Moncrieff drawled. "Yours was all anyone spoke about for several days. It was decadent."

The duke hummed his agreement. "Those rumblings almost overshadowed that you were missing."

Moncrieff smiled. "Say you will attend, Stannis, and that your mishap overboard has not scarred you from sailing."

"Nonsense," Daniel drawled. "I will be there."

"You should get the same chef he had," Beswick said. "The food was divine."

A knot tightened inside his chest and yearning stirred. Daniel ruthlessly pushed Georgianna from his thoughts, falling into the easy banter and camaraderie he shared with his closest friends.

Several minutes later, they entered the illicit party, greeted by beautiful ladies scantily dressed in silk peignoirs, wearing blue-and-gold half masks. Many of these ladies were women of high society with reputations to lose. However, Lady Helen, a marchioness who had been made a widow far too young, routinely hosted these scandalous parties where her guests were free to act on their baser and more decadent desires without fear of rebuke or discovery.

Moncrieff laughed as a lady rushed toward him and leaped into his arms. They kissed rather salaciously, and he murmured something in her ear that provoked a most startling blush.

Daniel chuckled, wending through the crowd, dipping his head to a few cronies who bowed in curtsy.

"Daniel," a voice gasped.

He leaned against the balustrade, shifting to face Lady Johanna. She peered up at him, her limpid gaze pooling with tears, her lush mouth trembling.

She came over, lifting a hand to his jaw. He caught it before her touch landed.

"My wife would not appreciate it," he murmured, dark amusement flowing through him.

She blanched. "Your *wife*? What do you mean? There has been no announcement."

"A rather risible situation only I would understand, I'm afraid."

Her shoulders relaxed. "I am terribly sorry, Stannis. I…I was inexcusably reckless, and I never intended for you to fall overboard. Please forgive me."

If not for your action, would I have not missed Georgianna? That thought struck him most forcibly. "Done."

She gasped at his easy capitulation, for it was evident she had not expected it.

The gentle air of anxiety visibly fell away from her. "Thank you, Daniel," Johanna said with a coquettish smile, delicately pushing her body against his. "Will you dance with me?"

He peered at her ravishing beauty, willing himself to be tempted by the raunchy delights her stare promised. Yet Daniel only saw golden-brown eyes brimming with laughter, sweetness, and passion. He hissed under his breath, scrubbed a hand over his face, and gently eased Johanna from his body. Even that she was pressed so against him felt like an offense and a betrayal.

"I am not interested. And to be clear, Lady Wimpole, you shoved me overboard in petty, thoughtless anger. I will forgive you, but your actions will not be forgettable. You not calling out to the captain or any member of the crew or staff after I fell, effectively leaving me to die in the frigid waters of the English Channel, has revealed a character that I can never let close to my circle ever again. Do not approach me going forward or you will feel the full measure of my displeasure."

Her eyes flared with her alarm, and before she could protest, Daniel walked away. Music and laughter blending into a canopy of sensual sounds, an invitation to relax and slide into pleasure, but he felt bored. The awareness did not startle him, and with a frown, Daniel realized he felt…empty.

I never once felt empty in Crandell.

Dark amusement wafted through him at the inane thought. That yawning boredom tugged at him, and he went outside onto the terrace window, lifting his face to the sky.

Footsteps padded closer, and Moncrieff stood a few feet from him, lazily lighting a cheroot. "You are not tempted to indulge?"

"No."

His friend cast him a considering stare. "You seem different."

"I am unchanged."

"Are you certain all your memories have returned?"

A humorless smile touched Daniel's mouth. "I am unchanged."

Repeating it did not make the distance growing inside of him lessen. Dipping into his pocket, he withdrew a cheroot and lit it, blowing out a plume of smoke.

"I have two delectable ladies awaiting my attention in a room upstairs. Join me."

"No." The sooner he could withdraw from this very tiresome affair, the better.

Moncrieff's low laugh felt like a mockery. "I am off to visit Lord Shelton's stud estate tomorrow. Will you accompany me?"

"I have other matters to attend."

"Matters more important than purchasing the most sought-after stallions for your famed stables?"

"Yes."

"Oh?"

"A visit to my wife is due, I'm afraid."

Shock slackened Moncrieff's jaw. "*What bloody wife?*"

A humorless smile tugged at Daniel's mouth, even as hunger and want trembled through him with such stunning force, he sucked in a harsh breath.

Yes, a visit to Crandell is needed.

CHAPTER SEVENTEEN

Mr. Hayle and Mrs. Hayle's large drawing room was filled with the elites of Crandell, all sipping champagne from elegant flutes and eating delicacies which Georgianna herself had prepared only a few hours earlier. The orchestra played quite beautifully, and several ladies and gentlemen stomped and hopped to the music, creating a lively, appealing atmosphere.

She scanned the crowd, hoping to catch a glimpse of her dear sister, who had far more honor than Georgianna could own to. Lizzie had not wanted to announce an engagement without Mr. Hayle's parents' blessings and had encouraged him to meet with them before the announcement to their guests. Mr. Hayle had at first resisted, but Lizzie had held firm in her beliefs.

A peculiar grief sat heavy against Georgianna's heart. According to Miss Beatrice, Mr. Hayle's younger sister, Lizzie, Mr. Hayle, and their parents had been locked away in the study for almost thirty minutes. That the Hayles ignored their guests in this manner suggested something serious or calamitous had happened. More than once, Georgianna had wondered if she should intrude on their private meeting, fearing Lizzie might need an advocate. Yet the memory of

Lizzie's plea this morning to trust her and allow her to navigate some waters on her own stopped Georgianna.

A footman walked by, deftly balancing a tray of champagne, and she snagged a glass, taking several sips to steady her nerves. She would not let them off if the Hayles forced their son to set Lizzie aside. But what power did she have to ensure they accepted her sister and their son's choices?

She emptied the glass, her thoughts furiously churning.

"It is quite decent of Mrs. Hayle to invite Miss Heyford tonight," Miss Lillianna Buford said. "After all, she is her *cook*, merely another servant."

Georgianna stiffened her spine at that snipe, leveling Miss Buford with a cool glare. The lady had not the grace to flush or look away but jutted her chin. Georgianna smiled tightly and walked away, hating that they spoke directly to her uncertainties.

Mrs. Hayle, while impressed with Georgianna's considerable skill and having been in raptures when she tasted her dishes and quite effusive in her praises, would only see Georgianna as a miss who worked. Mrs. Hayle would see no benefit in aligning their families, and worse, they had no father or brother or husband to speak up for their family. That familiar anger and sorrow snapped through her veins, and she walked along the edges of the ballroom, determined to find her sister and offer her support.

Georgianna faltered when Mrs. Hayle and her son entered the ballroom. A glance behind them did not reveal Lizzie, and concern curled through Georgianna. Where was her sister? Hurrying forward, she paused when Mrs. Hayle walked over, her expression delighted.

To see me? Georgianna blinked, hardly understanding when the lady held out her hand and took hers in a warm clasp.

"Lady Stannis, it is such a delight to know you graced us with your presence and your skill. I am so pleased."

Lady Stannis? The sudden tremble in her heart was appalling, and a terrible, weak-kneed feeling assailed Georgianna.

"I…" Her throat closed around the protest, and she snapped her gaze to Mr. Hayle, who stood, looking poleaxed. "I beg your pardon?"

"We were meeting with your husband, my lady," he said gruffly.

Her *husband*? "I beg your pardon?" She felt like a silly parrot.

"His lordship is speaking with Lizzie, and they should be along soon."

Oh God. Since the earl's departure from their manor a week ago, she had been waiting for the proverbial shoe to drop. Except she had not anticipated such a public appearance. What did he mean by this? Her heart hammered against her breastbone, and to her alarm, she felt faint. Georgianna took a deep, steadying breath, gently withdrawing her hands from Mrs. Hayle.

A familiar ache settled low in her stomach, and she *felt* his stare upon her. She glanced up, swallowing the gasp that almost pushed from her mouth as she unerringly found the earl in the throng. He was standing by the Corinthian column, his hawklike gaze pinned upon her. The earl cut quite a dashing figure in his black trousers fitted to his frame in a manner that suggested they had been tailored by the finest craftsman, a matching jacket that was immaculately tailored, and an exquisitely designed dark green waistcoat, a perfect complement to his eyes. He wore diamonds on his fingers and on his neckcloth, his narrow, heavy-lidded green eyes shockingly piercing upon her body.

How terribly handsome and coolly composed he seemed, indifferent to the awe and curiosity of Mrs. Hayle's guests as they stared at him and whispered behind their painted fans.

His gaze held hers captive, and Georgianna barely managed to subdue the flutters in her stomach. Everything was there within his gaze — the memories of their meetings, their kisses, and the provocative way he had made love to her for the long night.

It seemed as if the entire ballroom observed as they regarded each other, and the speculative whispers kissed over her skin in a dreadful warning. His lips curved ever so slightly in a mocking smile. Georgianna's heart began to hammer wildly, and her cheeks grew flushed. Mrs. Hayle bustled over to him, evidently preening to have such an important guest at her country ball.

An earl. The good people of Crandell would speak about this for years to come.

Mrs. Hayle proudly took him over to the squire for a formal introduction, and with a sense of desperation, Georgianna wrenched her gaze away. A ripple of murmurs went through the crowd, and several ladies stared at Georgianna with rank astonishment. It was then some of the whispers reached her ears.

"*Good heavens! Do you see the manner in which he stares at Miss Heyford!*"

"*Is he not the stranger who had washed ashore?*"

"*An earl! This surely could not be so!*"

"*They say he is Miss Heyford's husband!*"

"*Why would he marry her? He is so astonishingly handsome, and Miss Heyford is rather plain. Have you ever seen eyes so green and piercing?*"

"*I think her remarkably pretty…just not as fortunate as others in her connection.*"

"*Or more not so fortunate in her wardrobe. Her gown is ghastly and terribly outdated. Why would an earl's wife be garbed so poorly?*"

Her heart felt as if it would burst from her chest. The whispers swirled around her as she pushed through the throng, heading for the terrace window. Georgianna desperately needed a breath of fresh air. Of course, the entire populace of Crandell would recall that she had claimed him as her husband…and that he had lived with her for weeks…*alone*…without a doubt sharing the same bed.

Her entire body burned. *This is a disaster.* There was no room for her to step back, and she knew he would never pretend even for a moment she was his wife. Panic clutched at her throat, and she took several deep breaths once outside on the small balcony. Thankfully no one else lingered outside.

"Georgie?"

She whirled around at Lizzie's tremulous whisper. Then she blew out a sharp breath when her sister came into view. Georgianna hastened to grip her sister's hand. "Lizzie, what is happening?"

A shaky laugh escaped her sister, and she shook her head as if in a daze, yet her eyes sparkled with relief and joy. "It is all so incredible, I do not know where to start."

"At the beginning," Georgianna cried, glancing over her shoulder to ensure no one hovered. "Why is the earl here?"

"I gather Mr. Hayle had informed him of his mother's ball and the engagement announcement. I suspect the earl came, Georgie, because he knew without his presence, Mr. Hayle might waver, and his parents might never be persuaded to accept me."

Confusion and other complex emotions she could not name jumbled through her. "But he came as the earl...not as Mr. Stannis."

"I allow that when he was admitted to the library as Lord Stannis, I almost fainted. The Hayles are in rapture that they will be connected to a man of such consequences."

Dread dropped into her belly in an icy swirl. "But we are not connected to him, Lizzie! Did he say so or was it just presumed?"

Lizzie's brows furrowed. "When he entered the library, Mr. Hayle hastened to introduce the earl as your husband to his parents, and he...he then revealed he was the earl. Though there could not have been any doubt, considering his elegant dress and manners! His name is also well-known even in Crandell. The earl mentioned his loss of memory and that he is in full return of all his faculties. Mr. Hayle had been threatening Jonathan with cutting him off, and then everything changed once the earl interrupted our meeting without any prior announcement. Georgie, he has settled a dowry on me of ten thousand pounds, negotiated the marriage contract and settlement with Mr. Hayle, which is very generous to me in terms of allowance and widow's portion. I am sorry I did not wait on you to sign it. I was so overcome with relief and happiness I...I..."

Ten thousand pounds? Georgianna found herself caught between laughing, collapsing into a faint, and sobbing. "Why would he do this?"

Lizzie shook her head, tears glittering in her eyes. "Oh, Georgianna, I do not know, but I am so happy!" Her eyes widened. "His lordship is coming!"

Georgianna slammed her eyes closed, hating the way her heart pounded in dread and anticipation. An overwhelming ache throbbed behind her eyes. "I cannot face him!"

Lizzie made a hopeless gesture with her hands. Georgianna rushed past her sister and down the steps leading into the back gardens, grabbing the edges of her dress before breaking into a run. Georgianna slowed her momentum, taking deep steady breaths. She tried to organize her thoughts into a semblance of order before she faced him, for she knew he would follow.

He has regained his memories.

He has not expressed any anger or disdain but has ensured that Lizzie would be accepted by the Hayles.

Why would he do this?

Surely he will want recompense?

A ripple of awareness kissed over her skin, and her mouth dried. His wall of heat surrounded her, and Georgianna did not turn to face him but waited for him to speak, her heart shaking. There was a small rustle behind her, and she felt it when he dipped.

His breath was a piercing warmth at her throat as he leaned in far too close. "Have you missed me, wife?"

You wretch, she silently wailed, hating the mocking way he called her *"wife."*

Georgianna turned around, their proximity of such that her lips brushed his chin. She inhaled his evocative, masculine scent and felt the heat wafting from his body. She was overwhelmingly conscious of *everything* about the earl. The breadth of his shoulders, those brilliant eyes as he peered down at her, the harsh elegance of his cheekbones, and the firm sensuality of his lips. The intensity of his gaze almost sucked her down to a place she did not understand, and Georgianna realized how different he was from the man who had lived under her roof. This man was…coolly assured and powerful with the ability to crush her. They stared at each other in mounting silence, a perilous sort of tension coating the air.

"How odd," he said with scarce-veiled condescension, his eyes gleaming with an almost intimidating light. "I feel as if I've missed you, wife."

Her heart gave a painful squeeze inside her chest. "Why are you here, my lord? I am dull with comprehension as to your reason."

His lips quirked at the corner. "How brave you are. No apology, hmm?"

"I do not regret the necessity of having to deceive you. It saved my reputation and allowed me to recoup some of the losses *you* owed me." Georgianna allowed her mouth to curve into a polite smile. "I daresay we are now even, my lord."

"Prevarication in the vein of self-interest can be forgiven. We are even."

She jutted her chin higher. "How magnanimous of you."

"I am all sincerity and humility, wife." A beat of silence, then he murmured, "You look beautiful."

She gripped the edges of her skirt at the unexpected compliment. Though she had worn her finest gown and bustle and caught her hair in an intricate chignon with tendrils caressing her cheeks, Georgianna was quite aware she was only a small spark in the midst of glittering diamonds. Yet the admiration in his eyes pierced her with stunning warmth.

"Lizzie told me what you did. *Why?*"

"If Mr. Hayle had broken his promise and I put a bullet through his heart, she would have been broken," he said with a caustic bite. "Better to present a connection they cannot resist, hmm?"

"And when they find out I am not your wife in truth?" *I will be irrevocably ruined.*

"Plan to suddenly be a soul of honesty, do you?"

"I am to *pretend* to be your countess?" Incredulity rose her voice an octave. "Have you taken leave of your senses, my lord?"

The earl lowered his head, brushed his mouth slowly, deliberately across hers with devilish tenderness. "I'll generously allow the *faux* marriage, given the wondrous benefits."

"*Benefits?* There is naught but ruination."

Good heavens, she sounded like a squeaking rat.

A carnal smile touched his mouth. "Have you forgotten the consummation of our wedding night so soon, my sweet? Surely you did not think one night of hot fucking would suffice a gentleman of my carnal desires and a lady of your passion?"

Her throat dried, and her belly went frightfully hot. *Oh, for heaven's sake.* Despite the heat climbing into her cheeks, she held his provoking gaze. "You bloody libertine," she murmured, blushing at how husky and sensual she sounded. "I should plant you a facer."

He laughed, a low sound that might have warmed her if it hadn't infuriated her.

"Even your ferocity is endearing."

His gaze lowered to her mouth, his desire to kiss her a tangible thing. When he dipped his head, she did not move away but held herself still under his steady regard. The tightening of her belly was equal parts anticipation and nervousness.

"I am merely continuing the game you started, wife."

"This is different. The world cannot think I am a countess."

"The world?" he said bitingly. "I assure you, this little hidden piece of it will hardly make any ripple, and we will keep up our ruse only in Crandell, hmm?"

"Manners says I should thank you for what you did for Lizzie. But nothing is ever given for free," Georgianna said. "Surely it is not a pretend wife that you seek. There are no true benefits to you, my lord."

His chuckle warmed her lips, and she jerkily stepped back.

"What I want, *wife*—"

She put a hand over his mouth. "Don't you dare say it, my lord."

He licked her palm, and she dropped her hand as if burned. Oh God, he was too outrageous, and not a gentleman she could handle. She became so aware of the small distance between their bodies. In his arms, she'd found a hidden part of herself, and God help her wanton heart, she wanted to feel that excitement again.

Run, the practical part of her cried, yet she stepped closer to his masculine heat, wanting to walk that edge of madness once again. It was the cool watchfulness in his gaze that thankfully brought Georgianna to her senses. She took a measured step away from him, dipped into a curtsy, and hurried off, painfully aware of the heaviness of his stare on her shoulders.

She slipped inside the ball without catching the attention of anyone, for they were all keenly listening to their host announce the engagement of his son to Miss Elizabeth Heyford. There were a few startled gasps, then cries of congratulations and well-wishes.

Georgianna snagged a glass of champagne from a passing footman and cheered along with those gathered.

"Is she really a countess?"

"It cannot be believed! Surely there is some mischief afoot."

A tinkling laugh accompanied that whisper.

"Have you seen the earl? He would never deign to lower himself to marry one of the Heyford sisters. I am sure there is some sort of misunderstanding. Even Mr. Johnson had ended their attachment because of her inferior consequences, how dare we believe Miss Heyford would be married to an earl and society is not in an uproar?"

Despite Lizzie smiling and accepting those who surged forward to offer their felicity, from the flicker of wariness in her gaze, she had overheard some of the whispers.

Oh, Lizzie, do please ignore them.

Swallowing her champagne in a quick gulp, Georgianna set her glass down, slipped from the ballroom, and made her way toward the woodlands. Thankfully, the Hayles' manor was not so far from their humble abode, yet still it took her more than thirty minutes through the shortened path to reach home.

The younger girls were abed, and she thanked Mrs. Woods for overseeing their care before she trudged upstairs to her chamber. Georgianna removed her boots and clothes, climbing onto the sheets clad only in her stockings. Pressing her face onto the pillows, she allowed her shoulders to shake with her sobs, her heart squeezing with unfathomable longings for that wretched earl.

Why can I not root you from my heart and thoughts?

CHAPTER EIGHTEEN

Your presence is requested at 19 Berkeley Square, London. This is not a request you are able to decline, wife. I would urge you to not test my patience, though I have great forbearance for anything you do. I hope to discuss an advantageous offer.

    Yours,

    Daniel Rutherford, the Earl of Stannis.

"The arrogance of this man! And why does he still call me *wife*?" Georgianna cried, waving the letter that had been delivered by special courier. "He's vexing! And he dares to summon me and implies I cannot refuse!"

She rose from the sofa, walked over to the windows, tugged back the heavy drapes, and glared outside. "And what does he mean by this!"

Lizzie lowered the novel she'd been reading and ventured over to stand beside her. "I cannot fathom the earl's thinking, Georgie — you know and understand him best."

"*I* know the earl? I do not know him at all," she said incredulously. "Surely his generosity comes with strings, the kind that will wrap me up into impossible knots I will not be able to untangle."

What if he should demand what she was not willing to give? *I must resist all overtures from the earl, whatever they might eventually be.* The quivery feeling low in her belly mocked her silent plea.

"While his actions are befuddling, I do not think Lord Stannis might be so devious—"

She waved her hand, cutting off her sister. "How can you even think so for a moment, Lizzie? He *is* trapping me in his web by contriving to make me beholden to him and sinking me into his debt! It is enough that he has sent the two hundred and eighty pounds, so why must he go this far? I do not understand it. I have fired the scullery maid, the cook, the lady maid, and the man of all work that descended on us yesterday, and they have ignored my commands as if I am not the mistress of my home."

Lizzie cleared her throat delicately. "They did say it was your husband who hired them. I for one am grateful for the governess who has taken Anna and Sarah in hand. Mrs. Wimbotton is a Godsend, and the girls already adore her."

Her sister winced under the glare Georgianna cast in her direction.

"Will you go to London?"

"No," she said stubbornly, hating the surge of uncertainty that gripped her heart. Whatever did he mean by his actions? It was not a declaration of any sort of affections, for she was not foolish enough to ever think a man of his consequences

would want to be attached to her. The earl ruthlessly gambled with her reputation, though she
guiltily realized she had done the same by insti-
gating this mad ruse.

"Perhaps now that the entirety of Crandell
thinks you are his countess, Lord Stannis has to
keep up appearances by sending servants here,"
Lizzie murmured, her eyes gleaming as if the entire sordid mess was a vast source of
entertainment. "We must admit Mrs. Hayle would
be highly suspicious otherwise. Perhaps all of
these good graces will be withdrawn once
Jonathan and I are married."

That practical supposition from her sister cen-
tered Georgianna. "I will still be deeply in the
earl's debt, and I know he will collect," she whispered.

"How?"

She blushed, and her sister's eyes widened.

"Georgie, whatever are you thinking!"

She groaned and dropped her hands into her
palm. "I have lost all reasoning and good sense. I
am not thinking anything important."

Except she knew men like him seduced women
like her into being their mistresses, wooing them
with power and money and charming arrogance.
Georgianna reached into the envelope and withdrew the first cabin ticket aboard the train,
departing tomorrow. "There is no return ticket."

Lizzie seemed uncertain, then she said, "You
should go."

"Why?"

"Because you want to."

Shocked, she snapped her gaze to her sister, who stared at her with more awareness of the situation than Georgianna had allowed. She swallowed tightly and closed her hands over the envelope, crumpling the paper. There was much inner turmoil she kept from her sister, fearing it would burden her shoulders. Georgianna no longer wanted to hide anything from Lizzie. "I am afraid the earl will ask me to be his mistress."

"I know," Lizzie said softly, "especially when it is clear to me you want so much more."

Those words were a harsh blow to her heart, and she staggered away from the windows to sink into the sofa. "Are my desires so written plainly on my face?"

"No, but you did come alive when you saw the letter was from the earl. You burned…like a star, Georgie. I have never seen you so."

Flushing, she looked away and briefly closed her eyes.

I'll not be any man's soiled dove. Standing, she stooped to pick up the ticket that had fallen from her clasp. "I shall go and pack."

Lizzie grinned, and ignoring her, Georgianna swept from the room, hoping she was not making a most egregious mistake.

. . .

Daniel leaned back in his high wingback chair, reading over the points he wanted to argue in the commons for the reformation of the marriage act, especially as it concerned giving married women full autonomy over their personal assets and property. Lowering the sheaf of papers, he rubbed the back of his neck.

Inevitably, his thoughts turned to Miss Heyford. He'd sent the first class ticket to Georgianna a few days ago now, and he wondered if she would take up his challenge and attend to him in London. What he wanted was to offer her a job catering for his grandmother's birthday dinner to be hosted a week from today.

A knock sounded, then his butler entered to announce the grand dowager duchess had arrived along with his younger brother. Setting down his drink on the mantel, Daniel made his way from the library to the drawing room where his nana waited with his brother. A fierce rush of love filled him upon seeing her, and Daniel shook his head, wondering how he had ever forgotten, even for a moment, this indomitable woman.

His grandmother was garbed in a dark purple gown with a matching turban decorated with small white feathers. Her ears and neck dripped with diamonds, and she did not own the appearance of a lady approaching her seventieth birthday. She still gave the allure of a handsome and quite formidable woman, confident in her societal power. Daniel must have made a sound, for she looked up, her gaze narrowing.

"So you've returned, have you?"

"Ah, my great love has visited me," he murmured, walking over to press a kiss to his grandmother's cheek. "I heard you did not mourn my missing."

A very decided glint entered his nan's dark green eyes. "And I heard that you lost your memory and was cuckolded into believing you were a husband to some chit. Is there any truth to that story or is it some outlandish tale to cover up a debauchery you know will likely send me to the grave?"

He chuckled, even as he sent his brother a narrowed glance of retribution over Nana's shoulders. Stephen grinned before bowing and melting from the drawing room. They had never been able to lie to their nana, and ever since they were lads, only with one gimlet stare, she'd always been able to pull the truth out of them.

"It is the truth, Nana."

Her jaw slackened, and her fingers curled over the ebony head of her cane. "Someone *pretended* that you were her husband? For what purpose would such a scheme be conceived, Stannis?"

"Revenge," he murmured caustically.

His nana's eyes narrowed even further. "I am not sure if I should be outraged at this woman or admire her gumption."

"Do not admire the wretch."

His grandmother lifted a brow at his

uncharacteristic show of ire, green eyes very much like his own richly gleaming. "How interesting."

"I was away for three weeks, madam, missing our weekly chess matches, and walking along the Serpentine. Were you truly not at all worried about my whereabouts?" he teased.

"You've gone missing longer, knee deep in your debauchery and whatnot," his mother, the Countess of Stannis, retorted scathingly as she entered the drawing room.

Bloody hell. His nana and mother had planned this ambush. It was already hard enough dealing with one, but both of them and their machinations was likely to drive him to bedlam.

His nana fairly cackled and pressed a kiss to his cheek before hugging him, and in that hug he felt the echoes of her worry. Daniel rested his chin atop her head for a few moments before releasing her.

"I missed you, my boy."

Truly, only his nana, who could barely wrap her arms around him, would call him *"boy."*

"Let me see you," his mother demanded quite imperiously.

His grandmother released him, and he turned to his mother. Her gray eyes were somber as she ran her assessing gaze over him.

"You seem to have survived the ordeal."

Daniel kissed her cheek in greeting, and when he made to move away, she held onto him and hugged him rather fiercely. Sighing, he returned the hug and murmured, "I am quite well, Mother."

She released him, sauntered over to his grandmother, and sat on the well-cushioned sofa. His mother then sent for tea and a few pastries. Daniel took the lone wingback chair by the fire, crossing his leg at the knee, a move that was ungentlemanly and one he had picked up at Crandell.

His nana spluttered. "Are you aware of the uncouth manner in which you are sitting, Stannis?"

Bloody hell. The infernal rules that govern the aristocracy had not lived within his thoughts for the entirety of his time in Crandell. Gentlemen were never to sit in this indolent manner, especially in the presence of ladies. He lifted a brow, amused at her outrage. "I find it comfortable."

She huffed, then a very decided glint entered his nan's eyes. "In the time you were gone, your mother and I had to suffer the distress at thinking you were without an heir."

His brother choked on his tea and glared at their nana. Daniel chuckled, not surprised they would find a way to twist this nonsense to their advantage. "Stephen is the presumptive heir should any misfortune befall me, Nana."

"That young fool is only one and twenty and not likely to grant me any time soon the desires of my heart."

Stephen's expression grew pained. "Nana... have pity on my vanity. Am I no longer your favorite?"

"*Bah*," she said crossly, her hands curving over the head of her cane.

"Your birthday is next week, Nana," Daniel said, standing to walk over to the windows. There was a restlessness upon him that he did not like.

"I am exhausted with balls and all these society nonsenses. A celebration this year is not needed. I wish…" She sighed, the sound heavy and forlorn. "I have lived for so long, there is little in this world that enchants me. How I long for the days I would travel to Rome and Austria with your grandfather. I am weary of balls and soirees."

His mother frowned, touching his grandmother's hand with light concern.

"What do you wish for, Nana?" he asked quietly, recalling that she had mentioned her love for traveling more than once, and how she had missed those adventures his grandfather took her on in her younger days.

Daniel almost withdrew the question at the sharp, probing look of triumph she sent his way.

"I will not select a bride as a birthday present," he said drily, lifting his drink to take a long, needed swallow.

"It is not every day a lady turns six and seventy," she retorted. "I might keel over and die tomorrow."

"Nonsense. The scheming live long."

His mother choked on the sip of her tea before loosing a peal of laughter. When his nana sent her a chastising glance, she sobered and added her voice to the entire farce.

"Your grandmother is very correct in this regard, son. You are a nobleman of almost thirty years with immense holdings and responsibilities. It is your nana's fondest wish, and mine, too, to see you with a son…or a daughter before we hie off to our rewards." His mother gave him a smile that felt almost feral in nature.

"There are rumors about town that you are stepping into the political arena," his nana said, delicately biting into a scone and awaiting his reply.

"Hmm, it has reached the drawing room, has it?"

Her gaze sharpened. "So it is true?"

"Yes."

Triumph gleamed in her eyes, and he canted his head. "Nana—"

"Good, we have been waiting for you to get involved in more serious pursuits."

"I am glad you approve," he said drily.

"You know to become a successful political orator and a credible influential voice in our society, you need a wife."

Of course he had neatly walked into her diabolical trap. His mother shot his nana a look of scandalized delight.

"Yes," his mother breathed, "an eligible lady with a spotless reputation and good connection. Now, son, remove that severe frown from your brows. A wife is an inevitability, and the requirements would have been the same for your illustrious lineage. We are only suggesting moving your marriage alliance ten years forward. We have heard you say it enough that you'll get married when you are forty. To be a voice of influence in the House of Lords, your dastardly reputation will also need reform, and the perfect way to do that is by procuring a countess...*now*."

How badly Daniel wanted to wipe the smugness from their faces with a caustic reply, yet the change within him that he did not fully understand urged him to remain silent. He had not entered into the fray lightly. Working for the country in the House had always been a part of his duty, but he had never been serious about it and had always been very offhand with his arguments made on the floor, arguments written by lawyers and his secretary.

Except for the last few days, Daniel had been reaching and drafting his own motions, where even his damn lawyer had claimed his recent arguments were brilliant and needed no editing. "I will give this serious consideration."

His nana snapped her spine straight and stared at him as if he were a rarity. Even Stephen's jaw had slackened.

"My boy, you are entirely serious," his mother breathed.

His nana pushed to her feet and thumped her cane. "I knew you had it in you to be sensible, I—"

She paled, swayed, then tumbled over. Daniel dashed forward, catching her against his chest. "Nana!" He glanced at his brother. "Summon Dr. Andrews. He is needed immediately."

Stephen rushed from the drawing room, and he gently eased his grandmother to sit on the sofa.

"Bah, stop all of this fussing. It is merely a dizzy spell."

"You fainted twice last week," his mother said gently, holding her hands.

Dread pooled in his gut. His nana had fainted twice last week? He sat beside her, and she rested her head against his shoulders.

"Would you like to retire to your chambers, Nana?"

"I am not feeling up to the journey."

Daniel stood, hugged her to him, and lifted. A shocked sound came from his grandmother, and she slapped his shoulders.

"You will put me down this instant!"

He chuckled and walked with her from the drawing room, down the hallway, and up the winding staircase until he reached the large and elegant chamber she often stayed in whenever she visited his townhouse. He lowered her into the center of the bed, not liking how wan and frail she suddenly appeared. What the hell was going on?

Without taking off his shoes, he reposed on the bed beside her, and his mother sat in the single armchair close by.

"Incorrigible and impudent," his nana

muttered with great vexation, "to have lifted me so in your arms. The last person to hold me like that was your grandfather." A beat of silence, then she said, "You look very much like him."

"So you've said."

Daniel smiled when she shifted closer to him.

"What are you thinking about?" his nana asked, patting his hand.

At first he thought about diverting her, but somehow the truth came out. "Peach orange wine."

She made a small huffing noise low in her throat. "Is there such a thing?"

"Yes."

"Surely it could not have been palatable to the senses."

"Perhaps it was the company I had when I drank it," he murmured, those hot memories washing over him, stirring his blood…and an ache inside his chest. While he enjoyed the scent and taste of a woman, their sensual and comforting company, he had never missed a lover after parting. Yet he bloody yearned to see Miss Georgianna Heyford again. "However, it was the best wine I ever drank."

His mother straightened in the chair, and he saw the curious glance exchanged between his mother and grandmother.

"Who is she?" Nana demanded imperiously.

"My fake wife."

"That impudent wench who had you sitting with your leg crossed at the knee?"

He almost laughed.

"What are her connections?" his nana asked in accents of alarm. "From any family we know?"

"No one you know," he said.

"What is this creature's name?"

"She is inconsequential, Nana."

A small silence reigned, and he narrowed his gaze at the calculating glint in his mother's eyes.

"I'd like to see you happy with a family of your own before I die," Nana said.

Dread clutched at his throat. "You are not dying."

He was acquainted with death, having lost his grandfather and then his father a number of years ago. His nana had lost her husband and then son, but her formidable will had seen her meandering on without wilting. Daniel knew the ravages of grief would lessen upon losing loved ones, especially when the life mourned had been well lived, but he was not ready to lose his nana. *By God, not yet.*

"It is inevitable, my boy. I do not fear it. But I would like to see you settled…a great-grandson or a great-granddaughter in my arms before I go to my Artie."

"I will consider a match," he said gruffly.

"Truly?"

"Yes."

"Good. Your mother will provide the list of ladies I would consider perfect for you."

"Manipulative," he said fondly.

"A family trait you possess in too much quantity," she retorted. "Do not begrudge me my tiny amount."

His nana started to breathe evenly, and he slipped from the bed and tugged the coverlet to her chin. Seeing her, swallowed by the large four-poster bed, a dark fear washed through him. His mother touched his shoulder lightly, and he departed the room with her. They walked in silence down the hallway, then down the stairs.

"How long has Nana been sick, Mother? And why was it kept from me?"

"She has been feeling out of sorts these last few months. Your absence did not help," she said tartly. "Your grandmother fainted twice upon reading the news in the scandal sheet that you might be dead."

A cold feeling gripped him. "Has she seen any physicians?"

"Yes," his mother said with a small sigh. "Dr. Andrews said it was worry that had caused it. I am very thankful you returned. You know she dotes on you to an alarming degree." She pulled something out from her pocket. "Here is the list we made."

An emotion he couldn't quite identify twisted through his gut. "Been planning my demise long, have you?"

"For the last five years," she said smugly. "You are already over five and twenty, and it is an essential duty. Your nana is not getting younger,

Daniel. She does not have the time to wait for you to marry and have children…and you do know it is her fondest wish to have great-grandbabies to dote on."

His mother pressed a sheaf of paper into his hand. "I will send for you when the physician arrives."

He nodded and went into the library, taking a seat by the fire.

Daniel assessed the list of potential brides his nana and mother had made for his perusal. Instead of tossing it into the fire, he considered all names mentioned. His grandmother's list was terribly concise.

Lady Katherine Winslow, Daughter to the Duke of Leighton

Lady Emeline Prendergast, Daughter to the Earl of Wakefield

Lady Sarah Walcott, Daughter to the Earl of Stanford

The ladies were all from fine families, with suitable dowries, impeccable bloodlines, and spotless reputations. Daniel was familiar with them all and knew none had lush lips and brilliant, golden-brown eyes.

"Damn it to hell," the snarl ripped from him. "Will you forever haunt my damn thoughts?"

Of course, there was no answer, and as he folded the letter, he recalled the unexpected frailty of his grandmother who had almost been swallowed by the large four-poster bed. Daniel accepted it was time for him to find a countess and fulfill his duty as the Earl of Stannis.

CHAPTER NINETEEN

Georgianna's arrival at the earl's townhouse had been met by a housekeeper, Mrs. Chambers, who directed her to a lavish guest quarter fit for a lady. She had felt the housekeeper's curious stare but had been grateful no question had been asked. Georgianna had been allowed to rest and freshen up after her long journey before receiving a summons from the earl to meet in his library.

Taking a steady breath, she knocked on the large oak door and opened it when she was bid entry. She closed the door behind her with a snick, her gaze unerringly landing on the earl.

"Ah, wife, you made it."

A ripple of awareness kissed over her skin, and her mouth dried. She dipped into a quick but elegant curtsy. "Lord Stannis, please, my lord, do not refer to me as such. I shall not be able to explain if you are overheard."

"Very well. Miss Heyford it shall be then? Hmm?"

It felt silly, given their remarkable intimacy, but it was safer. "Yes, my lord." Georgianna cleared her throat. "How…how are you? Have your headaches stopped?"

"Yes. There have been no ill effects since the return of my memories."

"Good."

They stared at each other for a beat, and her belly knotted. What was this terrible tension? "Why did you ask me to come to London?"

He stared at her for a moment, that unwavering regard almost pushing her into a squirm. She jutted her chin, and his lips tugged, that look in his eyes gleaming even brighter.

"Was the journey pleasant?"

She tucked a wisp of hair behind her ears. "The accommodation was wonderful, thank you."

"Good."

He stood, padded over to the side mantel, and poured golden liquid into two glasses. "Are you to stand by the door, Miss Heyford?"

A dart of amusement went through her, and she sauntered closer. It would not do for him to think her unsure, even though she quaked inside…not from fear but the shattering awareness he evoked. He handed her the glass, and she took it to her lips for a bracing sip.

"I would like to hire you to cater my grandmother's birthday dinner in a few days."

Shock stole her words for a few moments. "Hire me?"

"Yes."

"I do not know what to say," she said softly, for this was the last thing she had expected. *Why would you do this, Daniel?* "Why me?"

"Are you not a brilliant chef?"

"I am incomparable," she said, smiling.

"I recalled what you said about learning cultures through your food. Do you have much experience preparing delicacies from other countries?"

She stilled, her heart stuttering in a rather odd manner. Excitement unfurled through her. "I... Some. My mother has several recipes, but I have never been able to try them because...well, because my resources are lacking, my lord. But once I have everything I need...the space, the kitchen help, and the ingredients, I can create anything."

"I want my grandmother to be transported through these dishes, fulfilling that hole created by being unable to travel anymore. A seven-course meal, Miss Heyford, each course something exquisitely unique from a different country. Can you do this?"

She struggled to show an unaffected composure when she wanted to hug him.

Georgianna had dreaded their meeting on her train journey, thinking he would want to exact his pound of flesh for her deception. She had been so sure the earl she would meet was the proud, conceited man who had heartlessly tossed her off his yacht. *Who are you?* she silently whispered, and a part of her knew the man without the memory was also the earl. Still, his offer felt remarkable and in the realm of fantasy, and her heart squeezed at the realization he was fulfilling some of her dreams.

"Yes, I can!"

"Good. Name your price."

Oh! "Five hundred pounds."

A brow lifted. "Five hundred pounds?"

It was an outrageously expensive sum. "Yes, of course. I have subtracted the aid you provided by hiring workers and sending them to the manor in Crandell. I was…alarmed when they mentioned their wages have been paid in full for a year."

Humor deepened the green of his eyes. "So you are saying you've already provided me a discount?"

She smiled and lifted an elegant shoulder. "If you feel I am taking advantage of your generous nature, by all means, let us haggle, my lord."

His low chuckle washed over her senses, and she dug her toes into the shoes.

"How unflinchingly bold you are, Miss Heyford. I agree to all your terms. Your skills are worth even more."

His acquiescence unrooted her, and she flung herself at him, hugging him around the waist. It was reckless and impetuous, and Georgianna could not say what pushed her into his arms, but the earl did not ease her from him but returned her hug. They stayed like that for an endless moment before she untangled from his body and peered at him.

A hunger was brewing inside for his touch, and she did not want to deny its existence or argue it away. Only then did Georgianna realize she was still looking to see the naked longing within his eyes whenever his gaze rested on her. And there it was, burning dark and wanton. She leaned against the bookshelves, aware of the slight trembling in her body. *Oh, Georgianna, do not do this!*

"I've missed you," he murmured, using his fingers to caress her cheek.

"Have you?" she asked, aware of the breathless ache in her voice.

"It is a befuddling awareness."

Yes, her heart sang. *Yes, yes, yes.* "This is not wise," she murmured, pressing a hand to his chest.

His hands lifted to her jaw, and her head tipped back. "Why not?"

His tone was rough with want, and she realized he might expect them to be lovers. *Oh God. The wretched, dissolute rakehell!* "Should I indulge in an affair with you, I might develop an inconvenient attachment, my lord."

"There is nothing about you that would ever be inconvenient to me," he said roughly.

Her heart started to race. "I am already falling in love with you."

He faltered into astounding stillness.

"Would you love me in return, my lord? Or is it not in men of your consequences to love women as...inconsequential as those from small towns in the countryside?"

A shadow touched his eyes, and his expression grew unfathomable. "How direct you are."

"Is that not the only way to deal with a gentleman with your power and influence?"

"I have not thought beyond knowing I want you more than I have ever wanted anything or anyone. That is a simple truth, Miss Heyford."

Longing halted Georgianna's breath. And then pain forced her to exhale. It was not a confession of anything that had meaning, and looking at the elegant, powerful man before her, she knew she could never be more to him than a lover…or a cook. The social divide between them and the evident wall around his heart were simply too great, and she understood now how ladies had become mistresses to men whose consequences and power far outweighed theirs. Her heart had been entangled, but they were a star in the sky she could not touch no matter how recklessly and boldly she reached.

Georgianna knew that despite this sensual passion and attachment between them, the earl would not dare offer for someone of such reduced circumstance or connection to the *ton*. However, agony still pierced her chest, and she worked to mask the feelings. "Ground rules," she said shakily. "There must be rules in our working relationship."

"What rules, wi…Miss Heyford?"

His thumb feathered over her cheek, and she closed her eyes, letting that tender touch sink into the crevices of her body that had been cold since he last held her in his arms. It took immeasurable strength, but she stepped away, needing the space from his nearness.

"No ravishment," she said, lifting her chin. "No seduction. If you can...promise this, I will gladly avail to reside under your roof for the duration of our agreement. If not, I will take lodgings at a hotel in St. James at your cost."

His eyes gleamed with amusement and an expression she could not identify. The earl was so physically beautiful and appealing that he was dangerous to any person's willpower. *I can be a lady of stiff, moral rectitude*, she silently wailed, then had to bite her lip from laughing at her absurdity.

"I'll not touch you under this roof."

She heard the distinction in his promise and recklessly thought it enough. "I also require half of the amount before I start working, my lord."

"Done."

His eyes were far too watchful and gleamed with a cunning sensuality that made her wonder if she had entered a trap. The earl walked over to his desk, wrote a bank draft for two hundred and fifty pounds, slipped it into an envelope, and handed it to her.

"Thank you, my lord."

"You are welcome, Miss Heyford."

"When is your grandmother's birthday?"

"In four days."

She gasped. "There is not enough time, my lord!"

"I have full confidence in you, Miss Heyford."

How wretched her heart was to flutter so. "How many people must I cater to?"

"Thirty."

"Are you so certain of the numbers?"

"No one will refuse this invitation, Miss Heyford, and my guests will be from society's most distinguished and influential families."

"You trust me to do this, my lord?"

His eyes darkened as they searched her face. "Yes, Miss Heyford, I do," he said softly.

A knot of impossible feelings tightened below her breastbone. "I must head to the kitchens right away and start planning!"

This appeared to startle him, but he dipped his head, led her outside, and introduced her to his staff. Though she wanted to dance and twirl, Georgianna kept her expression serene when he informed the housekeeper that whatever she wanted from the markets and butcher would be procured at all costs. This was the perfect opportunity to provide food that would see her worthy of the patronage of the *haut ton*'s most distinguished families. There must be no room for mistakes or distractions.

The earl went to his library, and Mrs. Chambers took her to the kitchen where she met the earl's cook, a gentleman who stared at her with some suspicions but soon relaxed after he realized her presence in his space would only be for a brief time. The kitchen itself was magnificent with a large workspace in the center. The kitchen boasted several cabinets and a gas range stove. A far cry from the wood cookstove she used in

Crandell. Excitement thrummed through her.

Georgianna fitted an apron and worked on the courses she hoped would delight his grandmother. That evening, with a wonderful kitchen staff to assist her, she prepared roasted quail, thin slices of braised pork, vegetables, delicate chicken-filled pastries, and fish in a crème sauce. It was carried out to the earl at dinner, and she watched from the doorway as he forked a piece of the pork. Ecstasy transformed the earl's face at the first bite. She dipped her head and hid her smile even as pleasure burst inside her chest.

"Compliments, Miss Heyford. Do you plan to remain hidden in the doorway and watch me eat all evening?"

How had he known she was there? Georgianna ventured forward.

"What is it?" he asked after taking another bite.

"Braised pork."

A dark brow winged upward. "I am certain I have eaten this before, but this taste is new somehow."

"The secret is in the spices," she said with a small smile. "I would like to add these as traditional English fares to the grand dowager's courses, considering some might find the other food too rich and diverse."

"Have you thought of a menu?"

She dipped into the pockets of her dress, withdrew a paper, and handed it over.

He held the list toward the light. "Bisque of

prawns, oyster soup. Goose, à la flamande, partridge pie… What is this note beside the pie?"

Georgianna hid her smile. "It is a spicy dish and uses white sauce and cayenne pepper. Does your nana like pepper?"

"She does," he murmured, scanning the rest of the menu. "Salmon served with lobster tail and chopped truffles. À la Claremont, braised beef with mushroom sauce, veal with allemande sauce, neck of lamb served with a while Toulouse ragout, calf feet braised in blanc served with potato croquettes and calf feet fried in batter and served with Italian sauce." Daniel glanced at her. "You have a thing for feet, hmm?"

She laughed, leaning closer to peek at the extensive list. "Do you also approve of the longevity noodles? It is really called yi mein, a noodle that is served with oyster sauce, garlic chives, and mushrooms. It should hopefully remind your nana of her travels to the east. It symbolizes longevity, prosperity, and good fortune."

The earl lowered the list to the table, holding her regard. There was a wealth of emotions in his gaze she could not interpret, and Georgianna's heart squeezed. He shifted and his fingers barely brushed her wrist, yet small tingles of sensation shot through her skin and her nipples tightened.

"I shall leave you to review the list," she said softly, stepping away.

"I am certain my grandmother will enjoy these, thank you."

Glancing away from his probing stare, she cleared her throat delicately before meeting his eyes once again. "I have an early morning, my lord. If you will excuse me, I must retire for the night."

"Very well, Miss Heyford, I wish you a restless and tormenting sleep."

The laughter pealed from her before she could restrain it, and he smiled, lifting his glass to her in a silent toast. She could feel his stare upon her as she left the elegant dining room. Once in her room, she leaned against the door, easing a long breath from her lungs. Georgianna removed her clothes, tumbled onto the bed, and hugged the soft pillow.

Four days...I only need to manage for four days, then we will part, and I will never have to think about him again. Perhaps if they ever encountered each other again in Crandell or the streets of London, they would exchange a polite bow...a curtsey, and nothing more.

Yet that promise to her silly, stubborn heart felt empty, for as she fell into a restless slumber, he stole into her sleep, haunting her dreams with impossible wants and desperate hunger.

• • •

I am already falling in love with you.

Daniel had no idea what to do with that soft confession, and as he lay in the dark staring at the ceiling, a smile tugged at his mouth as Georgianna thumped her pillow once more, her frustrated curse reaching through the walls.

Just deserved, Miss Heyford, for I am bloody well similarly tormented and unable to sleep.

However, she needed her rest. He was aware that she had woken before the rest of the household this morning and went to the kitchens. She would perhaps faint if she realized he had placed her in the countess's chamber and that the connecting door led to his rooms. Daniel had to fight the ruthless need that urged him to get up off the bed, open that door, take her into his arms, and kiss her until she allowed him deep into her body. His cock throbbed in greedy want, and he resisted the urge to fist his erection and squeeze to alleviate some of the ache.

He groaned, gritting his teeth as he gripped the sheets. How could one woman twist him into such knots? Hissing, he pushed from the bed to stand by his windows. It was early yet, barely minutes to midnight; he could venture out for a night on the town and find a number of willing women to slake the lust crawling through him. Daniel dropped his forehead with a *thunk* on the cool windows, never a man to willfully delude himself.

The only woman he wanted lay beyond that door and—

"That vexatious, dissolute blackguard has cursed me!"

Daniel stilled, then he chuckled, padding over

to the door. "What have I done, Miss Heyford, to deserve such censure?"

Her gasp reached through the connecting door. Turning his back, he folded his arms and leaned against it, closing his eyes. She said nothing for a beat, then he heard her footsteps as she drew closer.

"Are you behind this door?" she whispered in outrage.

"No," he said drily. "I am underneath your bed."

Another long beat of silence.

"You are not," she said irritably.

His brow winged upward, and his mouth twitched. "Did you by chance check, Miss Heyford?"

"It was entirely possible," she said. "One can never tell how far a rake would go."

He laughed and scrubbed a hand over his face. "Did you by chance bring any orange wine with you?"

"Of course not."

He did not perceive the whisper of her feet which would inform him she had returned to her bed. No…Georgianna was still standing right at the door.

"Are you still there, my lord?"

He smiled. "Aye."

"This is rather silly, is it not, that we are conversing so?"

"I could always open the door."

The low sound she made was desperate, and he laughed when he heard the distinct turn of the key he had left in the door.

"The wretch," she murmured.

The fond humor in her tone had his heart stuttering.

"A wretch, am I?" he asked, wondering at the compelling sensations winding through his body.

I am already falling in love with you. That aching whisper dug into him. Dismissing Miss Georgianna Heyford from his thoughts was more complicated than he'd thought possible. "You cannot sleep, hmm?"

"I cannot."

"A drink might do the trick. I have a decanter of whiskey here."

"Is that an invitation to join you in your chambers for a drink, my lord?"

"I promise to be the soul of propriety."

She made another low sound of disbelief. "You'll make no attempts at seduction?"

"Of course I will, but I shall stop the instant you resist."

"You wretch!" she gasped, then her sweet laughter pealed through the door.

"So you've said." He padded over to the side table by his bed, grabbed the decanter, and went back to the door. Daniel took a healthy swallow. "If you open the door, I'll pass you the brandy."

The key twisted, and his heart thumped with anticipation. Still, he restrained himself, only smiling when the door barely opened and a slim hand pushed through. He placed the carafe in that hand and watched it draw back, the door closing again. Amusement rushed through him, and he lifted a brow when the door cracked again, and she held out the brandy. They did that several times, drinking in companiable silence, Daniel ruthlessly fighting the desperate hunger crawling through his veins for her.

"How are the girls?" he asked, leaning his head on the door.

Her sigh whispered through the oak. "Excited that Lizzie is getting married in a few weeks. Lizzie has asked if they…if they could reside with her and Mr. Hayle at their new home in Derbyshire. It is a lovely manor there, with more modern conveniences. Lizzie says they will also be able to better afford…caring for the girls, given the income Mr. Hayle has secured working as a barrister for a marquess and the dowry you provided."

Her voice throbbed with suppressed emotions.

"You are saddened by this."

She was unnaturally quiet, then she chuckled ruefully. "Would I not be selfish to be? Sarah and Anna deserve the best life has to offer. I am learning to trust my sister with some of my burdens. It is not my responsibility alone to love and care for our family."

"But now you'll be alone."

Several beats passed, and when the door

opened, he merely pressed the decanter in her hands. When she passed it back, it was empty.

"I'll visit them often," she finally whispered, then hiccupped. "*Oh, dear.*" Then a muffled giggle and an odd thumping sound.

"Georgianna?" When she made no reply, Daniel ventured through the connecting door to see her lying on her back on the lush carpets, staring at the ceiling. Her heavy tresses spilled over her shoulders in a stunningly beautiful fan. Usually she wore a buttoned-up dress that hugged lushly to her curves but was still drab and far too plain. Her hair would be tightly pinned into a bun at her nape that accented the graceful line of the shape of her neck, and if she thought that severity of style diminished her loveliness, it was impossible to dismiss from one's awareness of her unique beauty.

Now she looked like a delicate, sensual creature of such ravishing loveliness, his mouth dried. He assisted her to stand, and when she wobbled against him, laughing, he swung her into his arms. Her small, sharp gasp brushed the skin of his throat. She yawned rather indelicately and snuggled closer into his chest. Daniel pressed a kiss to her forehead, wondering at the need that compelled him to do so.

"I miss the taste of you." The words came from him before he had the presence of mind to censure his desire. Another pulse of silence that felt fraught with perilous tension coated the air.

Her long lashes fluttered on her cheeks, which

had pinkened.

"Missing is all you shall do while I am in your employ, my lord," she said tartly, a very decided twinkle in her eyes.

Georgianna was rather lovely in a mischievous sort of way with the tilt to her mouth and the dimples winking in and out of her cheeks.

"I have my skillet with me, husband. Under my pillows."

Husband. He almost stumbled when she gripped the muscles of his forearms and squeezed. Did she even realize her fingers were trailing over his naked chest, her caress light, sensual, and so very tender? "Do you?"

Her lips curled upward like unfurling rose petals. "Yes, my weapon of choice to resist your ravishment."

His wif...*fuck*, Miss Heyford was a delight foxed. Her reaction had filled him with humor, and something far more tender and elusive. There was something charming and quite unpredictable about Miss Georgianna Heyford. This fire had been hidden before because she had perhaps feared revealing too much of herself. Daniel gently placed her onto the bed, gritting his teeth when she slid her hands upward to wrap around his neck. In the darkness of the room, her golden gaze smoldered like a low-burning ember. She touched his jawline with a single finger, and it hooked a raw sensation inside his chest.

"I want to run...so far away from you, my lord,

but I also want to run into your arms."

It felt like the earth shook beneath him. Her words were an evocative whisper of heat that settled hot and heavy against his cock. Daniel felt like he was falling from dizzying heights, his damn head spinning, his heart shaking, even though he logically knew his legs were firmly planted and braced on the ground.

Why in God's name do I feel so much for you?

That finger traced his lips, and when Daniel nipped it, she drew it back, laughing. Then she promptly fell asleep. He stood there in the dark of the room, staring at her for endless minutes, almost astonished by the warm sensation filling his chest. He seriously considered setting her up under his protection.

No…Miss Georgianna Heyford deserved better than to be any man's mistress.

He scrubbed a hand over his face and blew out his breath. She was simply digging too far under his skin, and he merely needed to slake this need he had for her, so when they parted he would not damn well be haunted by her. Yet there was this small niggle deep in his mind that he might need years to uproot her from the place she had sunk into him. Daniel felt…unmoored, and he did not like the feeling of not understanding this…whatever the hell this was.

Who am I really when I am with you?

CHAPTER TWENTY

For two days, Georgianna did not encounter the earl, buried in the kitchen, preparing the menu meant to delight the grand dowager's taste buds. The rest of the house itself seemed in an uproar as the servants busied themselves with cleaning and planning for a most elegant dinner party to take place in two days. She worked, experimenting on various dishes from as early as five in the morning to trudging upstairs to her bed around seven each evening. She was grateful she did not contend with the earl and his far-too-enticing charm.

If only he would spare my dreams.

Georgianna stifled a yawn, wiping her hands on the apron as she awaited his presence in the dining room. He entered, his veiled gaze sweeping over her in a searching glance.

"You are exhausted," he said, frowning.

"The opposite," she said smiling. "I feel challenged and invigorated, my lord. I have never before had so many ingredients at my fingertips to work with. I shall miss your kitchens dreadfully."

Georgianna walked to the five dishes she had prepared. She beckoned him over. "I thought of the places your grandmother traveled to in her youth, those places you mentioned she missed. Rome, Shanghai, Jamaica/the West Indies...New York..."

She lifted the spoon to his mouth. "Close your eyes, my lord."

"Why?"

"I want you to appreciate the taste of what I am about to offer." God, why did she sound so sensual? "Eating asks us to engage all our senses—sight, smell, taste. Have you ever truly savored a bite and wondered what really makes up the food you eat?"

His lips hitched in a small quirk, then his lashes fluttered closed. She held up the spoon to his mouth and his lips parted.

"Do taste all the flavors as they roll over your tongue," she whispered.

His gaze snapped down, ensnaring her. The earl took the food into his mouth, slowly chewed, the green of his eyes appearing almost black. He made a sound low in his throat, one she was unable to interpret.

"What is it?"

"It is roasted duck," she said softly, delighted by his pleasure.

"I've had duck before, Miss Heyford... This is not that."

She smiled. "It is the sauce that distinguishes the taste. Your nana spent an entire year in Russia almost two decades ago and has not returned. This particular sauce is from Russia. It contains tarragon, parsley, chervil, horseradish, sugar, a pinch of pepper, lemon juice, and a little mustard."

He swiped his tongue on his bottom lip, and she looked away, almost resenting the heat that flared in her belly. She hurried over to the small soup bowl, lifted it to him. His eyes gleamed when she tipped it to his mouth, and he took a large swallow.

"Oxtail soup," he murmured.

"Yes…a delicacy those who live on the island of Jamaica love, and it is said that Chef Francatelli prepared it for our queen."

"It is rich and flavorful," he said roughly.

"It is the meat itself and the mignonette pepper." She turned away, her movements jerky. *Two more days*, she reminded herself. Georgianna waved him over to the other dishes. "Please avail yourself of a taste. This is a dish that will let your nana taste the east along with a taste of Vienna. Unusual, I know, but they complement each other well."

"Ah, I was taking such pleasure in you feeding me. Afraid of being too close, hmm?"

Her mouth twitched, and she suppressed the smile. She waited, clasping her fingers before him as he tasted all nine dishes she laid out. When he had finished, he leveled his gaze on her.

"You've outdone yourself."

She grinned, warming at his praise. "Do you think the grand dowager will enjoy herself?"

"Yes, these are dishes fit for a queen. My nana will want to meet the chef, of course."

"I…yes. I will stay in the kitchen until—"

"You'll attend the dinner party as my honored guest."

The breath stilled in her throat. "I cannot, my lord!"

He lifted a brow. "Is not this the opportunity you wanted?"

It is. Georgianna's thoughts reeled with the possibilities and the number of clients she might secure.

"I've already commissioned a dinner gown for you...with assorted frippery and unmentionables, along with a shoe."

Her lips parted, but no words emerged. She understood his intentions. The earl did not want to hide her in the kitchen but proudly have her display the artwork of food she had created for those who had questions.

A small smile tugged at his mouth. "They have been delivered to your room."

A simple glance into Daniel's eyes was enough to tear her open, allowing inside the unbearable longing. Her heart was pounding so loudly that she could hear nothing else. "I...I do not know what to say."

"There is no need to say anything, Miss Heyford." He dipped into a small bow and walked away.

"My lord!"

He paused without facing her.

"Thank you," she said softly.

The earl made no reply and continued on to

his meeting. Georgianna tore off the apron and hastened above stairs to her guest chamber. Three large boxes were laid out on the bed. Her fingers prickled, and she curled them into a fist to fight the temptation to rip into the boxes. She took her time, lifting the lid of the first to stare at the most exquisite golden gown she had ever seen. It was made of soft, flowing silk with silk satin and a darker golden draper. The bodice was even lined with ecru silk taffeta. It must have cost the earl a fortune to have something this lovely commissioned in such a short time. Georgianna suspected that he might have started the commission before he even invited her to town.

The second box revealed silken stockings, a beautiful pair of dancing shoes, supple hand gloves; even a bustle had been set up in the corner of her room.

She sat heavily on the bed, an ache rising inside her throat, silent tears trailing down her cheeks. *Oh God, I wish you…me…I wish we were real.*

• • •

Georgianna had never appeared more beautiful. Earlier as she'd stared at herself in the cheval mirror, awe had suffused her body. The gown delivered by the earl fitted her body perfectly, and she'd appeared resplendent, sheathed in the dark golden ballgown that hugged sensually to her figure, and her rich, dark chestnut hair piled high atop her head in an artful coif.

Taking a deep breath, she entered the palatial dining room, hovering in the shadows, keenly observing. A small orchestra set played music in the background of the large drawing room that had been reorganized for tonight's feast. There were at least thirty people present, ladies and gentlemen arrayed in splendor. No doubt it lingered in Georgianna's mind that they belonged to the elite families of the *haut ton*. Nerves pitched through her, and she took a deep breath. The visual beauty of the food was arresting. Murmurs of appreciation swept through the small crowd, and the grand dowager's expression was one of genuine delight.

Smiling, she sauntered over to the two long tables that had her array of food on tasteful and exquisite display. There were several undercooks in the kitchen, waiting to carry out the dishes that could not have been arranged in a *service à la francaise* fashion.

"This is most incredible," the grand dowager duchess said, delight glowing in her green eyes. She glanced at the earl. "I have never seen a feast presented so beautifully. Praises to the chef."

"You may compliment the chef in person, Nana."

Daniel turned to her, and awareness kissed over her skin at the flare of heat in his gaze. The earl stared at her, and she blushed when his grandmother arched a brow, her lips forming a moue of curiosity as her stare volleyed between them.

"Nana, allow me to present our chef for tonight, Miss Georgianna Heyford. Miss Heyford, the Grand Dowager Countess of Stannis."

She dipped into an elegant curtsy. "Very pleased to make your acquaintance, your ladyship."

Green eyes so much like her grandson's landed on Georgianna. "I am simply astonished and impressed by your talent, Miss Heyford, and your graces."

"Thank you, your ladyship."

The countess came over, and similar introductions were affected. Georgianna felt as if she floated as she met several members of the *haut ton*, who flattered her creativity and skills. The champagne flowed along with the laughter and facile chatter of the guests. The earl paid no particular attention to her, but she could feel his gaze upon her body as she made the rounds with his guests, answering their questions about the food and the tastes they were experiencing.

A Mr. Gervase, a hotelier visiting from the United States of America, offered her a job.

"I beg your pardon?" she asked, peering at him in shock.

He briefly bowed, most charmingly. "Miss Heyford, the gentleman I work for would pay you a fortune should you choose to work for him."

For a long moment, she had no notion of what

to say. "This job would be in America?"

"At the Willard's City Hotel in Washington, a place of quality that embodies the finest luxury experience."

She smiled. "This is highly unexpected. I never envisioned leaving England shores." Or her family. Yet the desperate desire to travel and explore the world opened inside her. There she could learn so many new foods, including new experiences.

Mr. Gervase retrieved a card from his jacket pocket and handed it to her. "Please, do consider it, Miss Heyford."

Georgianna nodded, and he bowed before melting into the small crowd to mingle.

The earl's grandmother walked over to her, waving an imperious hand to capture Georgianna's attention. "I want you to create another lavish and exotic fare in the vein of this birthday meal, Miss Heyford."

Pride burst in Georgianna's chest, and she wanted to scream her delight. "It would be my honor, your ladyship."

"It is a most momentous occasion, and the presented table should show it." Her ladyship's eyes gleamed with an almost cunning light. "Is there any special food that is designed for engagement announcements?"

Georgianna's heart jolted. *Engagement announcements?*

"Yes, my grandson will soon announce an

engagement, and I believe I shall host a small, intimate dinner for this special day."

Her heart squeezing, Georgianna said, "I
would gladly cater for this dinner, your ladyship."

She nodded regally. "The countess will make
the necessary arrangements, Miss Heyford. Allow
me to say again how excellent your food is, the
artistic presentation memorable. I shall not forget
this birthday feast anytime soon."

Georgianna dipped into a curtsy, her heart
heavy as she watched the dowager countess saun-
ter away. Which grandson did she refer to? The
earl? Or the honorable Lord Stephen, whom she
had met earlier?

The countess announced there would be dancing in the smaller drawing room, and the guests
laughingly ventured from the dining area. She did
not join them, overwhelmed by the success of the
night and feeling as if she did not truly belong in
that drawing room with them as they danced.

Worse, her awareness of the earl felt too in-
tense, and Georgianna had not missed the
lingering glances many of the guests made between them. A few had been bold enough to
enquire if she would remain as the earl's guest for
a number of days. The soft speculation in their
tone had not been missed, and her heart
squeezed.

Tonight, in front of such elite guests of the *haut
ton*, he hadn't treated her like a servant or worker
in his household, and there had been those who

had noticed. Everyone had been cordial and respectful of her talent and art; however, to remain as his guest after tonight might start whispers, and her hopes of maintaining her respectability and business would be dashed. She knew she had to prepare her heart to bid the earl farewell.

Georgianna feared she was already deeply ensnared in the coils of love and lust, and it would be imprudent to stay even another night under the earl's roof.

One more night, the desperate, empty heart of her whispered.

Needing to feel the cool night air on her skin, she went outside, her feet taking her down one of the graveled paths, away from the laughter of the guests and strains of the orchestra. Georgianna sought the sanctuary of hedges that seemed to offer shelter from the world inside where she did not belong. She sat on a bench in the shadows, which provided the comfort of the hedgerows at her back to lean against.

Could she really dare to spread her wings and accept Mr. Gervase's offer? Leaving England would ruthlessly cut the attachment she owned for the earl. Georgianna closed her eyes, hating the ache in her throat. What was the sense in feeling this keen want for a man who was forbidden to her?

There was a deliberate crunch of footsteps drifting closer, and coldness unspooled in her belly to be replaced with a different kind of tension. She knew it was the earl. Georgianna gripped the edge of the stone bench and waited. When he appeared, the breath left her in a soft gasp. Down low in her abdomen, something heated in response. There was something faintly disreputable about his appearance. She stood but faltered when a lady joined him.

"My lord," the unknown lady murmured.

His shoulders tensed, however the earl's expression remained hidden in the darkness. "Lady Katherine. Why have you followed me?"

"My lord…I…" She stumbled closer to him, and Georgianna could not say what happened given the meager light, but somehow the lady was in his arms, coiled around the earl.

"Ah," he said bitingly, "it is one of these scenes?"

The lady gasped prettily and peered up at him. "My lord! We will soon be discovered and—"

"I'll still not marry you, so you should hurry inside."

She swayed, and Georgianna stepped forward only to falter when the lady seemed to gather herself. "Would you be so cruel, my lord? My reputation would be ruined."

"Not too well thought out, hmm?"

Perhaps it was fate or the lady's own machinations, but footsteps sounded. The earl made to walk away, and she gasped, "Lord Stannis, *please*!"

Unfortunately, her voice carried. Quite deliberately. The young lady's hand then fluttered to her throat, and she waited, evidently rioting with nerves yet hopeful.

"Are you gambling on my honor?" he asked, then coolly withdrew a cheroot from his pocket and lit it. "How naive. Even if you were to be found naked in my arms, Lady Katherine, I would not marry you."

Shock snatched the air and retort from the lady's throat, only a small squeak emitting from her. The footsteps moved closer, and Lady Katherine hurriedly patted her hair, clasping her fingers before her as the Countess of Stannis emerged. The earl remained indifferent, drawing on his cheroot as if there was not a compromising plot afoot.

The countess's eyes widened upon seeing her son. She stared at him, clearly aghast when she saw Lady Katherine. Another lady emerged, gasping, "Katherine?"

The girl dissolved into sobs and flung herself into her mother's arms. "Oh, Mama!"

Silent communication passed between the countess and the lady who held her sobbing daughter. She whisked her daughter away, leaving the countess with her son. Georgianna wished there was somewhere she could slip to escape being a part of this sordid scene.

"I expect you will do the honorable provision," the countess said tightly. "The duke will not take kindly to any marring of his daughter's reputation. A marriage announcement must be made."

Shock tore through Georgianna's heart, and

she stepped forward in instinctive denial.

The smile that touched Daniel's mouth was cruel and indifferent. "There is no force that can persuade me to go against my own convictions, Mother."

Georgianna was decidedly curious about that dangerous throb in his tone. There was a tightness across her chest that made it difficult to breathe. Observing the debacle before her, she was suddenly glad she had no ridiculous dream of wanting more with this man, who had the power to crush her heart beneath his boots.

"How long will you maintain this cruel reputation as a rake about town?" his mother demanded in accents of stinging rebuke. "Lady Katherine is on the list your grandmother made; would it be so unpalatable to make her your countess? It is evident that she went too far in her reckless admiration, but she is a very amiable and wonderful girl."

"I will think about it," he said, his expression impenetrable. "From the list Nana provided, I had thought Lady Katherine would be the first choice to be my wife."

The word from his lips speaking about another woman ridiculously pierced her. Georgianna felt as if something cracked inside her chest, the feeling so visceral that she shuddered.

"Good. I shall speak with the duchess." His mother vented a weary breath before turning away and retreating back inside the townhouse.

Georgianna waited for the earl to leave, but he only tipped his face to the sky, appearing far too stark and lonely in that silhouette.

"Ah, wife, we are finally alone, and outside."

She drew in a deep sustaining breath, alarmed that he had known she was observing. The words were coated with flirtatious heat. "I did not realize my presence was known."

"I can feel you whenever you are near. It is as if something invisible ripples over my skin."

Georgianna was painfully aware of him taking several slow, measured steps closer, yet she did not flee or offer any protest when he came so scandalously close.

"I did not mean to intrude on your business, my lord."

"It was no intrusion."

Georgianna wrapped her arms around her waist. "Will you marry her?"

He stiffened, and his mouth tipped sardonically. "I will consider the advantages of an alliance with the duke's family."

Georgianna's heart throbbed with painful intensity. "Of course, she is perfect for you."

"Far from perfect," he said with chilling indifference. "That I am an earl with wealth is all that matters to the ladies who wish to be my countess."

She blinked. "Does it happen often, a compromising situation?"

"Frequently enough where I once even made a list of the traits I would seek in my countess when

I eventually take a wife."

Curiosity hitched through her heart. "Dare I ask what those requirements might be?"

"A good family, with a suitable financial standing. In that way, I could be certain it is not my wealth why my wife wants me. I want the real, honest character of the woman I am to marry, and I will give her mine, even with all the flaws."

Georgianna swallowed past the frightful squeeze inside her chest. "That is logical."

"My countess does not have to be a great beauty. I am pretty enough."

She choked on her outrage, and deviltry danced in his eyes. There came that slow smile again, laced with promises of pleasure and potential heartbreak. They stared at each other, and she couldn't help noting how dangerously virile he appeared at the moment.

"I am leaving tomorrow. I…your nana seemed delighted with the menu, and I…" She swallowed at the reminder of the words, her tongue suddenly thick in her mouth. "Why do you stare at me so, my lord?"

"I want you as my lover, Miss Heyford."

Georgianna bit her lip hard to contain the ragged sound that wanted to whisper from her lips. "Tonight only?" she asked shakily as jagged cracks appeared in her heart and composure.

An emotion flared in his eyes, there and gone before she could identify it. "No, days…weeks… perhaps months."

Do you feel this way with every lover? Surely this connection between them could only happen once in a lifetime.

You never made me any promises, Daniel…but how I hunger for you to make them.

Yet she could not ask them, for her pride and heart could take no more wounding. She released a tremulous breath. Men of such power and consequences did not marry country misses like her, yet somehow she had thought the peculiar connection and friendship they shared would see him spare her from such a humiliating proposal. Of course he would not think much of her, given how she had fallen under his wicked charm and allowed him into her body.

He placed a finger under her chin and lifted her gaze up. "What is this pain I see in your eyes?"

"There is no pain," she whispered. *Liar*, a small voice whispered.

She stared at his beautiful features, his coolly guarded eyes, high cheekbones and sinfully inviting mouth. Daniel's expression became inscrutable. They had never spoken of love or tender sentiments, yet Georgianna knew she was falling deeper and deeper under his charm.

"Are you afraid?"

She swallowed. "No."

He placed a thumb against her lower lip, exerting the slightest pressure until her lips parted. "If you walk away, I'll not chase or try to coax you against your inclination."

No…you'll allow me to slide into madness without any seduction so I cannot hate you for not loving me.

From deep inside the townhouse, the bows of the orchestra leaped to life, and the exquisite music of the waltz filled the room. He reached for her, tugged her in his arms, and spun her with grace and elegance. It was dangerous…so very dangerous to her heart, yet she allowed him to sweep her into the rousing dance under the stars, the faint strains of the waltz their music.

He was utterly beguiling, a degenerate rake, uncompromising in his belief and character. He would never see her as more than a lover…a mistress if she was weak enough to allow it, yet she did not resist when he cupped her chin, lifted her face, and took her mouth in a carnal kiss that sucked her under. Georgianna was tempted both to resist him and to surrender to his ruthless persuasion.

"Will you spend the night with me?" His voice deepened, softened, lowered. "Will you be my lover?"

She stared up at him. Georgianna fought the ridiculous desire to curl her body against his chest and listen to the rhythm of his heartbeat under her ear.

I am already in love with you.

The awareness was sharp and sudden and painful. He was an enigmatic man with power and wealth; it was inexcusably reckless that she kept dancing close to his dangerous fire.

"Yes." *But only for one more night*, she said silently.

A powerful heat flared in the depth of his gaze. Daniel dragged her up against his body almost violently and caught her mouth with his in a burning kiss, one that intoxicated her with immediate delight. The earl framed her face with his two hands, and suddenly the kiss was hot, hungry, and demanding. A small noise of pleasure broke from her throat at the wanton throb that he provoked between her legs. The fingers in her hair tightened even further, and he spun with her to press her against the Neptune fountain.

Daniel tugged at her gown, his fingers expertly undoing the buttons to reveal her breasts to the cool night air. He dipped his head and licked at her sensitive nipple, and she moaned out in the stillness of the night.

"Shh," he murmured, his breath fanning over the throbbing tip.

He licked it again, and she whimpered and curled her hands behind his neck, the move thrusting her breast further out in a perfect arch and more into his mouth.

"What are you feeling for, my wife? Slow and deep...or wild fucking?"

Molten fire dropped low in her belly, and sweat beaded on her brow. The earl's mouth was too filthy! Yet...God, the desire coursing through her veins felt unspeakable. Did he even realize he called her wife still? Something dark and wanton twisted tightly, low in her belly, drawing her taut like a bowstring. He stooped before her and slipped one hand beneath her dress. *Oh God!* Sensual weakness assailed Georgianna, and she leaned back against the fountain, uncaring it dug into the tender flesh of her hips. She trembled and bit into her lower lip as he stroked his hands over her calves, over her knees, and up the sensitive skin of her inner thigh.

Daniel unhooked her skirts, the small wire bustle, and removed her clothes. Only her ragged breathing and the rustle of his movements punctuated the space. Soon she was naked, and she surged forward to push his jacket from his shoulders, her fingers trembling when he tugged at his neckcloth.

He laid his jacket on the ground, dragged her up against his body almost violently, and caught her mouth with his. Yet his kiss was deep and tender…and perhaps a bit desperate.

She slid her hands over his muscled chest, reveling in the rippling strength underneath her palms. A knot of mingled grief and pain tightened her throat. Her eyes were damp with tears and her heart ached with regret. Kissing him, sucking on his tongue, and hitching her lips around his hips, allowing him to bear her down onto the jacket on the grass felt like a decadent, unsavory delight. A dark, hot lust slid through her veins, slow and heavy, and she trembled under its intensity.

How wonderful it would be to be your lover always…your wife and friend.

That thought was dragged from a place where she buried all her unfulfilled longings. There wasn't any chance she would ever be of equal consequences with anyone he could marry, but for a desperate, agonizing moment she allowed for the dream that it might be real. She allowed that dream closer into her heart, holding it there for the most precious moments before she released it, feeling the raw burn of tears in her eyes. Georgianna poured her love and longing into their kiss, surrendering for one more night, before she would disappear from his life like a thief in the night.

CHAPTER TWENTY-ONE

Daniel broke their hungry kiss, their ragged breaths puffing against each other's lips. Very gently, he stroked her swollen lip with his thumb. "I want to feel these lips on my cock. And you sitting atop me, riding my tongue."

Her mouth lifted at one corner, a wicked little smile of lust and anticipation. That she would explore this wanton heat between them with no fear or hesitation squeezed his heart. There was so much he wanted to say to Georgianna, but the words would not form. He took her lips, at first hungry and demanding, then gentle, for the need to worship her burned through him. He made love to her mouth for endless seconds before he feathered his kiss down. He nuzzled her collarbone and soft whimpers of need escaped her as he bit at her throat…right above her fluttering pulse.

"Daniel," she whispered.

He arched her to him, seized her nipple between his teeth before laving the sensitive flesh with his tongue. Her ragged moan settled along Daniel's cock like a kiss of pleasure. He rolled her nipples between his fingers, pinching and pleasuring her. His lover touched him all over, eager to explore him as he did her. Her fingers coasted over his shoulders to his buttocks, where she squeezed. Pleasure rushed through his veins in a fiery burn, and with a ragged groan, he lowered himself down to her splayed thighs.

"Such a lush, pretty pink pussy…and already wet for me."

"You're the devil," she whispered, looking scandalized.

"My words made you wetter, hmm?"

A choked sound came from her, which tapered into a small scream when he licked her soft folds, pressing his tongue against her clitoris before sucking that nub into his mouth. She arched against him, her fingers gripping his hair. His lover tasted like heaven. Her breath came in shuddering gasps, and she murmured his name, her tone strained and desperate. He slid his hand underneath her bottom and pulled her onto his mouth, licking and teasing until she unraveled with a cry. She sobbed his name, undulated her hips, whispers and hoarse cries ripping from her throat, yet he never released her from under the lash of his tongue. He showed her no mercy, driving her to climax three more times before he rose over her body.

Daniel's heart raced, and urgent desire coiled in his gut. He reached between their bodies, fisted his cock, and pressed it against her sex. A noise of pleasure broke from her throat. Hot, drowning pleasure gripped him when he started to push his cock into her quim. He held her gaze as he entered her slowly. She raised trembling fingers and touched his mouth. That small caress was scarcely a breath of sensation, yet it pierced his heart like a well-aimed arrow with feelings of tenderness and affection and something so profound, it felt unknown.

Georgianna was hot and wet and so damn tight, sweat beaded on his forehead. She shifted her legs, twining one around his hips and the other around his thigh. He withdrew so that only the tip of his cock nudged her snug entrance, and then he plunged. Her soft cry mirrored his deep groan.

"You're stretched so tight around me," he murmured.

Her nails dug into his shoulders before her hands crept around his nape and tugged him toward her raised mouth. A deep ache of want filled Daniel's soul. He kissed her with an almost violent passion, slipped one of his arms under her and gripped her buttocks, snapping his hips in a driving rhythm. His tongue glided sensually with hers, a provocative mimicry of how he rode atop her.

She clutched his shoulders helplessly, kissing him with torrid passion as he thrust into her clenching core with almost mindless fervor. He became lost in her scent, taste, and the feel of her beneath him. The need to release pulsed inside him, and Daniel snaked a hand between them and pinched her clitoris between his fingers. She clamped down on his cock so tightly, he groaned at the exquisite sensation.

"Daniel," she gasped against his throat, shaking as her release bathed his cock with wetness.

He rode her through her convulsions of pleasure, and soon he found his release deep within her body. For a beat, they lay unmoving, then he dipped his head and pressed the softest of kisses at the corner of her lips. They stayed like that for several moments until their breathing eased and her shivering stopped.

The distant sound of music and laughter reached them, and he gently eased from her body, assisting her to stand. They spoke no words as they helped each other to dress. Her hair tumbled over her shoulders, and when he tried to put it up, she laughed. The sound was shaky and throbbed with emotions he could not decipher.

Something tender and shockingly vulnerable settled on her face. "I shall slip inside through the side door leading to the music room. No one will see me."

He lightly fingered a loose tendril of hair on her cheek. "Go in my chambers—I will be up soon. We need to talk, and our night of loving is far from over."

Pleasure lit her expressive face before her expression shuttered. Georgianna stared at him for several moments, her throat working visibly to swallow. The pale moonlight illuminated the uncertainty etched on her lovely face. She pressed her mouth on the underside of his jaw, closing her eyes. Daniel felt the weight of that soft kiss, the minute tremble in the fingers that touched his jaw. Another whisper of a kiss feathered over his cheek, and he closed his eyes against the sensations.

"Georgianna?" he asked gruffly, not understanding why his heart jerked or what it was she silently communicated.

There is something. Daniel could feel the shifting tension invading her body. She let out another soft breath, almost a moan, yet it sounded pained. Something dark and hollow twisted inside his chest. They stayed pressed together for a beat, then she turned from him, nimbly slipping away into the darkness.

• • •

Grave matters such as a marriage alliance could not wait until the respectable morning hours, not when he might change his mind. Aware of the taste of his lover still in his mouth, Daniel stood a respectable distance away, annoyed that he would not deal with this nonsense.

The duchess, his grandmother, and his mother were seated on the sofa, all three appearing far too pleased with themselves. Almost an hour ago, his lover had slipped away upstairs to his bedchamber, and he wanted nothing more than to be with her, either drinking brandy and playing chess by the fire or engaging in another bout of torrid lovemaking.

By God, Georgianna Heyford had been perfectly, exquisitely fashioned for him.

Every kiss, conversation, and lovely laugh
spilled from her throat had endlessly teased
Daniel with possibilities he had never considered.
Being with her was the most honest and refreshing connection he'd ever formed. He couldn't
begin to think about their sexual attraction, or his
body might respond unpardonably.

A sound whispered through the night, and he
stiffened when he saw a slim figure hurrying down
the steps of his townhouse, a valise clutched in her
hand, the cowl of her cloak covering her hair. He
would know her shape and walk anywhere, and
for a moment, incomprehension muddled his
thoughts.

Daniel sucked in a harsh breath when he realized she was leaving, and the manner in which she
did so revealed she did not want to inform him.

By God, she truly is leaving.

A cold knot of dread invaded his heart. He did
not want to lose her.

Daniel recalled the agony that had burned her
eyes bright when he'd asked her to be his lover,
and she had taken a deep breath as if bracing
herself against some terrible wound. He recalled
the feel of that soft kiss on his jaw, and that he
had not understood she said farewell. Regret,
sharp and hot, spliced through his chest. He had
reduced her to this with his thoughtlessness,
sneaking away from a gentleman's townhouse as

if she were an unwanted, unloved burden. He had made her believe she was not worth more, that he would only ever see her as a woman he would use and then discard when she was.... Bloody hell, she was simply *everything*.

He pressed a hand over his eyes, squeezing his temples hard, as if that would center him against the desperate love rising in his heart. Daniel took a long, hard breath. Georgianna Heyford was a bright, living flame—passionate, kind, loyal, witty, creative, and dedicated to her passion and those she loved.

His heart hammered, and he released his pent-up breath. She was gone. It was not yet a damn second, and he felt that hole gaping inside his chest like a physical ailment. A hired carriage rumbled to stop before her, and she waited until the steps were knocked down before entering. A twisting pain squeezed deep into his body.

The hackney would have rattled away, taking her from his life, her actions informing him that this time, it was permanent, with no door open for her to return. They would indeed now be mere memories in each other's lives, a moment they would years in the future look back on, either with fondness or with the bitterest of pains. Recalling the haunted shadows in her expression and the bright burn of pain in her eyes, he knew Georgianna would never look back on their moments with anything akin to joy.

And who are you to be, wife? He briefly closed

his eyes. He had not shown the desperate feelings brewing in his heart for her, feelings that would only build and grow, for he had fallen for her with his entire heart. "I am a damn fool."

His grandmother frowned. "Whatever do you speak of, Stannis?"

"You will forgive me, Nana, Mother, Your Grace, I have an urgent matter to attend to."

"Stannis," his grandmother said sharply. "This is not a matter that can be delayed. The duke will expect—"

"As I already have a wife, I cannot imagine what the duke could expect of me. Of course, Lady Katherine would not have known this when she plotted her scheme. Everyone should be allowed the dignity of making their own choices, and your daughter tried to steal mine, Your Grace. Given the close association between our families, I will forget the entire matter, but I will not be forming any alliance with your daughter. Even if it is your dearest hope."

His grandmother spilled the tea down the front of her French gown, then swooned rather dramatically against the sofa. "What do you mean you are already *married*? To whom?"

The duchess gasped and surged to her feet, every line in her body taut with anger. She cast him a fulminating glare and marched for the drawing room, slamming the door.

"Who are you married to?" his mother cried. "What manner of cruel jest is this?"

Aware of their shock, a humorless smile tugged at his mouth. "Miss Heyford is my wife."

His grandmother's lips parted in a silent gasp. "You married the cook? *When*?"

A rough laugh escaped him, and padding over, he kissed her cheek. "The marriage was officiated by one Miss Sarah Heyford some weeks ago in Crandell. A pity you missed it; it was a rather lovely day, Nana."

His nana spluttered and snapped her spine straight. "I do not appreciate your jesting about matters of such serious importance…"

He leveled her with a stare that tapered her words and had her arching a brow.

"You mean a lot to me, Nana, but I will decide my future and countess. It took me a while to understand that what I feel for Miss Heyford is not just mere affection for a lover and friend."

"I knew there was something between the two of you," his mother gasped, a hand fluttering to her chest. "You are in love with that creature?"

The words settled between them, heavy and fraught.

"She wraps me in knots I do not understand," he said, providing the unvarnished truth.

"Does she have *any* suitable connections?" his mother asked, standing.

"Marianna," his nana snapped. "Do not encourage the boy to foolhardiness! Society will not forgive him for marrying a lady so decidedly inferior to him in background, reputation, and—"

"Fuck society, Nana," he said with deliberate and perhaps unforgiving crudeness. "I have the reputation of a libertine, yet I am accepted in their drawing rooms, fawned over in the hopes I will marry one of their daughters or befriend their sons. Now that I would marry a woman who is beautiful, clever, witty, and kind, do you think I would give a damn what they think? I only feel like the grandest of fools to not have realized that the leap in my heart whenever I see her smile means she is my beloved."

Without awaiting a reply, he stormed from the drawing room, calling for his horse to be readied. It would take at least fifteen minutes for his stallion to be carried from the mews and even longer for the carriage to be called around.

Daniel rushed toward the front door, the butler opening it without a command, and he hissed out a breath, for he no longer could distinguish her hackney from the dozens queuing away from the dinner party.

He searched for coaches that did not bear a crest or had the appearance of a hired carriage. Daniel saw three such equipages in the distance, and he broke into a run, knowing that he could not allow her to spend even a night thinking that he did not love or want her. The very notion cracked open his chest. He dashed down the street, uncaring of the people pushing their carriage curtains aside to watch him sprint.

The scandal of it all would drive Nana to

apoplectic shock, but that did not stop Daniel. He tried to flag down a carriage with no crest, but the coachman ignored him. He wrenched open the door, using the power and strength of his body to haul himself upon the top steps of a carriage that still raced ahead.

"Moncrieff!" a shrill voice cried out.

Daniel barely had time to process that his good friend, who had just been at his dinner party, was seated in a disguised carriage next to a veiled lady with a puppy clutched in her hand, for the damn puppy now morphed into a monster launching at him.

"For fuck's sake," he hissed, jumping down from the carriage and hurtling toward the other coach that had picked up speed.

Damn it all to hell. She needed to be in the next one, for his lungs and muscles burned with his effort; still, Daniel did not slow his steps.

The alarmed cry of, "Pug, stop!" pushed him to glance over his shoulder to see the damn dog racing at his heels, its jaw snapping.

"What the hell!"

Another snap and the little terror's teeth sank into his boot this time. Daniel never realized he could kick off a shoe with such ease, given the effort his valet took to help it off his foot.

The few carriages that he presumed moved away from his house slowed, and several faces of ladies and gentlemen of the *haut ton* peered out at the spectacle, wearing varying expressions of shock and alarm. And amid all this, the damn dog abandoned the shoe and still gave chase, painfully reminding Daniel of a cantankerous hen called Hetty.

Bloody hell.

• • •

Heartbreak tasted like a bitter lemon.

With each rattle of the carriage wheels taking her farther away, it was as if a knife sliced into her belly and twisted. Georgianna was aware of every ache in her body, the lingering feel of the earl's kisses, and the feel of him inside her body. She swiped the tears off her cheeks with trembling fingers. Had she made the right choice to leave without telling him how she felt?

"Would there be any point to it?" she whispered in the emptiness of the carriage.

Could I bear his indifference if I told him how much I loved and wanted all of him, just not for a few months?

Georgianna gripped the edges of the squabs until her fingers ached. There had been a deep fear upon her heart that if she wished him farewell, he would convince her to stay and be his mistress. This need for him was a burning flame, and surely he would eventually consume her until she lost all sense of herself.

Except she had never been a coward or shied from difficult situations. If that had been her character, she wouldn't have found the initial gumption to pretend to be the earl's wife. She rapped on the carriage's roof, intending to ask the coachman to take her back to the earl's townhouse.

The coachman did not seem to hear her, for there was some dreadful commotion outside. The carriage rocked precariously, the door wrenched open, and the earl spilled inside, breathing heavily. They stared at each other for a shocked, frozen moment. "My lord!"

She blew out a slow, measured breath even as her heart pounded. His déshabille state and uneven breathing informed her of what had happened, and she stared at him as if he were an unknown creature. "You *chased* the carriage?"

His gaze gleamed with that wicked, unapologetic light. "I know."

"You've started a scandal," she said faintly, aghast.

"What is one more in my arsenal?"

The emotions in his eyes stirred an almost painful, sweet ache deep inside her. "Daniel? Are you aware that you are only wearing one shoe?"

His humor faded but his gaze remained intent. "A determined dog has it, I'm afraid."

She squeezed her fingers until they ached. Georgianna was almost afraid to ask him why he was there. "I…"

"You are leaving."

"Yes. I…I felt as if we said our farewell. I…I

am thinking of going to America."

He grew still. "America?"

A nervous laugh bubbled from her, and she nodded. "This is perhaps the second time I am leaving Crandell."

"I know."

"Mr. Gervase offered me a job. I think...I think this is an opportunity I cannot give up. I might stay there for a year or two, then perhaps I'll visit Rome and..."

The earl's gaze lowered to her fingers, and he reached out, tenderly took her hands, and pried them apart. He then gently massaged her abused flesh. A sweet feeling flipped several times low in her belly. "Daniel?"

"I'll come with you."

The jumble of emotions hammering at her heart—shock, gladness, bewilderment—had Georgianna closing her eyes for a few seconds. "What do you mean?"

"Wherever you go, I'll be there. If you wish to return to Crandell and live at the manor, I'll be there."

"You would live in Crandell?"

"Yes."

"And you would come with me to New York?"

"Yes. Then Rome...Shanghai...wherever you wish. My estates are well managed, and my brother is brilliant. Communication has changed, and for a couple of years we can explore the world together, my sweet. If you want to explore forever, I am there."

"I do not understand what you are saying." Georgianna braced herself for an answer that might shatter her heart in its entirety, for if he said words in the vein of *traveling alone would better hide their affair*, she would smack him and pray for forgiveness afterward.

He leaned forward and brushed his fingertips along the curve of her throat. The strong feel of his fingers sliding over her skin sent her pulse racing. "My lord, I—"

"Marry me, Georgianna."

His offer was so terrifying that she froze, afraid his words were not real and a figment of her fevered imagination. "Marry you?" she choked. "I…"

"I should have never asked you to only be my lover when you are my beloved one. I wish for you to be my friend, my wife, my countess, the woman I laugh and dream with. Only with your hands clasped in mine, Georgianna, enjoying this life, will living be worthwhile," he said gruffly. "I am damn sorry that for even a moment I caused you doubt and pain. Forgive me, please."

Shock stole the air from her lungs, then she launched herself into his arms, hugging him tightly. "I love you," she said with a sob.

"I love you, too," he said, burying his face in her hair. "Marry me again, wife."

Laughter shook her shoulders, and she leaned back to see his expression. His eyes gleamed with a tender, sensuous light, and he cupped her cheeks with a reverence that brought a lump to her throat.

"Are you not to douse my fear with an answer?"

She dropped her forehead to his. "Yes, I'll marry you."

"Thank Christ. I could not have withstood a rejection after running down the street like a madman to catch your carriage."

"You could have found me in Crandell," she murmured. "I should warn you…society will think me a most unusual countess."

"I'll have it no other way. I think I've already created the scandal of the season chasing after you with a dog on my heels." He brushed his lips over hers, as light as a breath. "As for waiting, that was impossible, my love. I did not want you to even linger with the thought for an hour that you are not cherished…that you are not my beloved. For so long I've eschewed the idea of marrying, for to my mind, it has always been only a duty, one to fulfill so I might carry on my name and property, nothing more. You make me burn to live life, wife."

Her throat worked on a swallow, and a terrible ache formed behind her eyes. Daniel caught her against his chest and took her mouth with a deep kiss, and she sank into their embrace, wordless wonder, and unmatched happiness bursting inside her heart.

EPILOGUE

ONE YEAR LATER...

Dearest Lady Stannis,

Anna, Sarah, and I imagined you emitted an unladylike snort because I did not offer you salutations as Georgie. In our defense, Aunt Thomasina is smugly peeking over my shoulder as I pen this letter. She professes she always knew you would make a splendid match with one of the most sought-after bachelors of the season. Our aunt swears this to be true. While she bemoaned the scandal that rocked the haut ton, *after the earl was seen chasing you to profess his love, our aunt is magnanimous, and she has forgiven him for embroiling us in it, given the wonderful outcome.*

We dearly miss you and were heartened to receive your letter from New York. We are very eager to discover the new dishes you learned to create, and we were even more pleased by the praises the queen lavished on your cookbook. There is even a rumor that the chef of Buckingham Palace has used some of your recipes. The special news I wanted to inform you of, Georgie, is that Mr. Hayle and I will be expecting our first child in a handful of months. Only yesterday, the physician confirmed it to us. Oh, Georgie, I cannot adequately express my joy. We are very happy.

Anna and Sarah are doing well, and they miss you and Lord Stannis dearly. They were very happy when I told them they would reside with you and the earl, upon your return to England, at his principal estate. Anna claimed Midge, Nellie, and Hetty would be most pleased by the copious lands they would now have to roam. In my next letter, I shall update you on all the latest gossip milling about in society. I send good wishes and tidings to you and the earl.

Your sister,

Mrs. Elizabeth Hayle.

Smiling, Georgianna folded the letter and pushed it into the deep pockets of her dress as hands slipped around her waist. A fierce rush of love clutched her heart, and she leaned back against the heated warmth of her husband.

"You are reading it again?"

"Yes," she murmured. "I miss them so. I did not reply to Lizzie, because I knew we would arrive before my letter reached her."

"They will be happy to see you."

Georgianna smiled, gasping when the ship dipped and water sprayed them on the top deck. "I will be so happy to be off this ship!"

His soft laughter curled around her. "We will dock in a few hours."

"Are you certain?"

"The captain confirmed it earlier."

Turning into the cage of his arms, she peered up at him. "Do you think the *haut ton* will still remember our scandal?"

His eyes gleamed with good humor. "I daresay, even in ten years, no one will forget that I chased your carriage wearing one shoe."

She laughed, burying her face against his chest. "It has been a year!"

Georgianna was not truly worried about their reception by society. While at the home Daniel had bought for them in New York, she had been shocked to receive a letter from the queen, praising her creativity and ingenuity with the dishes in her cookbook. The last year had been a wonderful experience and adventure for her.

They had scandalized everyone by officially marrying only days after Daniel proposed, then departing England's shore for New York within the month. She had not been outrageous enough to accept Mr. Gervase's offer now that she was a countess. However, she still visited his grand hotel and explored America, learning about their culture through food. Daniel had promised they could travel to Vienna and Italy afterward, but she missed her family dreadfully and knew that he missed his, too.

"If you are worried, Beswick wrote to me about some duel Moncrieff fought over a lady. I never knew he had it in him; nonetheless, that scandal seems to preoccupy society. I am sure they will have no thought of us."

Georgianna lifted her head from his chest. "A *duel*?"

"Yes."

"They have been outlawed for years. How could he partake so publicly that the *haut ton* knows about it?"

Daniel grinned. "It seems he has finally fallen in love, but the lady is not falling so easily under his charm. Good for her, I say."

She blinked, for he had regaled her with tales about his friends, the Earl of Creswick, the Duke of Beswick, and the Marquess of Moncrieff. Given the tales she had heard, the marquess seemed the one most unlikely to ever be caught in his own throes of love.

Daniel cupped her face, tilting it upward. He pressed a kiss to her mouth, swallowing her soft gasp. "You are going to scandalize the other guests!" she said.

"We are the only ones mad enough to be up this early, my love."

She giggled, for he had woken her quite early for them to catch the sunrise. Georgianna slipped her hands around his nape, holding him to her and returning his kiss with all the love she had in her heart. Pulling her mouth from his, she traced a finger over his brow. "You remember those gifts you were seeking for Nana?"

He groaned in mock horror. "Must you remind me that I have her wrath to face for being away for so long?"

Georgianna smiled. "I have the perfect gift to add to yours. I am certain she will be so happy."

"I am afraid nothing will be able to beat the pink diamond I got for her. That woman loves her jewelry."

"I think she would love her great-grandchildren even more."

Daniel froze, then he lowered his gaze to her belly. "Are you saying you are with child?"

"I am astonished that you are surprised, given how often we tup."

"Such crudeness," he drawled with a devilish smile. "Seems I have created a monster. It is a good thing that I love you so much, my wife."

She pinched his belly, and he laughed, tugging her into his arms to kiss her.

"Look," he murmured against her mouth.

Georgianna turned around, gasping at the splendor of the rising sun. She leaned back against her love, basking in the fiery beauty of a new morning.

"I love you, wife," he said, playfully nibbling her ear. "I am very happy we will have our first child soon."

"I love you, too, Daniel."

Her heart brimming with love and happiness, Georgianna and Daniel held each other as they gazed at the rising sun with promises of a new dawn.

ACKNOWLEDGMENTS

I thank God every day for loving me with such depth and breadth. To my husband, Du'Sean, you are so damn wonderful. You read everything I write. Your feedback and support are invaluable. I could not do this without you. Thank you to my wonderful friend and critique partner Giselle Marks. Without you, I would be lost. Thank you to Stacy Abrams for being an amazing, wonderful, and super-stupendous editor.

To my wonderful readers, thank you for reading *An Earl to Remember*. I hope you enjoyed Georgianna and Daniel's journey to love and happily-ever-after as much as I enjoyed writing it.

Special THANK YOU to the Historical Hellions, who always root for me, and everyone who leaves a review—bloggers, fans, and friends. I have always said reviews to authors are like a pot of gold to leprechauns. Thank you all for adding to my rainbow one review at a time.

AMARA
an imprint of Entangled Publishing LLC.